A Beguiling Ruse

Lords & Ladies of Mayfair

Laura Beers

Chapter One

England, 1813

Miss Rosamond Hendre had the most remarkable change of fortune. She went from living a quiet life in the countryside to being prepared to be presented into the highest echelons of Society. This was a life that she had never even considered a possibility that she could have, but here she was. It felt like a dream, and if she was, in fact, dreaming, she hoped she would never wake up.

The sun was shining, the birds were chirping, and she knew that today was going to be a wonderful day. She threw back the covers and tossed her legs over her bed. She had no doubt that Lady Anne would chide her on her exuberance, but she did not care. She vowed that she wouldn't waste this opportunity that she had been given. After all, it wasn't every day that a daughter of a seaman would be mingling with people in high Society. It was a secret that would ruin everything if it ever came to light.

She sat down at the dressing table and began to brush down her blonde tresses. After she put the brush down, she placed her hair into a tight chignon and fingered curls to frame her face. In a place that everything was done for her, she enjoyed doing the little things for herself.

A knock came at the door, but before she could say anything, it opened and Lizette stepped into the room with a bright smile on her face. Ever since she had gotten married over a week ago, her sister was rarely seen without a smile, which was a testament to how happy she truly was.

"Good morning," Lizette greeted. "I came to see if you would like to accompany me to breakfast."

"I would be happy to." Rosamond walked over to the wardrobe and retrieved a pale blue gown. "I am surprised that you didn't request a tray to be sent to your room."

"Tristan went riding with Roswell, and I wanted to spend time with my favorite sister," Lizette responded as she lowered down on the settee.

"How very thoughtful of you," Rosamond said as she held the gown up for Lizette's inspection. These gowns were so impractical since the ornate buttons sewn into the back required a lady's maid to help her dress. She did miss her simple country dresses that allowed her to dress herself.

As if on cue, her aunt, Mrs. Betsey Everly, stepped into the room. "Shall we get you dressed, Dearie?" she asked.

"Yes, please," Rosamond said as she placed the gown onto the bed. "I do feel rather silly that you tend to me as a lady's maid."

Aunt Betsey waved her hand in front of her. "It is truly my privilege to care for you and Lizette."

"I know, but..." Rosamond started.

"No buts," Aunt Betsey said, speaking over her. "I assure you that there is no place that I would rather be."

Lizette spoke up. "I would save your breath. Tristan even offered to let Aunt Betsey retire to the countryside, but she declined his offer."

Aunt Betsey gave Lizette a chiding look. "You know you

shouldn't call me that. What if one of the other servants over-heard you?"

"I think we are safe in the privacy of Rosamond's bedchamber," Lizette responded.

"Regardless, it just boggles the mind that Mr. Westcott even suggested that I retire to the countryside," Aunt Betsey said with a shake of her head. "Why would I leave my two nieces to go reside in the middle of nowhere?"

"He was trying to be nice," Lizette pointed out.

"You two are the only family I have left, and I have no intention of ever leaving." Aunt Betsey went to pick up the dress. "Now, let's get you dressed before you miss breakfast."

Rosamond removed her dressing gown and slipped the pale blue gown on.

As her aunt buttoned the back of the dress, she asked, "Are you excited for your ball this evening?"

"I am," Rosamond admitted. "I would have never thought a simple country girl like me would be having a coming out ball."

"You are hardly a simple country girl. Besides, you have been preparing for this for a whole month now," Lizette remarked.

"I do hope I don't let anyone down," Rosamond said.

Lizette rose from her seat. "That is unlikely to happen," she responded. "Just be yourself and everything will work out precisely how it should."

Rosamond smiled. "I daresay that our aunt is starting to wear off on you. That was a right proper encouraging speech."

Aunt Betsey laughed. "I am pleased that Lizette is carrying on my legacy, especially since I can't always be the one that gives encouragement."

A knock came at the door before it was opened, revealing Lady Anne. She stepped into the room with a tight smile on her lips. "I am glad to see you are dressed. But we have much to do today," she said. "Come along, girls, do not dally."

As soon as she uttered her words, Lady Anne departed from the bedchamber.

Lizette came to loop arms with Rosamond. "I have learned it is best to do as Anne says," she advised as she led her sister into the hall.

Lady Anne was waiting for them. "First, we will eat breakfast, and then we will begin Rosamond's lessons until we take our midday meal," she said. "After a short rest, we will have another lesson before we adjourn to prepare for the ball this evening."

Rosamond resisted the urge to groan. She didn't think she could stand any more lessons. Lady Anne had been relentless in her teachings, but she was forced to acknowledge that she had so much to learn. She knew she had no right to complain since she refused to squander this opportunity.

Lizette leaned closer to her and whispered, "I would limit what you drink since it sounds like you won't have time to visit the water closet."

Lady Anne arched her eyebrow and asked, "Do you have something to add, Lizette?"

"I was just merely providing encouragement," Lizette replied with mirth in her eyes.

"Very good," Lady Anne said. "We need to do all that we can to support Rosamond on her special day."

While they walked down the stairs, Rosamond saw the stoic butler at his post in the entry hall. She tipped her head at Brownell. "Good morning," she greeted. She made it a point to acknowledge all the household staff and learn as much as she could about them. It was important to her that she never got to the point where she took the people that served her for granted.

Brownell gave her a kind smile. "Good morning, Miss Hendre."

"How is your mother faring?" she asked.

"She is well, and I thank you for asking."

Rosamond continued on to the dining room and saw Lord Ashington sitting at the head of the table, reading the newssheets. Despite having a commanding presence, the white-haired marquess had been nothing but kind to her since she had arrived at his doorstep.

Lord Ashington rose when he saw them enter. "Ladies," he murmured.

Lady Anne waved him back down. "Father," she said. "We are only here for a quick breakfast and then we will adjourn to the drawing room."

"A cup of tea and crust of bread, then," Lord Ashington teased.

Lady Anne frowned. "Today, of all days, should be taken most seriously."

"My apologies," Lord Ashington said, appearing unrepentant. "I would imagine you intend to inundate Rosamond with lessons today."

A footman pulled out a chair for her and Rosamond sat down.

Lady Anne placed her napkin onto her lap as she said, "Rosamond is making excellent progress but there is so much that she must learn."

"I do hope you are being patient with her," Lord Ashington remarked.

"But, of course," Lady Anne said, looking the epitome of innocence.

Lord Ashington grinned as he turned his gaze to Rosamond. "I hope you are having some time to enjoy yourself."

"Lizette and Tristan have been kind enough to take me on rides through Hyde Park," Rosamond shared as she reached for her cup of chocolate.

"Only in the early morning hours since Rosamond hasn't

come out yet to Society," Lady Anne remarked. "She will have much more freedom after tonight."

"Speaking of which..." Lord Ashington's voice trailed off as he brought the newssheets up. "Rosamond's ball has made the Society page."

"As well as it should," Lady Anne declared. "This will be the event of the Season."

Lord Ashington extended Rosamond the newssheets. "Do you wish to read it for yourself?"

"Father, I would be remiss if I did not remind you that a lady does not read newssheets in front of a gentleman," Lady Anne chided lightly. "It is vulgar."

"Very well," Lord Ashington said as he placed the newssheets down.

"Well, my curiosity has been piqued." Lizette reached for the newssheets and opened them up to the Society page, earning a disapproving look from Lady Anne. "It would appear that Rosamond has caused quite a stir."

Lizette lowered the newssheets as she explained, "Everyone is quite riveted by Lord Ashington's new ward, especially since her dowry is rumored to be at twenty thousand pounds."

At the mention of her dowry, Rosamond sucked in her breath. She was already immensely grateful for what Lord Ashington had done for her. But to offer up such a large sum of money for her dowry? It was unthinkable.

As she opened her mouth, Lord Ashington put his hand up, stilling her words. "I know what you are going to say, Rosamond, and my answer will always remain the same."

"It is just too much," Rosamond breathed.

Lord Ashington held her gaze. "Because of your actions, Lizette was returned home to me, unharmed. This is the least I can do to show you my gratitude."

"But you already named me your ward. Is that not enough?"

"No, because no ward of mine will be presented to Society without a respectable dowry."

"Twenty thousand pounds is more than respectable," Rosamond argued.

Lord Ashington's eyes crinkled around the edges. "This dowry will allow you to have your choice of suitors, giving you the freedom to marry for love."

"How can I ever thank you?"

Shoving back his chair, Lord Ashington replied, "Just live your life and be happy." He rose. "If you will excuse me, I am needed at the House of Lords. That place is filled with entirely too many misfits."

Rosamond watched Lord Ashington as he departed from the dining room and her heart felt heavy. She didn't want to disappoint him, but she was afraid that Society would see right through her. What if they declared her a country bumpkin and she brought shame upon Lord Ashington?

Lizette's voice broke through her musings. "You need not fear."

"How can I not?" Rosamond asked, wondering how her sister knew precisely what she was thinking. "There is so much riding on tonight. What if the *ton* recognizes me for who I truly am?"

"And who is that?" Lizette inquired.

Rosamond glanced at the footman before saying, "An upstart that has no business being Lord Ashington's ward."

"What poppycock!" Lady Anne exclaimed. "No one will dare to think that once you walk in on Lord Ashington's arm."

"And if I trip on my gown when I walk into the ballroom?" Rosamond asked.

"Then you will pick yourself back up and hold your head high," Lady Anne said. "Besides, that scenario is entirely improbable."

"What if someone notices how similar in appearance Lizette and I are?"

Lady Anne smiled. "That is to be expected since you two will be introduced as cousins," she said. "I assure you that no one will dare assume anything else since you are Lord Ashington's ward."

Rosamond bobbed her head. Lady Anne was correct. There was no way that anyone would guess that she and Lizette were actually twins. They weren't identical and they had many differences, including the color of their hair.

But that didn't mean she could stop herself from worrying about the ball. She needed tonight to go perfect so she could feel as if she did belong in this world; a world that was unfamiliar to her. In order to fit in, she knew it wouldn't be enough to act herself, she needed to change everything about herself.

Lady Anne pushed back her chair and rose. "Shall we adjourn to the drawing room?"

Rosamond glanced down at her nearly full plate before she rose. "I think that is a grand idea." Perhaps her nerves would calm down before the midday meal.

Malcolm Barrington, the Viscount of Brentwood, exited his coach and adjusted his top hat. He had been at the club when he had received his father's urgent message. What could possibly be so important that he had to be interrupted when he was with his friends?

He approached his family's whitewashed townhouse and the door was promptly opened by his tall, heavy-set butler.

"Good afternoon, my lord," Osborne greeted him.

Malcolm removed his top hat and extended it to Osborne. "Is my father in his study?"

"Yes, and Lord Everton has been expecting you."

He didn't want to keep his father waiting so he proceeded to the rear of the townhouse. As he stepped inside of the study, he saw his white-haired father was sitting on the settee with a drink in his hand. His cravat was untied, hanging loosely around his neck, and his jacket had been removed.

His father looked up at him with bloodshot eyes. "It is about time you graced me with your presence," he said gruffly.

Malcolm didn't enjoy a close relationship with his father so he took no offense to his critical words. Frankly, he had learned to disregard most of what the aged earl said to him.

"Isn't it a little early to be drunk?" he asked.

His father harrumphed. "Not after the morning that I had, and I am hardly drunk."

He walked further into the room and asked, "Now, what is so important that you sent a messenger to retrieve me from the club?"

Bringing the glass up to his lips, his father revealed, "We are ruined, Son."

"Pardon?" he asked, fearing he'd misheard the earl.

"What is there not to understand?" his father demanded. "We have lost everything and it is only a matter of time before the debt collectors come to call."

Malcolm felt like he had been punched in the gut and it took him a moment to recover. "How is this possible?"

"Our money was tied up in the stock market and it took a turn for the worse."

"What of our country estate?" Malcolm asked. "Does it not turn a profit?"

"It hasn't for years. Until we secure the funds to update our farming equipment, it will continuously lose money."

Malcolm ran a hand through his hair as he tried to think of some solution. "Can we sell any properties off to get the funds?"

"All of our properties are entailed."

"What of our townhouse?"

His father blinked. "Where would we live?"

"We could return to our country estate."

"During the middle of the Season, I think not," his father declared.

Malcolm walked over to the drink cart and picked up the decanter. His father was a proud man, and he knew it would take much convincing on his part to have the man leave Town when the House of Lords was in session.

"Regardless, I borrowed against our townhouse so there is little value in selling it," his father revealed.

After Malcolm poured himself a drink, he took a sip as the realization hit him. They were in an impossible situation, and he could see no way out of it.

His father leaned forward and placed his drink down. "There is only one way to save us," he said.

"Which is?"

"You could marry an heiress."

He huffed. "I think not," he replied. "I have no desire to fall prey to the parson's mousetrap at this time."

"You are nearly thirty years old. By the time I was your age, I had already sired two children."

Malcolm grew solemn at the thought of his younger sister. Enid had thrown her life away when she had eloped with Mr. Longbourn. It had been two years, but the memories of that fateful night still haunted him.

"If you don't marry, what will become of your mother?" his father asked.

Now his father wasn't playing fair. He knew he would do just about anything for his mother. She had endured much at his father's hand and he had always been the one to protect her.

Malcolm tightened his grip on the glass. "Even if I wanted to marry an heiress, they are in short supply this Season." Not that he had looked before. He was far more interested in spending time with the young ladies that expected nothing in return from him.

His father leaned forward and picked up a newssheet from the table. "I have taken the liberty of finding a most suitable one for you."

"Wonderful," he muttered before he took a sip of his drink.

Holding up the newssheet, his father shared, "Lord Ashington's ward has a dowry of twenty thousand pounds and her coming out ball is this evening."

"I detest debutantes." They had all filled their heads with nonsensical notions about love and whatnot. They would bat their eyes unceasingly and attempt to send messages with their fans. It was infuriating and not at all what he was looking for.

"Not this one," his father said. "With twenty thousand pounds, we could save our floundering estate and have enough to carry us through."

"What about the next time?"

"We won't find ourselves in this situation again because we will ensure our estate starts thriving," his father replied.

Malcolm walked over to the window and stared out. He no more wanted a wife than he wanted a thorn in his boot. He had seen his parents' marriage crumble over the past two years, and he vowed that he would never have that happen to him.

His father rose and walked over to him. "There is no other way, Son," he said as he extended the newssheet towards Malcolm.

He accepted the newssheet and his eyes landed on the article about Miss Rosamond Hendre. Little was known about her other than she was Lord Ashington's ward and, most importantly, that her dowry was set at twenty thousand pounds. He had little doubt that every fortune hunter had their caps set on Miss Hendre.

"Even if I wanted to marry Miss Hendre, I can assure you that I won't be the only one vying for her attention this Season," Malcolm said.

"It is imperative that you get her to marry you, and quick-ly," his father asserted. "Once word gets out about our change of fortune, the invitations will stop coming and it will be much harder to secure her hand in marriage."

"What if she doesn't want to marry me?"

His father looked at him like he hadn't considered this possibility. "Why wouldn't she wish to marry you?" he asked. "You are heir to an earldom."

Malcolm handed the newssheet back to his father. "I will think on it."

"Do not think too long because your future depends on this union, as well," his father said. "If you don't marry Miss Hendre, then the country estate will fall further into disrepair and you will stand to inherit nothing but debt."

"But what if Miss Hendre is unacceptable?"

"Meaning?"

"What if she is unfortunate to look at?" Malcolm replied. He did not want to be saddled with an ugly wife. There were some things that he could just not abide.

His father placed a hand on his shoulder. "I'm not asking you to fall in love with this girl. I just want you to marry her. Once you gain access to her dowry, you can pack her up and send her to our country estate."

"What a lovely thought," he muttered.

"It is merely the plight that gentlemen must endure. Not every woman is handsome enough to tempt us, but we must look past that." His father dropped his hand and took a step back. "You could always take a mistress. It is perfectly accept-able for men of our station to do so."

Malcolm tensed. "I would never do something so despicable."

"It gets rather lonely in a loveless marriage." His father's words were undeniably sad, but it did little to deter him.

Turning towards his father, Malcolm said, "You made your choice. I have yet to make mine."

"But I know you will do the right thing and pursue Miss Hendre," his father responded. "Furthermore, having Lord Ashington's ward as your wife will advance my position in the House of Lords."

"Well, then I have no choice," he mocked.

"Lord Ashington wields a lot of influence in Parliament and you would be wise to remember that."

"I care little of politics."

"One day you will." His father walked over to the table and picked up his drink. "I have catered to you long enough. It is time to do your duty and marry for the sake of our family."

Malcolm tossed back his drink and placed the glass down onto the windowsill. Was he a fool to even consider what his father was proposing? But what option did he have? If he didn't marry Miss Hendre, then their family undoubtably would face ruination.

His mother stepped into the room. "Am I interrupting something?" she asked, glancing between them.

"What is it that you want?" his father snapped.

Ignoring his father's sharp tone, Malcolm walked up to his mother and kissed her on the cheek. "Good afternoon, Mother," he greeted. He was sad to notice that the lines on her face were starting to deepen, and her once dark hair was turning silver.

She smiled up at him. "How are you, Son?" she asked. "I haven't seen you in days."

"I'm afraid I have been rather busy," he replied.

"No doubt you have been carousing with your friends," she said knowingly.

"Perhaps," he responded as he returned her smile. He preferred to spend his time with his friends than remain at home, with his father.

"Well, you should slow down and make time to have dinner with me."

His father spoke up. "Did we receive an invitation to Lord Ashington's ball this evening?"

The smile disappeared from his mother's lips as she turned to address her husband. "We did, and I plan on attending."

"Good, good," his father muttered. "I will join you, as will Malcolm."

"Why the sudden interest in this ball?" his mother asked.

His father walked over to the drink cart as he replied, "Malcolm intends to pursue Miss Hendre."

If his mother was pleased by this news she did not appear so. "Have you met Miss Hendre?" she questioned.

"I have not," Malcolm said.

"Then why would you wish to pursue her?" his mother pressed.

Malcolm was debating how he should answer when his father spoke first. "Mind your business, Diane."

His mother pursed her lips. "You are being especially cantankerous today, George."

"Do you not have somewhere else you have to be?" his father asked.

Turning to face Malcolm, his mother said, "I will be looking forward to having you join me this evening."

"As will I," he responded.

After she departed from the room, Malcolm frowned at his father. "You could have been nicer to Mother."

"For what purpose?" he asked. "It is not as if she can help us."

"You are unbelievable," Malcolm muttered.

"No, I am pragmatic."

Malcolm shook his head as a thought occurred to him. Perhaps he'd just found a way to help his mother, as well. "If I do go along with his madness of pursuing Miss Hendre, I will expect something in return."

"More than a twenty thousand pound dowry?" his father asked in disbelief.

14

"Yes." He hesitated before saying, "I will expect you to be pleasant to Mother."

"Pleasant?" his father repeated. "But I have tried being pleasant with her and that is why you are here."

Malcolm resisted the urge to look heavenward. "Do be serious."

"I am, and I resent the fact that you think you know what is best for your mother and me."

"You two are hardly civil to one another."

"That is the way it has been for two years now," his father said.

"It doesn't make it right."

His father picked up the decanter and poured himself a drink. "You worry about yourself and I will see to your mother," he remarked dismissively.

"No."

"No?" his father asked. "You would dare to defy me."

"In this case, yes," he replied.

His father grew silent. "You win," he spat out. "I will make an attempt at being cordial to your mother and you will marry Miss Hendre."

"Assuming she will have me."

"She better, for your sake." His father walked over to his desk and placed his glass down. "The sooner you marry her, the better."

"Yes, Father," Malcolm said before he turned to leave the room.

As he headed towards his bedchamber on the second level, he knew he needed to resign himself to the fact that he would do whatever it took to convince Miss Hendre to marry him. It was far preferable to being ruined.

He would have this Miss Hendre beguiled with him in no time.

Chapter Two

Rosamond felt as if she were in a fairy tale. She was dressed in an exquisite ballgown that she could hardly afford, a strand of pearls hung around her neck, and she was waiting to be announced at a ball that was being held in her honor. It all seemed so magical.

If only her mother could see her now, she thought. What would she think of her transformation from a country girl to a lady? She imagined her mother would be proud of her, no matter her place in Society.

Lord Ashington held his arm out. "Are you ready?"

She accepted his arm as she asked, "Do I have a choice?"

He smiled and kindness reflected in his eyes. "Your whole life is about to change."

"Again?" she asked. "I daresay that my life radically changed the moment I arrived at your townhouse."

"With good reason," Lord Ashington said. "But the moment we walk through those doors, you will have suitors lining up to vie for your attention."

"I doubt that very much."

Lord Ashington gave her a knowing look. "Just wait," he said as the doors were opened by two footmen.

As they walked into the ballroom, it was eerily quiet, despite the hordes of people that were present, and Rosamond could feel their eyes upon her. She had never been one that felt comfortable being the center of attention, but she had little choice in the matter now. The only sound she could hear was her heart pounding in her chest, and she feared that it was so loud that others might hear it.

"Breathe," she whispered to herself.

The ballroom had been decorated with an abundance of flowers which contrasted nicely with the dark blue-papered walls. The oversized, gold chandelier that hung in the center of the hall was lit with hundreds of candles and a chalked design of the marquess' crest was laid out on the dance floor.

Her eyes roamed over the hall until they landed on familiar faces. She let out a sigh of relief as she saw her sister, standing by Lady Anne, near a column. Never had their presence been more welcomed.

Lord Ashington led her over to Lizette and dropped his arm. "That went well," he acknowledged.

Rosamond nodded. "I agree since I managed to not fall on my face in front of everyone."

"The night is still young," Lord Ashington joked. "If you will excuse me, I will leave you in the capable hands of my daughter and Lizette."

Lady Anne spoke up. "Where are you going?"

"I need to speak to Lord Everleigh about a bill that was introduced into Parliament this afternoon," Lord Ashington explained.

"You need to do so tonight, of all nights?" Lady Anne asked.

"It is the perfect time to do so."

Lady Anne gave him a chiding look. "Very well, but don't be gone for too long. Rosamond needs her guardian."

"That is why she has you," Lord Ashington said with a wink.

As the marquess walked off, Lady Anne turned to face Rosamond with a smile on her face. "You did well. I could see the looks of envy on the women's faces when you stepped into the ballroom."

"Why do I wish them to be envious of me?" Rosamond inquired.

"Have you learned nothing from me?" Lady Anne asked. "To be the diamond of the first water means you are far superior to the other debutantes."

"But I am not superior to anyone, and I do not have such lofty expectations to believe that I will receive such an honor."

"We shall see," Lady Anne murmured.

Lizette shook her head, causing the curls that framed her face to sway back and forth. "Just be yourself and try to enjoy yourself this evening," she advised.

"That is precisely what we don't want," Lady Anne said. "A young woman does not simply enjoy herself at a ball. It is a strategic game to determine who will come out on top."

"But I do not want to come out on top," Rosamond contended.

"With every interaction, every smile, you will prove to Society that you deserve your place amongst them," Lady Anne explained.

Rosamond knew there was no point in trying to argue with Lady Anne since it would get her nowhere. She had learned that Lady Anne was a proud woman with strong opinions, but her heart was usually in the right place.

Her eyes left Lady Anne's and she scanned the hall. All the women were elegantly dressed, and many wore exquisite diamond necklaces around their necks. Just one of those necklaces would feed her village for a whole month, she surmised. Even the pearls around her neck would fetch a pretty penny, but she had borrowed them from Lady Anne. The only thing of value that she had was her mother's thin gold wedding band that she wore on her right hand.

Lady Anne's voice drew back her attention. "Here comes Lady Brighton and her son, Lord Brighton. He would make a fine match for you."

Rosamond followed Lady Anne's gaze and saw Lord Brighton. He was a short man with a thin mustache. His ears fanned out from his face and his cheeks were noticeably red.

Lady Brighton and her son came to a stop next to Lady Anne and she said, "Good evening, Anne."

Lady Anne tipped her head in acknowledgement. "Amelia," she greeted.

"My son was hoping for an introduction to Miss Hendre," Lady Brighton said, gesturing towards him. "Weren't you, Son?"

Lord Brighton bobbed his head ardently. "Nothing would please me more," he replied, his eyes not straying from Rosamond.

"Very well," Lady Anne said. "Lord Brighton, allow me the privilege of introducing you to my father's ward, Miss Hendre."

Knowing what was expected of her, Rosamond dropped into a low curtsy and murmured, "My lord."

Lord Brighton bowed. "Enchanted."

They stared at one another, awkwardly, before Lady Brighton said, "My son was hoping to dance with you on the next set."

"Mother," Lord Brighton grumbled, "I can speak for myself."

"Then do so," Lady Brighton responded, her lips pressing into a thin line.

Lord Brighton offered Rosamond an apologetic smile. "My mother is rather zealous, but she wasn't wrong in her assumption that I would like to dance with you. Dare I ask if you are available for the next set?"

Rosamond graciously smiled. "I would be honored, my

lord." She felt elated at the thought she had secured her first dance.

"Wonderful. I will return to collect you when the next set begins." Lord Brighton turned towards his mother and offered his arm. "Shall we, Mother?"

Lady Brighton accepted his arm and they disappeared back into the crowd.

Leaning closer to Rosamond, Lady Anne said, "That went very well. Don't you agree?"

Rosamond shrugged. "Lord Brighton seems like a nice enough man."

"A nice enough man?" Lady Anne repeated. "He is influential in Parliament, and it is rumored that he has an income of ten thousand pounds a year."

"Yes, but what sort of man is he?"

Lady Anne looked baffled by her question. "Why does it matter what sort of man he is?" she asked. "He is a viscount."

"I am more concerned if he is kind," Rosamond pressed.

"He does not appear to be *un*kind," Lady Anne replied.

Rosamond turned to her sister for help. Would Lizette understand why she was asking these questions?

Lizette's eyes held compassion. "You will have to excuse Anne but she is of the mindset that titles are of the utmost importance."

"That is not entirely true. Need I remind you that I married for love, and not a title?" Lady Anne said. "Furthermore, I would have never invited Lord Brighton if I could not vouch for his character."

"Pray tell, tell me one thing you know about Lord Brighton, other than he is a viscount?" Lizette asked, a teasing tilt to her voice.

Lady Anne conceded with a sigh. "Perhaps I don't know much about the man, but I know his mother. Is that not good enough?"

"Not in this case. Rosamond deserves a man that will love

her above all else, regardless of his position in Society," Lizette replied.

"Why can she not have both, as you have?" Lady Anne asked.

As Lizette went to reply, Tristan approached them with his friend, Lord Roswell, by his side. He came to a stop next to his wife and kissed her cheek.

"I see all that worrying on Rosamond's part of falling did not come to fruition," Tristan teased.

Rosamond grinned. "I have yet to take the dance floor."

Lord Roswell chuckled. "I have faith in you," he said. "You do not strike me as a young woman who would lose her footing on the dance floor."

"Thank you," Rosamond said. She was grateful for the easy friendship that she had developed with Lord Roswell since he had helped save her and Lizette from her ex-fiancé.

Tristan interjected, "We saw you were speaking to Lord Brighton and we hope you do not seriously entertain him as a suitor."

"That is rather presumptuous to assume he would be interested in me, considering we just met," Rosamond said.

Tristan shifted in his stance before saying, "Lord Brighton placed a bet in the book at White's that he would secure you as a bride by the end of the Season."

"Why would he do such a thing?" Rosamond asked.

"Some men can't help themselves," Lord Roswell replied. "They truly believe there is no harm or foul by placing a bet in the book since it is only seen by the members of the club."

"That is despicable," Rosamond muttered.

"We won't disagree with you there," Tristan said.

Rosamond glanced in the direction that Lord Brighton had disappeared. "Surely I can't be expected to dance with him now."

"But you must!" Lady Anne urged. "By not dancing with

him, you would be doing yourself a great disservice. You would look petty."

Lizette nodded. "I agree with Anne."

"You do?" Rosamond asked.

Her sister gave her an amused look. "I don't know why you sound so surprised. Anne is right. By not dancing with Lord Brighton, Society dictates that you forego dancing with anyone this evening, and it could greatly diminish your chances of finding a suitor."

"Am I just to pretend that I know nothing about the bet?" Rosamond asked.

"Precisely," Lizette replied. "Go on being your charming self, and once the dance is done, you don't have to ever engage with Lord Brighton again."

"I am not very good at pretending," Rosamond said.

With a knowing look, Lizette responded, "It begins to become easier with each passing moment when you know what it is that you are fighting for."

Rosamond knew that it was time to concede. She would just have to pretend that all was well when she danced with Lord Brighton. After all, the next set was the quadrille so there wouldn't be much chance to converse anyways. She just had to keep a smile on her lips and be mindful to keep things cordial.

After all, this is what she had wanted- to be a part of Society. And she didn't want to let anyone down, including herself.

Malcolm was pleased. Miss Rosamond Hendre was a beautiful young woman with blonde hair, fair skin and high cheekbones. But as he watched her from across the room, he was convinced that she smiled entirely too often to be of a serious nature. Most likely, she just had a pretty face, but not much substance to her. Which was fine by him. He wasn't looking for a love match. He just needed to marry her.

The pesky question that was on his mind was how he was going to secure an introduction. He didn't know Lord Ashington or his daughter, Lady Anne, well enough to approach them for one so he would need to seek out one of his friends to do the honor.

He had great confidence that he could charm Miss Hendre once he spent some time with her. Women were all the same. All they really cared about was flattery. They were vain creatures, and he knew what it took to garner their attention. It was a tried-and-true formula for him. It was a shame how easily it worked to secure a woman's affection.

Malcolm leaned against the column as he watched Miss Hendre dance a set with Lord Vaughn. He wasn't worried about him. Lord Vaughn was tall and slender, reminding him of a scarecrow, and possessed only a rudimentary intelligence. Miss Hendre was no doubt dancing with him out of obligation and not because she could actually fall for the unfortunate-looking man.

A servant passed by with flutes of champagne and Malcolm reached out to claim one. He brought the drink to his lips and tried to think of all the things that he could say to Miss Hendre that would capture her attention. He could always compliment her dress. No, she had no doubt already heard that one many times over the course of this evening. He could tell her how alluring she looked this evening and wait for her to blush demurely.

His eyes scanned over the crowded ballroom, and he saw many young women glancing his way, and offering him coy smiles. He knew all too well that he was considered one of the most eligible bachelors and he enjoyed the attention that came with it. Ladies would whisper enviously behind their fans as he waltzed with the most beautiful women in the room.

But now his priorities had shifted. He turned his attention

back towards Miss Hendre and saw her laugh at something Lord Vaughn had said. No doubt she was being polite because Lord Vaughn was rather dull.

Lord Brighton came to stand by him and followed his gaze. "She is quite lovely, is she not?"

Malcolm feigned ignorance. "Whom are you speaking of?"

"Miss Hendre," Lord Brighton replied. "She is a rather remarkable young woman that I had the pleasure of dancing the first set with."

"You don't say," Malcolm muttered.

"We had an undeniable connection and I asked for permission to call upon her tomorrow," Lord Brighton shared as he puffed out his chest.

Malcolm glanced over at the viscount. He didn't count Lord Brighton as one of his friends, but he was rather an acquaintance… an infuriating acquaintance. "Why exactly are you telling me this?" he asked.

"Because I have decided to take Miss Hendre as my wife."

"Interesting." Malcolm couldn't resist taking a jab at him by asking, "Does your mother know this?"

Lord Brighton bristled. "Mother has no say in the matter."

He doubted that was the case, but he decided to take pity on the man. "Regardless, I also intend to pursue Miss Hendre."

"You will lose."

"And why is that?" Malcolm asked.

Taking a step closer, Lord Brighton said, "Once Miss Hendre hears of your reputation with the ladies, she will want nothing to do with you."

Malcolm gave him a bored look. "What do you know about my reputation?"

"All I know is that you are rather fond of the ladies."

"Are you not?" Malcolm asked.

Lord Brighton tilted his chin haughtily. "I am looking for a woman above reproach to be my viscountess and Miss Hendre fits that bill."

Malcolm grew tired of Lord Brighton's pretentious attitude. "I daresay that once Miss Hendre hears about the special bond you share with your mother, she won't want anything to do with you."

"There is nothing wrong with the relationship I have with my mother," Lord Brighton contended.

"Well, you have nothing to worry about, then," Malcolm said before brushing past him. He didn't truly consider Lord Brighton a threat to his goal of marrying Miss Hendre, but he could cause some problems, especially if the man revealed his affinity for the ladies. He wasn't a rake by any means, but he did enjoy spending time with beautiful women. And there was no shame in that, either.

The music wound down and Malcolm watched as Lord Vaughn escorted Miss Hendre off the dance floor. The moment she reached her aunt, she was once again surrounded by her legion of admirers.

"How pathetic," he muttered under his breath. These men were fawning over Miss Hendre, and she no doubt was enjoying every minute of it.

He saw Lord Roswell was standing back and he was speaking to Mr. Tristan Westcott. Perhaps it was time for him to be introduced to Miss Hendre and lessen the competition. Once it was evident that he set his cap on Miss Hendre, he had no doubt many of the gentlemen would bow out.

He crossed the room and came to a stop next to Lord Roswell as he waited to be acknowledged.

Lord Roswell turned towards him. "Good evening, Brentwood," he greeted. "Have you met Mr. Tristan Westcott, heir presumptive to Lord Ashington?"

"I have not had the pleasure," he said as he tipped his head at Mr. Westcott.

Mr. Westcott responded in kind before he walked off.

Malcolm lifted his brow at Lord Roswell, hoping for an explanation.

Lord Roswell chuckled. "You will have to excuse my friend, but he is a man of very few words," he shared.

"It would appear so." He hesitated before saying, "I saw you conversing with Miss Hendre earlier. Would you be so kind as to introduce me to her?"

Lord Roswell grew solemn. "No, I do not think that is a good idea."

"Whyever not?"

"Miss Hendre is an innocent and I have great respect for her," Lord Roswell said. "I do not think she is interested in a dalliance with you."

"I am not looking for a dalliance. I'm looking for a wife."

Lord Roswell crossed his arms over his chest and his critical gaze swept over Malcolm. "What of Lady Susan?" he asked. "Did you not set your cap on her?"

"I did, but my circumstances have changed."

"Meaning?"

"I would rather not say," Malcolm replied. He didn't wish to reveal that his family was in dire straits.

Lord Roswell's eyes left his and swept over the room. "There are plenty of other young women in this very room that would love to be a countess one day. Why not bother one of them?"

"I would prefer Miss Hendre."

"Why is that, exactly?" Lord Roswell pressed.

"My reasons are my own." Why was his friend being so blasted stubborn about providing an introduction? He had never had such qualms before. Did Lord Roswell want Miss Hendre for himself?

Lord Roswell uncrossed his arms and brought them to his sides. "You should know that Miss Hendre is a clever young woman and will see through any blarney that you attempt to throw her way."

"Does this mean you will provide the introduction?" he asked hopefully.

"Are your intentions truly honorable?" Lord Roswell asked.

Malcolm nodded. "They are."

Lord Roswell sighed. "Very well, but don't make me regret this." He waved his hand as he started walking away. "Follow me."

Malcolm was elated by the prospect of being introduced to Miss Hendre. It was only a matter of time before she was enamored with him.

Lord Roswell stopped next to Miss Hendre and waited for a moment as she conversed with another gentleman.

Once she stopped speaking, she turned her attention towards Lord Roswell and smiled. "Lord Roswell," she greeted cordially.

Lord Roswell returned her smile. "I have not forgotten about the dance you owe me."

"Neither have I."

Gesturing towards him, Lord Roswell said, "Miss Hendre, I would like to introduce you to my friend, Lord Brentwood."

Miss Hendre dropped into a curtsy. "Lord Brentwood."

He bowed. "It is a pleasure to meet you."

"Are you enjoying yourself this evening?" Miss Hendre asked as her steady gaze held his.

"I would enjoy it more if I could dance with you," he said.

Miss Hendre gave him an apologetic look. "I'm sorry, my lord, but my dances are all spoken for this evening."

"I am sure that I can convince one of your admirers to forego his dance with you so I might have the honor," he said flirtatiously.

"That would be intolerably rude of me to allow such a thing."

"But it isn't uncommon to do such a thing," he pressed. To

further entice her, he smiled his most dashing smile; the one that always worked on the ladies.

Miss Hendre smiled sweetly. Almost too sweetly. "Yes, but, unlike you, my word means something, Lord Brentwood."

As he opened his mouth to respond, she shifted her gaze towards another gentleman and started speaking to him.

What had just happened? Miss Hendre had just dismissed him out of hand.

Lord Roswell placed a hand on his shoulder and leaned in. "Your mouth is open, Malcolm," he whispered.

Malcolm closed his mouth and stormed off. How dare Miss Hendre speak to him in such a fashion. She may be Lord Ashington's ward, but he was heir to an earldom and demanded respect.

He walked onto the veranda and rested his hands on the iron railing that encircled it. What a pretentious young woman! He deserved far better treatment than what she had shown him.

Lord Roswell's voice came from behind him. "I tried to warn you about Miss Hendre."

"You could have warned me that she was so pretentious."

"Pretentious?" Lord Roswell repeated with a shake of his head. "No, that does not describe Miss Hendre at all."

"How would you describe her, then?"

"Kind. Loyal. Stubborn."

"She wasn't very kind to me."

Lord Roswell came to stand next to him. "You were asking her to rid herself of a dance partner so she could dance with you," he said. "I know most of the women of your acquaintance would do such a thing, but not Miss Hendre."

"Does she not know who I am?"

"Frankly, I don't think she cares," Lord Roswell replied. "Titles mean very little to her."

"That is absurd and couldn't possibly be true. Everyone cares about their position in Society."

"If you really are interested in Miss Hendre, you will need to make more of an effort," Lord Roswell advised.

Malcolm pushed off from the railing. "I have never had to work to secure a woman's affections before and I refuse to start now."

With a shake of his head, Lord Roswell said, "Then you are associating with the wrong women, and I strongly encourage you to stay away from Miss Hendre."

"Why is that?"

"Because Lord Ashington is not a man that I would want to trifle with."

As his friend walked back into the ballroom, Malcolm stared at his retreating figure and wondered if he had approached this all wrong. Lord Ashington was a very busy man and he doubted that he had time for a ward to be underfoot. He would meet with the marquess and he would ask for Miss Hendre's hand in marriage. He had little doubt that Lord Ashington would promptly recognize what an advantageous match it would be for both of them. With any luck, he would be able to post the banns that very day.

Miss Hendre may have dismissed him this evening, but he would like to see the look on her face when Lord Ashington told her that they were engaged.

Chapter Three

Rosamond reluctantly blinked her eyes open as the sun streamed into her bedchamber. She had danced well into the morning hours, and she was exhausted. But she knew what was expected of her and she needed to prepare for callers.

A thrill of excitement coursed through her at the thought she would have gentlemen callers. She had met the most delightful gentlemen last night and had savored every glorious moment of her coming out ball. It had been surreal and even Lady Anne was pleased with her performance.

The only plight had been when she was introduced to Lord Brentwood. What an arrogant man! He was rather handsome with his strong jaw, straight nose and broad shoulders, but she had little doubt that he used his attractiveness to achieve his purposes. He had thought she was so weak of a woman that she would do his bidding upon his request. Fortunately, after she had dismissed him, she saw him leaving the ball shortly thereafter. Good riddance. She hoped that she would never have to see Lord Brentwood again.

The door opened and her aunt stepped into the room. "Good morning... er... afternoon," she greeted. "I daresay that you have slept the day away."

Rosamond sat up in bed and rested her back against the wall. "In my defense, I didn't go to sleep until very early this morning."

"You do not have to explain yourself to me."

"But I feel as if I must."

Walking over to the wardrobe, Aunt Betsey retrieved a pale green gown. "Lady Anne has requested your presence in the drawing room," she informed her niece.

Rosamond went to place her feet over the side of the bed. "Have there been any callers for me?"

"Yes, and they are waiting for you to make an appearance."

Rosamond blinked. "They are here? Now?"

Aunt Betsey smiled. "Why do you sound so surprised?" she asked. "I thought you told me that your ball was a roaring success."

"It was, but I didn't dare to presume gentlemen callers would arrive so early."

"It is hardly early."

Rosamond rose and removed her dressing gown. "Then we must hurry. I do not want to make them wait too long."

As her aunt began to dress her, she said, "You weren't very talkative this morning when you were preparing for bed."

"That is because I was utterly exhausted," Rosamond admitted. "All I could think about was closing my eyes and going to sleep."

"I am glad that you had such an enjoyable evening."

"It was more than that. It was... perfect."

Her aunt stepped back and walked over to the dressing table. She patted the back of the chair, encouraging Rosamond to sit down.

Rosamond did her bidding and sat down. "I do not think I could have planned a more lovely evening," she revealed. "I met the most remarkable gentlemen, and they were all so attentive to me."

"Well, it was your ball," Aunt Betsey teased.

"It was more than that," Rosamond said. "I felt like a princess last night. I now know how Princess Charlotte must feel like every day."

Her aunt picked up a brush and began to work on her long, blonde tresses. "Did you find a gentleman that you favor?"

An image of Lord Brentwood came to her mind, but she quickly banished the thought. Where had that thought even come from? He was the last man that she would ever favor. His cockiness appeared to know no bounds.

"It is too early to tell, but last night proved promising," she replied.

Her aunt placed the brush down and started pulling her hair into an elaborate chignon. Once she was finished, she took a step back and said, "It is time for you to greet your suitors."

"They are hardly my suitors." Rosamond rose and smiled as a thrill of excitement coursed through her. "Wish me luck."

"Just be yourself and everything will work out precisely the way it should be," her aunt encouraged.

"You always make it sound so easy."

"Life is hard, but if you greet it with a grateful heart, life has a tendency of working itself out for your benefit."

Rosamond gave her aunt a grateful smile before she departed from her bedchamber. As she started to descend the stairs, she couldn't believe the sheer number of flowers that filled the entry hall. She felt as if she belonged in a flower shop.

Brownell stepped into the hall with a bouquet of flowers in his hand. "It is good to see you out and about, Miss. I trust you slept well."

"I did," she replied.

Brownell placed the flowers onto a side table. "I will place the rest of the flowers in the parlor, if you have no objections."

"There are more of them?" she asked in disbelief.

With a decisive nod, he replied, "Yes, Miss."

"The parlor will work just fine, then."

Rosamond continued on to the drawing room but came to a stop outside of the door. She put a hand to her stomach as she attempted to calm her nerves. She didn't quite know why she was suddenly nervous. This is what she had been preparing for from the moment Lady Anne started giving her lessons on propriety nearly a month ago.

Taking a deep breath for courage, she stepped into the drawing room and saw Lord Vaughn, Lord Brighton and Mr. Stone sitting around Lady Anne.

Lady Anne glanced over at her when she walked into the room. Her eyes flickered with relief. "I am so glad that you could join us," she said.

The men promptly stood and turned to greet her.

After she politely greeted them with a tip of her head, she went to sit down next to Lady Anne and the men returned to their seats.

Lady Anne shifted on the settee and said, "Lord Vaughn was just telling me the most delightful anecdote about his sister."

"Is that so?" Rosamond asked as she turned her attention towards Lord Vaughn.

Lord Vaughn puffed out his chest. "Yes, my sister received an autograph from none other than Lord Byron."

Rosamond brought a smile to her face, but it was forced. She had never understood the fascination of collecting autographs, but it was a pastime that some women preferred. Knowing that Lord Vaughn was waiting for a reply, she settled on, "That is remarkable." She hoped her words sounded somewhat believable.

"My sister is tickled pink," Lord Vaughn said.

"As well as she should be," Lady Anne remarked. "I am sure that his autograph is a boon to her collection."

Lord Vaughn nodded. "She has also written to Wellington but she has yet to receive a reply."

"That is not surprising since he is busy fighting a war," Rosamond said.

"Perhaps, but I know my sister will be terribly disappointed if he doesn't reply," Lord Vaughn responded. "I would hate for it to discourage my sister, especially since it is best for young women to remain busy while they are in pursuit of a husband."

Rosamond fought hard not to frown, but she found it nearly impossible to do so. "May I ask how old your sister is?"

"She is seventeen," Lord Vaughn replied.

"Do you not worry that she is too young to get married?" Rosamond asked.

Lord Vaughn furrowed his brow, as if he had never considered this before. "It is best for women to marry young so they haven't had time yet to develop pesky traits or become too opiniated."

Rosamond pressed her lips together as she resisted the urge to tell Lord Vaughn that he was utterly ridiculous. He spoke as if a woman having an opinion was akin to a disease. Why couldn't women express their opinions without the risk of being labeled as difficult or a bluestocking?

As she wrestled with her thoughts, a maid walked in with a tea service and placed it on the table in front of her.

"Would you care for me to pour?" the maid asked.

Lady Anne shook her head. "No, thank you," she replied. "Miss Hendre will see to serving her guests."

The maid dropped into a curtsy and departed from the room without another word.

Rosamond moved to sit on the edge of the settee and poured three cups of tea. As she handed them to the gentlemen, they murmured their gratitude.

For a few moments, no one spoke as they sipped their tea, and Rosamond was grateful for that. She hoped that Lord

Vaughn was done spouting nonsense. She didn't know how much longer she could hold her tongue.

Lord Brighton leaned forward and placed his teacup down onto the tray. "My mother had wished to accompany me today, but she had a previous commitment."

"That is most unfortunate," Lady Anne said. "Please inform your mother that she was dearly missed."

"I will pass along your well wishes," Lord Brighton responded.

Mr. Stone spoke up. "Would you be so kind as to play a piece for us on the pianoforte?"

Rosamond gave him an apologetic smile. "I'm afraid I have only started on my lessons for the pianoforte so my abilities are limited."

"How unfortunate," Mr. Stone muttered as he brought the teacup up to his lips. The displeasure was clearly written on his face.

"My mother is rather proficient at the pianoforte and has even been known to compose her own music," Lord Brighton shared.

"That is quite the feat," Lady Anne acknowledged.

Lord Vaughn leaned back in his seat. "May I ask what occupies your time, Miss Hendre?"

"I adore gardening," Rosamond replied.

With a disapproving look, Lord Vaughn said, "My sister would never do something that would soil her hands."

Rosamond knew what would appease Lord Vaughn since Lady Anne had shown her the many pastimes that were appropriate for ladies, but she didn't care much for this pretentious lord. He had behaved quite differently last night at the ball when they were dancing. But now that he was here, she had little doubt that they would not suit.

Before she could speak, Lord Brighton remarked, "My mother enjoys toiling in her garden at our country estate. She says it provides her with a sense of peace."

She knew that Lord Brighton was coming to her rescue, but she did not need his help. Furthermore, she did not think she could listen to one more comment about his mother. Did he even realize that he kept talking about her?

Lord Brighton held out his teacup. "May I have more tea?" he asked. "I have been rather parched as of late."

Rosamond accepted his teacup and poured him more tea. As she handed him back the teacup, their fingers brushed up against one another and she was quite certain that Lord Brighton did so on purpose.

Lord Brighton took a sip of his tea, then said, "My mother would greatly approve of this tea. She does not enjoy bland tea."

Four. That was the fourth comment that Lord Brighton had made about his mother. Did he not hear himself speak?

The long clock chimed in the corner and Rosamond didn't think this afternoon could get much worse.

Malcolm exited his coach and took a moment to admire Lord Ashington's grand three-level townhouse. It was one of the finest ones in Town with the red-brick arches over the sash windows complementing the brown brick.

He approached the main door and used the knocker to tap on the door.

The door was promptly opened and the butler greeted him with a solemn expression. "May I help you?"

Malcolm retrieved the calling card from his waistcoat pocket and extended it towards the butler. "Is Lord Ashington available for callers?"

The butler accepted the card and opened the door wide. "Please come in, my lord," he encouraged. "If you will wait in the entry hall, I will be just a moment."

Malcolm stepped inside and glanced up at the mural on the ceiling. He had never been inside of Lord Ashington's townhouse before, but he had heard about the grandeur of it. The butler disappeared down a hall, his heels clipping on the polished marble, and he was left alone.

He heard voices drifting out of a room that was just off the entry hall and he was curious to see if he could catch a glimpse of Miss Hendre. He walked over to the door and peered in. He saw Miss Hendre was sitting next to Lady Anne on a settee and she had three gentlemen callers that seemed to hang on her every word.

No doubt, she loved being the center of attention, he thought. After all, women were nothing if not predictable. They reveled in their own vanity.

The butler returned to the entry hall. "Lord Ashington will see you, my lord," he said before he spun on his heel.

Malcolm followed the butler down the hall that was lined with gold-framed portraits. The butler stopped outside of an opened door and indicated he should go inside.

As he stepped into the room, he saw Lord Ashington was sitting at his desk and he had books opened in front of him. The marquess had his head down and he was writing something.

"Give me a moment," Lord Ashington said, not bothering to look up.

Malcolm stepped further into the room and came to a stop in front of the desk. Lord Ashington appeared rather busy, and he knew this boded well for him. After all, he had no time to tend to a ward since he was hailed as a champion for the poor and needed to focus on politics.

Lord Ashington put the quill down and looked up. "How can I help you, Lord Brentwood?" he asked.

Malcolm went to sit down on an upholstered armchair. "I am not sure if you know who I am, but I am the eldest son of Lord Everton."

"I know who you are," Lord Ashington responded, "but my question is- why are you here?"

"I was hoping to speak to you about your ward, Miss Hendre."

Lord Ashington closed one of the books in front of him. "I see, and what do you want with Miss Hendre?" he asked in an annoyed tone.

Malcolm shifted uncomfortably in his seat. The marquess was not being particularly welcoming but that didn't mean he wouldn't welcome what he had to say.

"I find myself in a position that I require a wife," Malcolm started, "and I have come to discuss the possibility of a wedding contract between me and Miss Hendre." There. He had said what he had intended to say. Now, he just had to sit back and wait while Lord Ashington considered it.

To his surprise, Lord Ashington promptly said, "No."

Malcolm's brow shot up. He hadn't expected to be dismissed so readily. "My lord, if I may, I will be an earl one day and…"

Lord Ashington put his hand up, stilling his words. "I do not care if you are a prince," he said. "I am not arranging a marriage for Miss Hendre. I wish for her to marry for love."

"Love?" he huffed. "Surely, you cannot be in earnest?"

"Miss Hendre is a remarkable young woman and I trust her judgment on the matter."

"You cannot allow a woman to make such a serious decision. They are fickle creatures, and they use their emotions entirely too often."

Lord Ashington leaned back in his seat, his expression giving nothing away. "I see that you are not acquainted with Miss Hendre."

"I spoke to her briefly at the ball last night."

"She must have left a lasting impression on you for you to be here."

"You could say that." He decided to leave out his true

thoughts on Miss Hendre and her questionable behavior last evening.

The marquess considered him for a moment before saying, "If you want to marry Miss Hendre, you will need to convince her yourself."

Malcolm frowned. This was not the outcome he was hoping for, but he wasn't ready to concede. He would just try a different argument. "My lord, you are a busy man and you do not have the time for a ward. I think we both can agree that a marriage between Miss Hendre and me would be advantageous. By agreeing to this union, you can wipe your hands of Miss Hendre and I will take her."

Rising, Lord Ashington walked over to the drink cart and asked a question of his own. "Would you care for something to drink?"

"No, thank you."

Lord Ashington picked up the decanter and poured himself a drink. Once he picked up his glass, he asked, "Why do you believe I wish to wipe my hands of Miss Hendre?"

"You are generally regarded as a champion for the poor and are engaged in important work in Parliament. I have no doubt that occupies all of your time." He hoped by stroking the marquess' ego that he would see the validity of his argument.

Lord Ashington took a sip of his drink, then said, "You are not incorrect in that assumption, but my daughter has been tending to Miss Hendre. So you see, there is no rush to marry off Miss Hendre to the first gentleman that proposes marriage."

"If Miss Hendre married me, she would one day be a countess."

"I am aware, but that means little to me." He lowered his glass to his side. "And I have no doubt that it would mean less to Miss Hendre."

Malcolm reared back. "Does she wish for a loftier title?"

The marquess chuckled. "No, you misunderstood me. Miss Hendre does not aspire for a title. She is far more interested in finding a love match this Season."

"I think that is foolish."

"And why is that?"

"Love is fleeting. For what is there one day, will be gone the next," Malcolm said. "It would be far better for Miss Hendre to marry for security."

"Is that what you are offering then- security?"

"It is," Malcolm said.

Lord Ashington's eyes grew reflective, and his words grew purposeful. "I want more for my ward. And as for love being fleeting, you are wrong. The moment I laid eyes on my wife, I was smitten. She took my heart with her when she died."

"My lord, I did not mean to imply that love does not exist, but it is rare in our circles."

"Yet it is obtainable, but one must first make an effort."

Malcolm rose. "I do believe that Miss Hendre and I would suit," he lied. He didn't think he could ever fall for a young woman such as Miss Hendre. He doubted she had a serious thought in her head.

Lord Ashington walked over to his desk and moved the books to make room for his drink. "My answer remains no, but that doesn't mean you can't take matters into your own hands."

"In what way?"

"You must convince Miss Hendre to marry you."

Malcolm stiffened. "I do not have time for games."

"Neither do I, and that is precisely what I think you are doing," Lord Ashington said. "If you had any real affection for Miss Hendre, you would be in the drawing room right now, and not bothering me with this nonsense."

"If I may—"

The marquess cut him off. "No, you may not. As you so eloquently pointed out earlier, I am a busy man, and I don't have time for this." He reached for the quill. "You are dismissed, Lord Brentwood."

Malcolm stared at the marquess for a long moment before he departed from the study. He was astonished that Lord Ashington was allowing Miss Hendre to choose her own husband. Did he not care for her future at all? To allow a lady to select her own husband was ludicrous. She would be distracted by emotions and those had no place in a marriage.

He intended to leave but his feet faltered in the entry hall. He was still in the same position that he was last night. He needed to marry Miss Hendre or else his family faced ruination.

Botheration.

He no more wanted to go into the drawing room than he wanted to chew glass. Trying to compete for a woman was beneath him. Women usually flocked to him, and he could have his pick of them. Except none of them had a dowry of twenty thousand pounds. Only Miss Hendre did, and that was extremely vexing.

Malcolm knew he would eventually need to marry to produce an heir, but he was not yet thirty. He had many years ahead of him to bear a son. But he was now in an impossible situation, and the only way out of it was to wed Miss Hendre.

As he muttered a few curse words under his breath, the butler approached him and asked, "Would you care for me to announce you, my lord?"

How did the butler know that he intended to see Miss Hendre? "Yes, that would be preferable," he replied.

The butler stepped into the drawing room and announced him. Malcolm reluctantly walked into the drawing room and saw Miss Hendre was watching him with pursed lips. She didn't look eager to see him and the feeling was mutual.

He bowed. "You are looking lovely, Miss Hendre," he said, hoping to disarm her with flattery.

She tipped her head demurely. "It is good to see you again, Lord Brentwood."

Liar. So that is how she was going to play this game.

Malcolm walked over and sat down on an upholstered armchair. The conversation went on around him and it was nothing short of boring. Lord Brighton was discussing his mother and how she loved Hyde Park during the Season.

He watched Miss Hendre as she nodded along, but she didn't appear to be that interested in what Lord Brighton was saying. Her eyes may have been looking straight ahead, but she seemed far away.

Her eyes darted to his and he realized that he had been caught staring. He cleared his throat and turned his attention towards Lord Brighton.

Lord Brighton stopped speaking and waited for Miss Hendre to respond.

She smiled. "You appear to have a rather close bond with your mother."

"I wouldn't say that," Lord Brighton said. "We are no closer than any son and mother are."

"Of course," Miss Hendre remarked graciously. "I just find it admirable that you love your mother so much that you know her favorite flower that grows in Hyde Park."

Lord Brighton puffed out his chest. "That is because I listen to what women are saying. My mother says I am an excellent listener."

Malcolm resisted the urge to look heavenward. Miss Hendre was just playing to Lord Brighton's vanity, and he was foolish enough to believe it was sincere.

Miss Hendre shifted her gaze towards him and asked, "Do you by chance know your mother's favorite flower, Lord Brentwood?"

"I do not, but I know about things that truly matter," Malcolm replied.

"Do you not think knowing your mother's favorite flower matters, then?" Miss Hendre pressed.

Malcolm shook his head. "In the grand scheme of things, knowing someone's favorite flower is a trite detail."

"You may consider it a trite detail, but to that person, it means a great deal," Miss Hendre argued.

"I assure you that my mother does not care a whit if I know what her favorite flower is."

"Then your mother is an anomaly," Miss Hendre said as she dropped his gaze.

Malcolm was not about to let Miss Hendre dismiss him again and have the last word. "We are in agreement since there is no one like my mother. She does not fall prey to the emotional trappings that befall most women."

Miss Hendre's eyes flashed with something that he perceived was annoyance. "Pray tell, what emotional trappings are those, my lord?"

"Women feel too deeply, and they are foolish enough to make decisions based upon those emotions," Malcolm said. "It is much more sensible to think like a man."

Mr. Stone lifted his teacup. "Hear, hear," he muttered.

The lines around Miss Hendre's lips tightened. "Why is it when a woman makes an argument that a man doesn't agree with then she is ruled as emotional?"

"Women have no place in trying to argue with a man since he uses reason, not emotion, to win," Malcolm said.

The same blasted sweet smile from last night came to Miss Hendre's lips. "Forgive me, but I'm afraid I must go lie down. I find that I have an adverse reaction to stupidity."

Lady Anne gasped. "Rosamond, that was uncalled for," she murmured. "You must apologize to Lord Brentwood."

"I apologize," Miss Hendre said without a hint of remorse. "But since I am a member of the weaker sex, I tend to speak before I think."

Miss Hendre abruptly rose and all the gentlemen stood.

Malcolm brought a hand up to his chest, feigning innocence. "I did not intend for my words to offend you, Miss Hendre."

"Of course not, Lord Brentwood," Miss Hendre said. "To do so, it would mean that I value your opinion."

Lady Anne jumped up and began to usher Miss Hendre towards the door. "I must insist that Rosamond retires for a spell. She is clearly not feeling like herself."

Malcolm watched as Miss Hendre walked out of the drawing room with her head held high. What a vexing woman. He knew that he had provoked her with his comments, but it was no less than she deserved.

Unfortunately, that was not how he intended the visit to go. He was supposed to be trying to convince her to let him court her, not push her away.

Chapter Four

With every step she took, Rosamond found herself growing increasingly agitated by that infuriating man- Lord Brentwood. What right did he have to come into her home and insult her so soundly? Was it because she had dismissed him last night?

She opened her bedchamber door and stormed inside. "Vexing, vexing man," she muttered under her breath.

Lady Anne spoke up from behind her. "Pray tell, what has gotten you so riled up?"

"It is that maddening man."

"I assume we are speaking about Lord Brentwood."

Rosamond tossed up her hands. "Who else would we be talking about?" she asked. "He was rude and arrogant and... impossible!"

"Yes, he was all those things but why did you let him get to you?"

"What am I supposed to do?"

Lady Anne sighed. "Do you not recall your lessons?"

"I could not just sit there and let him insult me so soundly," Rosamond said. "I would bet that *toshers* have better manners than that man."

Walking over to the settee, Lady Anne sat down. "There will always be men and women like Lord Brentwood but you must not let them win. By losing your composure, it reflects poorly on you, not them."

"Why did Lord Brentwood even come to call if he intended to act as he did?"

"Perhaps he felt slighted when you declined his offer to dance last night," Lady Anne suggested.

Rosamond placed her hand on her hip. "He wanted to rid me of one of my dance partners. I would never have done something so intolerably rude."

"I will agree that you did the right thing. Lord Brentwood put you in a difficult situation and you acted honorably."

"Yet that maddening man did not think so," Rosamond said. "He walked off in a fit."

Lady Anne patted the seat next to her on the settee. "Regardless, you cannot treat your guests with such curtness."

Rosamond sat down, being mindful to keep her back rigid. She knew Lady Anne did not approve of her slouching, for any reason. "I cannot abide that man."

"I do believe he was trying to get a rise out of you, as you attempted to do to him." Lady Anne gave her a knowing look. "Why else would you ask what his mother's favorite flower was?"

With a slight shrug of her shoulders, Rosamond responded, "Lord Brighton had no qualms with that."

"If Lady Brighton had her way, her son would be attached to her hip."

"He did mention his mother fourteen times during the course of our conversation."

"Oh, my, I hadn't realized it was quite so often."

Rosamond reached for the pillow that was behind her and placed it in her lap. "Truth be told, I was not enjoying myself even before Lord Brentwood arrived."

"Why is that?"

"Those gentlemen were awful," Rosamond said. "They rambled on with their stories and I was forced to grin and bear it."

"They acted no differently than the other gentlemen of the *ton*."

Rosamond groaned as she leaned back. "That is what I was afraid of. Frankly, I preferred when I danced with them because we spoke so little. The more I engaged with them, the more I wished they would stop talking."

"If you want me to feel sorry for you, then you will be sorely disappointed," Lady Anne said. "Besides, you are in the remarkable position of being able to choose your suitors. Not every lady is as fortunate as you."

"I know, but I just wish there was an easier way to wade through all the prospects."

Lady Anne gave her a chiding look. "A lady does not slouch, my dear."

Rosamond reluctantly straightened up in her seat. "I just hope that I never have to see Lord Brentwood again."

"I think that would be for the best for everyone." Lady Anne rose. "Now that is settled, shall we return to the drawing room?"

"Must I?"

"Do not let one person distract you from achieving your purposes," Lady Anne advised. "You have worked too hard to give up now."

"I don't want to give up, but I could use a break."

Lady Anne held her hand out. "Ladies are the epitome of grace and are excellent hosts, even at the expense of themselves."

Rosamond tossed the pillow behind her and slipped her hand into Lady Anne's. She knew that Lady Anne was just trying to help her, but she just wanted to wallow in self-pity for a moment. "I will go, but I do so under protest."

"Under protest it is," Lady Anne said as she helped Rosamond rise. "I assure you that this is for your own good."

"I must admit that it is much simpler to find a suitor in the countryside."

Lady Anne gave her a curious look. "May I ask how you met George or is that too hard to think about?"

"I do not mind," Rosamond replied. "A part of me will always love George, despite what he did to Lizette. Is that wrong of me?"

"I do not believe so. The heart is not one to easily forget."

Rosamond offered Lady Anne a grateful smile. "George and I met at a country dance," she said. "It was not nearly as fancy as the one that the gentry put on, but it was held at the local coaching inn. They cleared out the tables and brought in people to play music."

"You danced in a coaching inn?" Lady Anne asked, aghast.

"We did, and it was such a fun evening," Rosamond replied. "After that, George and I were inseparable for the next month or so. We became engaged shortly thereafter, but my mother did not approve of the union."

Lady Anne started walking towards the door. "What were her reasonings?"

"She did not think George was worthy of me, even though he was the grandson of a vicar," Rosamond replied. "She asked for us to wait to get married until we were absolutely certain that is what we wanted to do."

"Aren't you glad that she had the foresight to suggest that?"

"I am now, but at the time I was furious," Rosamond said. "Shortly thereafter, my mother started to show signs of sickness. She visited the apothecary in the next village over and he suspected that she had cancer."

Lady Anne placed a hand on her sleeve as they walked down the hall. "I remember watching my mother wither away right in front of me. It is not something that I would wish on my worst enemy."

"Nor I," Rosamond said as her heart grew heavy. "At times, I just miss her so much."

"I was forced to say my goodbyes to my mother over and over again as her mind slowly deteriorated."

"That sounds awful."

"It was, but I was not prepared to live a life without her." Lady Anne removed her hand and placed it on the railing as she descended the stairs. "I do hope that I will one day be as great as my mother was before the dementia consumed her."

Rosamond grew quiet. "I guess I should be grateful that my mother did not suffer towards the end."

"That is a blessing, at least in my mind."

As they walked into the drawing room, she saw Lord Brentwood standing next to the window, looking out towards the street, and his hands were clasped behind his back. What was he still doing here? Did he not have the good sense to leave as the other gentlemen did?

Lady Anne leaned in to her and whispered, "Behave, Rosamond."

Rosamond stopped and clasped her hands in front of her. "Lord Brentwood," she greeted, hoping her words sounded somewhat cordial, "what a pleasant surprise that you are still here."

Lord Brentwood turned to face her and bowed. "I couldn't leave without first offering my deepest apologies for how I acted earlier."

She wasn't fooled by his sudden transformation. What was he trying to achieve from apologizing?

As she tried to dissect what his nefarious plan could be, he took a step closer to her and said, "Say that you will forgive me."

Rosamond knew that he had put her in a most difficult position... again. If she refused to forgive him, then she looked petty and rude. He sounded genuine enough, but his eyes told a different story. They appeared to be challenging her to make the next move.

Well, she refused to be outplayed by such an infuriating man. If Lord Brentwood thought she was a simpering miss that he could control, then he would be wrong.

Bringing a smile to her face, she replied, "You are forgiven, Lord Brentwood."

His lips twitched. "Wonderful," he said. "May I be so bold as to ask you on a carriage ride with me tomorrow during the fashionable hour?"

Drats. She had no desire to spend additional time with him, but she could think of no polite reason to turn him down.

With her smile intact, she said, "I would greatly enjoy that."

"As will I, Miss Hendre." The smallest of smirks came to his lips, as if this had been his plan all along. "Until tomorrow, then."

She dropped into a curtsy. "Good day, Lord Brentwood."

He bowed and offered his goodbyes.

Once he had departed from the room, Rosamond walked over to the window to see if she could get a final glimpse of Lord Brentwood. She watched as he removed his top hat before he stepped into his awaiting coach.

What was he about? She suspected he no more wanted to go on a carriage ride with her than she wanted to go with him. So why had he asked her to go? And why during the fashionable hour?

Lady Anne came to stand next to her. "It would appear that Lord Brentwood wishes to become your suitor."

"Then he shall be sorely disappointed."

"He is rather handsome."

"Yes, vexingly so, but I am looking for more than just a handsome face."

Lady Anne let out a soft laugh. "It is ironic that the one man you want nothing to do with is the first man that invited you on a carriage ride."

"It isn't funny," she asserted. "He didn't invite me out of the kindness of his heart. He wants something; I am sure of it."

"Of course he wants something. You are an heiress. Any man would be lucky to marry you."

"I can assure you that the last person I would ever even consider marrying would be Lord Brentwood."

"I believe you," Lady Anne said, taking a step back. "Now, let us prepare to receive more callers."

"What if no one else comes?"

As if on cue, Brownell stepped into the room and announced, "Mr. Whitmore and Mr. Moore have come to call for Miss Hendre."

"Please send them in," Lady Anne ordered as she moved towards the settees.

A moment later, the two gentlemen walked into the room with bright smiles on their faces. They both appeared to be rather eager to be there.

"Welcome, gentlemen," Lady Anne greeted. "Once Miss Hendre takes a seat, we will invite you to join us for a cup of tea."

Lady Anne gave her an expectant look and Rosamond knew what her duty was. She was to pour the tea, smile and engage her guests in polite conversation. But she realized that she would never truly get to know a gentleman by discussing the state of the gardens or the weather.

It was becoming increasingly difficult to play the part of a lady when she had the strangest desire to buck tradition.

Malcolm had set out what he had intended to do. He had secured a carriage ride with Miss Hendre for tomorrow, during the fashionable hour. By doing so, his intentions would not be called into question, and he could begin to enact his plan to have Miss Hendre's heart turned towards him.

Now, he just needed to play the part of a devoted suitor. He would charm her so profusely that she wouldn't even know what happened. But first, he had to prepare himself for tomorrow. He found he quite liked antagonizing Miss Hendre, but he couldn't continue to do so if he wanted her to fall for him. He would need to play nice and remember that she was just a means to an end. This was not a love match by any means. He just needed a wife with a large dowry.

He walked up the steps of his townhouse and the door was promptly opened. "Welcome home, my lord," Osborne greeted.

"Is my father home?"

"No, but he intends to be home before supper."

Malcolm removed his top hat and extended it to the butler. "Very good," he said. "Please inform me at once when he returns home."

"Yes, sir." Osborne accepted the hat and lowered his voice. "You have a visitor."

His eyes strayed towards the drawing room. "Who is it?"

Osborne paused. "Your sister- Lady Enid Longbourn."

Taken aback, he asked in disbelief, "My sister is here?"

"She is, but..."

Malcolm didn't wait for him to finish as he strode over to the drawing room. He stepped into the room and stopped. There was no one in here. Where was she?

Osborne's voice came from behind him. "Lady Enid is waiting for you by the servants' entrance."

Turning to face the butler, he asked, "What is she doing there?"

"She assumed that she wouldn't be welcomed in your home," Osborne replied.

Enid wasn't wrong. Their father had disowned Enid the moment he had discovered she'd eloped with Mr. Longbourn and would be furious to discover that she had the nerve to return home. But that didn't mean he couldn't go speak to her.

"Do not breathe a word of this to my father," Malcolm ordered.

A relieved look came to Osborne's face. "I wouldn't dream of it, my lord."

The quickest way to the servants' entrance was by going out the main door and approaching it through the small courtyard on the side of the townhouse. He exited the townhouse and rounded the corner.

His steps faltered when he saw his sister's haggard appearance. She was dressed in tattered clothing, her brown hair was disheveled and she had dirt smudged on her cheeks. Her face was much thinner than he would have liked and her eyes were sunken in. She looked nothing like she did before she had eloped. Even the light in her eyes was gone, leaving behind a bleakness to them.

As he walked slowly towards her, Enid refused to meet his gaze and she wrapped her arms around her waist.

He stopped in front of her, and he couldn't help himself from blurting out, "What happened to you?" There were so many things that needed to be said between them, but there were far more pressing matters at hand. How had Enid come to be in such a state as this?

In a soft voice that he hardly recognized, she said, "I know I am the last person you wish to see but—"

He didn't let her finish before he pulled her into a tight embrace. "I have missed you, Sister," he murmured.

"I have missed you, too," she responded, her voice choking with emotion.

Malcolm could feel her relax into his arms, but he was alarmed by her thin frame. He leaned back and asked, "How have you come to this?"

Tears welled up in Enid's eyes. "My husband died and I had no one to turn to," she revealed. "The creditors came and took possession of our home, leaving me with nothing but the clothes on my back."

"What of his family?" he asked. "Couldn't you have lived with them?"

"They turned their backs on me," she said. "They claimed they didn't have the funds to care for another useless female."

"When was this?"

"Two months ago," Enid replied. "I have been living at a workhouse since I couldn't find work due to my lack of experience. Furthermore, my worn dress was not fancy enough to work in a shop, leaving me with no options."

"You should have come here straightaway and…" he started.

Enid put her hand up, stilling his words. "I have only come because my child is sick and needs a doctor. But I don't have the funds to pay for one."

His eyes widened at what she had just revealed. "You have a child?"

"I do," she replied. "She is a year old, and she is all that I have left. I can't lose her."

"You won't. I promise that." Malcolm placed a hand on her sleeve. "Where is your child now?" he asked.

"A friend at the workhouse is watching her for me. I had to leave early this morning to walk here," Enid replied.

"You walked all the way here?" he asked, glancing down at the worn boots on her feet.

"I did, because I could hardly afford a hackney," she replied. "Frankly, I didn't know what kind of welcome I would receive."

That was a fair statement. If his sister hadn't looked like

she had just been dredged through a sewer, his reaction to seeing her would have been much different. He had been hurt when Enid had abandoned him to elope, without so much as a goodbye. He loved his sister and only wanted what was best for her. But he couldn't bring himself to believe that a marriage between her and Mr. Longbourn had been in her best interest. She deserved better, and he wished he'd had the opportunity to tell her as much at the time. Quite frankly, he cared little for the scandal it caused to their family, despite his father's insistence that it tarnished their grand reputation.

Malcolm felt the bones peeking out from under her skin, prompting him to ask, "When was the last time you ate a meal?"

Her eyes grew downcast. "I took a bite of the food this morning, but I gave the rest to Marigold."

"I must assume that Marigold is your daughter."

"She is," Enid confirmed. "I felt she needed the food more than I did."

Malcolm removed his hand from her sleeve and went to open the door of the servants' entrance. He wasn't about to let his sister starve, not when they had ample amounts of food to go around. "Let's get you something to eat," he encouraged.

"I couldn't possibly go in there," she argued. "What if word got back to Father about my visit?"

"I am far more concerned about getting you some sustenance than worrying about Father's reaction."

Enid looked unsure. "I don't wish to be a burden."

"Too late," he teased. "Come along. I am sure Mrs. Booth has something prepared that you can eat."

He could see emotions flickering across her dirtied face and he was worried that she would refuse him. But to his pleasant surprise, she stepped inside and he followed her.

The tall, round cook looked up from kneading bread in surprise. "Lady Enid?" she asked in disbelief.

Enid shifted uncomfortably in her stance. "Hello, Mrs. Booth."

Mrs. Booth stared at her for a moment before she sprang into action. "You look like you could use a good meal," she said, reaching for a bowl. "Go sit down at the table and I will bring you some of the soup that is simmering."

Enid sat down as she was directed.

Malcolm claimed the seat across from her and asked, "Why didn't you come to me when your husband died?"

Lowering her gaze, she replied, "I was embarrassed… and ashamed."

"So you suffered in silence?" he asked.

Fresh tears appeared in Enid's eyes. "I wouldn't be here if it wasn't for Marigold. I just need a few coins and I will be on my way."

Malcolm shook his head. "I'm afraid that is impossible."

Enid's eyes grew sad. "You won't give me any money?"

"No, you misunderstood me," Malcolm said. "I cannot let you go on as you have been. I want to help you."

"But we both know that Father would never allow that."

"Let me deal with Father," he said.

Mrs. Booth placed a bowl of soup in front of Enid and a plate with a piece of buttered bread. "Eat up," she encouraged. "There is more if you want it."

Enid eagerly reached for the spoon and started eating the soup at a fast pace. It wasn't long before the bowl was empty, and she had placed a hand on her stomach.

"Perhaps I shouldn't have eaten the soup so fast," Enid said. "I am not used to such rich food anymore."

Malcolm didn't dare ask what she had been accustomed to eating at the workhouse. He had read about the unsavory conditions in the newssheets and how people died at an alarming rate. Sadly, no one seemed to care enough to do anything about it.

Mrs. Booth came to stand next to her. "Can I get you another bowl, my lady?"

Enid looked up at her with a grateful look. "I would like that very much, please."

As the cook went to do her bidding, Malcolm said, "We will return to the workhouse and retrieve Marigold at once. Then, I shall secure lodgings for you at a boarding house until I can convince Father to let you return home."

"I daresay that is an impossible feat."

"That doesn't mean I won't try."

Enid reached for the bread and tore a piece off. "Father will never allow me to return home."

"But your circumstances have changed now since you have a child- his grandchild."

"That won't matter to him." Enid glanced around the kitchen before asking, "What if you were to give me a job? It would be far preferable to be working here than the workhouse."

With a shake of his head, he said, "I am not going to give you a job."

"Why not?" she asked with a hint of defiance that proved to him that his sister wasn't completely lost to him. "It would be the perfect solution."

"You are the daughter of an earl—"

She spoke over him. "That eloped with someone far below her station. I have made my bed and now I need to lie in it."

"What of Marigold?" he asked. "Does she not deserve a better life?"

At the mention of her daughter's name, Enid's shoulders slumped, as if the weight of her burdens were too great for her to carry anymore.

Mrs. Booth came to stand next to the table. "Do not let your pride be the death of you," she counseled as she placed the bowl down on the table. "Take Lord Brentwood up on his offer to help you."

"It isn't that simple," Enid contended. "What if Father disowns you, too?"

He gave her a smug smile. "I am his heir," he reminded her. "It would take an act of Parliament for that to happen."

Enid pressed her lips together. "Father is incredibly stubborn."

"As am I."

Enid picked up her spoon. "It would be nice for Marigold to sleep on a bed again," she murmured. "She has done nothing wrong to deserve such a terrible life."

Malcolm reached over the table and placed his hand over hers. "This is not who you are. You deserve better than this."

"But it is what I have become."

"Then we must change that," Malcolm said. "Once you are finished eating, I will escort you back to the workhouse and we will remove Marigold from that vile place."

"I should warn you that the workhouse is in an unsavory part of town."

"I assumed as much."

Enid bit her lower lip. "Thank you, Malcolm," she said in a shaky voice. "Frankly, if it wasn't for Marigold, I don't think I would have had the will to carry on after my husband died."

Malcolm withdrew his hand and responded, "I am most thankful that you had Marigold then."

"She is my greatest joy," Enid said. The tenderness in her voice that was present every time she mentioned her daughter's name proved to Malcolm just how much she loved her child.

"I am looking forward to meeting my niece."

After Enid took a few bites, she put the spoon down and turned her attention towards Mrs. Booth. "Thank you for the soup. It was delicious."

Mrs. Booth smiled. "I have taken the liberty of packing up some biscuits for your journey to the workhouse."

"That was most thoughtful," Enid said.

Malcolm pushed back from his seat and rose. "I will go inform Osborne that we will require the coach at once."

Enid went to rise, but he waved her back down. "You remain here. The fewer servants that know about you being here, the better."

His sister nodded. "That is wise."

Malcolm smiled at his sister, relieved that she was here with him. They still had much to say to one another, but that could wait. The most important thing was that his sister was safe and far away from that workhouse.

"It will all work out; you will see," he encouraged. His words were for his benefit just as much as they were for Enid. It would not be an easy path that he was forging, but it had to be done.

"I have never taken you for being such an optimist," Enid said, a slight teasing tilt in her voice.

"Usually, I'm not, but I find in this particular case I am."

As he went in search of Osborne, Malcolm knew this would be an uphill battle with his Father, but he refused to abandon his sister and her child. He would ensure they were set up in a boarding house and Marigold would receive proper medical care. At least until they could return home.

Chapter Five

Malcolm watched his sister as she stared out the window of the coach. He couldn't quite believe that she was here with him. He had been furious when she had eloped with Mr. Longbourn but he never wished ill-will to fall upon her. In the two years that she had been gone, he had often thought about Enid, but he never made an attempt to contact her. He couldn't. What she had done had brought shame down upon her and their family. But that didn't mean he could stand by and let her- and her child- remain at a workhouse.

He knew that it would be a fight with his father to allow Enid to reside with them at the townhouse. Perhaps his heart would soften once he knew that he was a grandfather. Although his father would have been much more pleased if he had a grandson, but that was neither here nor there. Marigold deserved a better life than what she had been given.

Enid shifted her gaze to meet his. "I know what you are thinking," she said softly.

"I doubt that."

"You think I was intolerably stupid for eloping with John."

"I wasn't thinking that, but it is true," he replied. "How could you have chosen him over your own family?"

"I had no choice."

"Everyone has a choice," Malcolm argued.

Enid started fidgeting with her hands in her lap. "I had fallen so deeply in love with him that I had no choice but to follow the dictates of my heart."

"Love is a useless emotion. It makes people do foolish things."

Enid gave him a weak smile. "You have never been in love, I see."

"Of course not," he replied. "I am a sane man that has no grand illusions about marriage, love and whatnot."

"Love is not that simple. It is unexpected and changes everything."

Malcolm shook his head. "You have always tried to use emotions to explain yourself, but I prefer reason."

"Love cannot be explained by reason alone since it consumes you, body and soul."

"That is a ticklish argument because no one should choose love over security. Love will not pay the bills or keep the creditors at bay."

Enid nodded. "You are right," she said. "For a short period of time, we were happy."

"Were you so unhappy at home?"

"That had nothing to do with my decision. From the moment I met John, I knew my life had changed for the better."

"Even though you lived in squalor?"

"If Father would have released my dowry, we would have been quite comfortable, but he refused to do so," Enid said. "He even threatened John that he would call the magistrate if he ever returned to speak to him."

Malcolm lifted his brow. "What did you expect Father to do?" he asked. "You were the one that eloped in the middle of the night, courting scandal to fall upon our family's reputation."

"I didn't marry John to spite you or the family."

"No, you were just thinking of yourself as you always have," Malcolm said dryly. He knew his words were harsh, but they were the truth, nonetheless.

Enid pressed her lips together. "As opposed to how you are living?" she asked. "On the rare occasion I was able to find the Society page in the newssheets, I would read how you and your friends were cavorting all over Town."

"There is nothing wrong with my behavior since I behave like a perfect gentleman."

"We both know that is not true," Enid said. "You have always had a fondness for the ladies."

"Not anymore. I have decided it is time that I get a wife."

"A wife?" she repeated back in surprise. "You, the man who vowed never to fall prey to the parson's mousetrap?"

Malcolm did not take offense to Enid's lackluster response since it was a fair reaction. He had made his opinion known, on multiple occasions, of his poor view of matrimony. But his circumstances had changed, and he had no choice but to marry.

"Yes, and I have selected Miss Rosamond Hendre to have that honor," he shared.

Enid's brow furrowed. "That is an odd way of putting it, Brother," she said. "Has Miss Rosamond been receptive to this 'honor'?"

"Not yet, but she will be once I begin to woo her properly."

"I see, and why did you select this particular young woman to be your wife?"

Malcolm adjusted his cravat as he replied, "Because she has a dowry of twenty thousand pounds and is the ward of Lord Ashington."

"And?"

He gave her a blank look. "And what?"

With a pointed look, his sister asked, "Do you hold any affection for Miss Hendre?"

"Not at this time, but she isn't completely intolerable. In due time, I do believe we will grow to care for one another." At least he hoped that was the case.

Enid's eyes turned sad. "Does Miss Hendre know that you are offering a marriage of convenience?"

"It matters not, because I am giving her the opportunity to become a countess. Most young women would fall over themselves to achieve such a title."

"How noble of you," his sister muttered.

Malcolm felt himself growing irritated by his sister's responses. Why did his sister care who he married, anyways? This was his life, and he would do as he saw fit. "I am not going to argue with you," he said. "I am putting duty ahead of my own wants."

"I daresay that is a mistake. Love is always worth the gamble."

"Says the woman that has nothing and is living at the workhouse with a child in tow," Malcolm huffed.

Enid's eyes grew downcast.

Malcolm regretted his unkind words the moment that they had left his mouth. His sister had been through so much and she didn't need for him to constantly be throwing that back into her face.

As he opened his mouth to apologize, the coach came to a stop in front of a blackened two-level brick building that had fallen into disrepair. Most of the windows were cracked and some of them even had a sheet to cover up the openings. A crooked sign above the door read- *Tatterman's Workhouse, established 1811.*

Enid went to exit the coach but he placed his hand on her arm, stilling her.

"Allow me to go first," he encouraged.

She sat back down and nodded her acknowledgement.

Malcolm opened the door and stepped down onto the filthy, trash-filled pavement. He reached back to assist his sister and she came to stand next to him.

"It might be best if I go in and retrieve Marigold without your assistance," she said. "I'm afraid that your presence may cause some unwanted attention."

He reached for her hand and brought it into the crook of his arm. "You do not need to concern yourself with that."

Enid looked as if she were going to argue, but instead just bobbed her head. "Very well, then."

Malcolm approached the main door and reached for the handle. As he opened the door, a horrific smell wafted out of the workhouse, and he attempted to appear unaffected by the offending odor that was invading all of his senses.

His sister had no qualms with the smell and proceeded inside the dimly lit hall. Tables were set up and women were standing next to them, their backs to them, and they were busy with their tasks. No one seemed to speak but there was an occasional cough.

As his sister walked down the center of the hall, a short, burly man with a cane went to intercept her.

"What do we have here?" the man mocked as he stopped in front of her. "Did Miss Prig finally return home?" He glanced over her shoulder. "And I see you brought a dandy with you."

Malcolm went to respond but Enid spoke first. "I am just here to retrieve my child and I will be on my way," she said in a reserved tone.

The man slammed his cane against one of the tables, startling everyone in the room. "What gives you the right to come and go as you please?" he demanded.

"Please, Mr. Goggins, I meant no disrespect," Enid murmured.

"Well, you have a funny way of showing it." Mr. Goggins

brought his cane up and pointed it at Malcolm. "Who is this person?"

Enid gestured towards Malcolm, but her gaze remained downcast. "This is my brother, Lord Brentwood."

Mr. Goggins narrowed his eyes. "You mentioned nothing of a brother before, especially one with such a lofty title. How do I know if you are telling the truth?"

Malcolm decided he'd had enough of this man. He was entirely too full of himself for having such a lowly position. Taking a commanding step forward, he said, "My sister will be collecting her child and we will be on our way."

"I think not," Mr. Goggins responded. "Enid is my responsibility and I take that duty very seriously. She cannot come and go as she pleases. There is a hierarchy, and I am on top."

Malcolm placed a hand on his sister's shoulder and encouraged, "Go get Marigold while I deal with this man."

Mr. Goggins swiped his cane down to block Enid's path. "She is going nowhere," he growled.

Malcolm took a step closer to Mr. Goggins. "Allow my sister to pass or I will have no choice but to return with the magistrate."

"Be my guest," Mr. Goggins mocked as he performed an exaggerated bow, "but you should know that magistrates don't come to these parts of town."

"Well, fortunately for me, I noticed the sign above the door reads 'Tatterman's Workhouse'. It would be a shame if I spoke to Mr. Tatterman about the ill-treatment that you showed me and my sister," Malcolm said.

Mr. Goggins' eyes grew hesitant. "You are bluffing. You couldn't possibly know Mr. Tatterman."

With a flick of his wrist, Malcolm remarked, "He is a dear friend and I have no doubt he will not react kindly to your rude behavior. Most likely, he will dismiss you from your position here."

Pursing his lips, Mr. Goggins lowered the cane to his side

and addressed Enid. "Go retrieve your urchin and never come back. You are no longer welcome here."

Malcolm tsked. "That was not very kind. Try again."

Mr. Goggins clenched his jaw as he forced out his next words. "You are always welcome here."

Without saying a word, Enid hurried towards a door at the rear of the hall and disappeared through it. Mr. Goggins continued to glare at him, but he cared very little what this man thought of him. If he had his way, he would never see him- or this workhouse- again.

After a long moment, Enid appeared with her daughter protectively in her arms. "We should go," she urged as she approached him.

Malcolm didn't need to be told twice since he was more than eager to depart. He tipped his head at Mr. Goggins. "Good day to you."

He scoffed in response.

They exited the workhouse and stepped into their coach. Once they were situated, the footman closed the door and the coach started rolling away.

Malcolm took a moment to admire his niece who sat in Enid's lap. She had a full head of blonde hair, fair skin, and green eyes that were similar in color to her mother's. However, her cheeks were an alarming shade of pink.

Enid wrapped her arms around Marigold. "Thank you for what you did back there. Mr. Goggins is a vile man, but I can't find it in my heart to despise him since he did put a roof over my head when I needed it the most."

"Why didn't you come to me straightaway?" Malcolm asked. He knew he had asked this question, multiple times, but he wasn't satisfied with her response. Why hadn't she trusted him enough to come to him? "I would have helped you."

"I couldn't stand the thought of how you would look at me," she hesitated, "just as you are doing now."

"How am I looking at you?"

"With pity," Enid replied.

As he went to respond, Marigold let out a raspy cough and he leaned forward to touch her warm cheek. "She needs to be under a doctor's care at once."

"That would be most appreciated," Enid said as she let out a yawn. "Excuse me, I was up rather early this morning."

Surprising even himself, Malcolm held out his hands. "Would you like me to hold Marigold while you sleep?"

Enid arched an eyebrow. "You?"

"I can hold a baby," he defended.

"Have you ever held one before?"

Malcolm shook his head. "How hard could it be?" he asked. "Besides, you look as if you need to close your eyes for a moment."

"I do." Enid extended Marigold towards him. "Be gentle with her."

He moved the child to sit on his lap and she promptly leaned her head against him. And that was all it took for him to be charmed.

***

Rosamond was tired of balancing a book on top of her head. She had been caught slouching... again, and Lady Anne felt she needed more time focusing on her posture. Most of the lessons that Lady Anne engaged her in were worthwhile and she was fortunate to have her as a teacher. But she would be grateful if she never had to balance a book on top of her head ever again.

Lady Anne sat next to her, and she was explaining the order of precedence that goes along with the seating arrangements at a dinner party. It was a lesson that she had heard before, multiple times, in fact. She was all too aware of who would be seated first and where they would sit at the table.

Her eyes strayed towards the windows. How she wished that she could forego this lesson and take a ride through Hyde Park. It would be much more enjoyable.

Lady Anne stopped her explanation and asked, "Are you listening, Rosamond?"

"I am," she replied as she brought her gaze back to meet Lady Anne's.

With a knowing look, Lady Anne said, "It seems you are rather occupied at the moment."

Rosamond gave her a weak smile. "I do apologize but I was woolgathering. I meant no disrespect."

Lady Anne's face softened. "Perhaps I am being a little overzealous on the lessons, but I want to ensure you are prepared for every situation."

"No one can prepare for every situation," she argued.

"What if you meet a duke and do not address him as 'your grace'?" Lady Anne asked. "You risk being ostracized by Society."

"For a simple slip of the tongue?"

"The *ton* is not known for being sympathetic."

Rosamond reached up and removed the book from on top of her head. "You need not fear. I would never do anything that would embarrass you or this family."

"I know you believe that, but what if you slipped and fell during a dance?" Lady Anne asked. "You would be ruined."

Lizette happened to step into the room at that moment and laughed. "I daresay that Rosamond is not clumsy enough to fall during a set."

Lady Anne put her hands up. "I am just trying to explain some of the ways that Rosamond could be ruined."

"Which are all silly reasons," Lizette asserted.

"I agree, but it doesn't change anything," Lady Anne said. "We need to ensure that Rosamond is putting her best foot forward, especially after her outburst in the drawing room earlier today."

Lizette gave Rosamond a curious look. "What happened in the drawing room?"

Lady Anne answered for her. "Rosamond chided a gentleman for his opinion, and she even declared that she had 'an adverse reaction to stupidity'."

"Who was this gentleman that she insulted?" Lizette asked.

"Lord Brentwood," Lady Anne said.

Lizette's lips twitched. "I would imagine he is not used to a woman speaking her mind to him."

"Of course not!" Lady Anne said. "He is a viscount and will one day be the Earl of Everton. Furthermore, he is considered to be one of the most eligible bachelors of the Season."

Rosamond leaned forward and placed the book onto the table. "I couldn't just sit there and allow him to insult me."

"What you should have done was just have a stiff upper lip," Lady Anne said. "You are supposed to be a lady, after all."

"Do all ladies pretend to be something they are not?" Rosamond asked.

"The smart ones do. They hide a part of themselves until they are married," Lady Anne replied. "No man wants to saddle himself to a woman that is disagreeable."

Rosamond reached for her teacup. "Is that what you did to get married?"

"It was very different for me and John," Lady Anne replied. "We were well acquainted with one another by way of our parents, and he was a smart enough man to value my opinion."

Lizette interjected, "Tristan respects my opinions, encourages them, even."

"That is what I want," Rosamond admitted. "Besides, I have no intention of ever marrying Lord Brentwood. He is the most maddening man."

"So you have repeatedly said, but you still must endure his presence once you go on a carriage ride tomorrow," Lady Anne said.

Rosamond let out an unladylike groan. "Do not remind me. No doubt he will use the time to say things that are intolerably stupid."

"Need I remind you that he will be an earl one day?" Lady Anne said.

"I do not care if he was an heir to a dukedom," Rosamond responded. "I just want to marry a man that will love me above all else."

Lady Anne nodded. "You are right. That is what I want for you, as well, but I'm hoping the right gentleman will come with a title."

"I do not need a title to be happy," Rosamond said. "I have managed to live my life just fine without one."

"You say that now but if you married Lord Brentwood then you would be inundated with invitations to social events," Lady Anne said.

Rosamond took a sip of her tea. "Please never put those words together in a sentence ever again. I assure you that I will never marry him."

Lady Anne sighed. "Very well, but do try to avoid insulting him tomorrow. Just smile and nod at whatever he is saying."

"I am not sure if I can do that," Rosamond said. "My mother did raise me to have a voice, after all."

"I'm not saying to not have a voice, but maybe you can just dim it down for a few hours," Lady Anne said. "You wouldn't want to get the reputation as being too opinionated."

Rosamond brought a hand up to her chest. "Heaven forbid that I have an opinion," she said, feigning outrage.

"There is an easy way and a hard way to navigate the trappings of the *ton*," Lady Anne remarked. "If you continue down the path you are on, you will find that some doors may be shut to you."

Lizette spoke up. "I must agree with Rosamond."

"Of course you do," Lady Anne said, softening her words with a smile. "I have never met more opiniated young women than you two."

"Why should Rosamond spend her time on gentlemen that she knows she will not suit with?" Lizette asked.

"If I recall correctly, you didn't have a favorable opinion of Tristan when you first met him," Lady Anne pointed out.

"That is true," Lizette replied. "He definitely grew on me."

"Precisely. Lord Brentwood might be a perfect suitor for Rosamond once she gets to know him," Lady Anne said.

Rosamond placed her empty teacup onto the tray. "Lord Brentwood is a vexing man who is entirely too cocky for his own good. We would never suit, and I do not know how many times I have to say that to convince you of it."

"That is a shame, then," Lady Anne said. "What of your other suitors? Have you found one that you favor?"

"I have not," Rosamond replied. "They were all rather draining to converse with."

Lady Anne shook her head. "I daresay that you might be entirely too picky. You hardly have spent any time with your suitors."

"I will not settle for the sake of obtaining a title."

Rising, Lady Anne said, "We are going in circles now and I find that I need to rest before the dinner bell is rung." She turned her attention to Lizette. "Will you remain in the drawing room in case Rosamond receives callers and requires a chaperone?"

"It would be my pleasure," Lizette replied.

After Lady Anne departed from the drawing room, Lizette met her gaze and remarked, "She means well."

"I know, and I am most grateful for her help, but I fear that we both want different things when it comes to me finding a suitor," Rosamond said.

"Just follow your heart," Lizette encouraged.

Rosamond winced. "I tried that once and it didn't quite work out."

"So does that mean you just give up?"

"No, but I will be more cautious when it comes to picking a suitor," Rosamond said. "I don't want to make a mistake."

"For what it is worth, it's never too late, or too early, to be whoever you want to be," Lizette said. "Once you determine that, it will be easier to pick a suitor."

"I know what I want to be," Rosamond responded. "I want to be a member of high Society and fall madly in love. Just as you did."

"Then marrying an heir to an earldom would suit your needs."

Not this again. How many times did she have to say that she would never, ever, suit with Lord Brentwood. "It would, but I do not favor him. Not in the least."

"All right, I believe you." Lizette cocked her head. "Are you enjoying yourself here in London?"

"Yes, why would you even ask such a thing?"

Lizette shrugged. "I found that I prefer the quiet life of the countryside than the hustle and bustle of living in Town."

"It is quite different living in London," Rosamond agreed. "But I am most grateful for everything that has been given to me."

"I don't doubt that, but do not be so caught up in the trappings of high Society that you forget who you are."

Rosamond glanced at the door before lowering her voice. "It almost sounds like you are speaking from experience."

"I may have been born into this life, but I was removed to the countryside for most of my life. I sometimes miss the simple life."

"Have you told Tristan this?" Rosamond asked.

Lizette bobbed her head. "After the Season, we will retire to my manor for a few months in Bridgwater. Tristan had the foresight to see to the renovations that were required to bring it up to snuff."

"That is most fortunate."

"It was," Lizette agreed. "It was at that moment that I first realized that Tristan had a kind heart."

"Tristan is a good man," Rosamond said. "He has been nothing but kind to me since the moment we first met."

Lizette smiled. "He knows all of my secrets and guards them fiercely. I have never felt more safe- or loved- than when I am with him."

"I am happy for you."

Lizette leaned forward and picked up the teapot. After she poured herself a cup of tea, she picked it up and took a sip. "Will you tell me about your suitors?" Lizette asked as she brought the cup and saucer to her lap.

"Lord Brighton constantly is speaking about his mother, and I don't believe he can help himself," Rosamond shared. "Lord Vaughn is an arrogant man. Mr. Stone is..." Her voice trailed off. "I don't know what quite to make of him yet."

Lizette laughed. "I do not envy you. Wading through the hordes of gentlemen to find a match can be exhausting."

"That is a good word for it- exhausting." She hesitated before asking, "What will happen to me if I don't pick a suitor this Season?"

"There is no harm in that," Lizette replied. "You can either retire with Lady Anne and Lord Ashington to their country estate or you can join me and Tristan at Bridgwater."

"I wouldn't wish to intrude."

Lizette gave her an amused look. "You do not need to fear about that. You are always welcome in my home, and I do believe Tristan has told you that on many occasions."

"That he has," Rosamond said. "I know this may sound silly, but at times, I feel so alone. You and Aunt Betsey are the only family that I have left."

Lizette placed her empty teacup down onto the tray. "I

knew that feeling all too well before I married Tristan. After I lost my mother, I felt lost, and I struggled to come to terms with my new life that I was thrust into."

Rosamond went to respond when the butler stepped into the room and announced, "Mr. Howard has come to call on Miss Hendre."

She forced a smile to her lips. "Send him in, please," she ordered.

Lizette moved from her seat and came to sit down next to Rosamond on the settee. "So it begins…" she teased.

Chapter Six

Malcolm sat in the darkened coach as it made its way down the congested streets towards his townhouse. They had been fortunate in finding a respectable boarding house that had a room available for Enid and her daughter. Once they had settled in, he had sent for the doctor and waited until he arrived to tend to Marigold.

To Enid's great relief, the doctor was quick to reassure her that Marigold would recover now that she was out of the damp and disease-ridden workhouse. He gave her some medicine and promised to return tomorrow to see how Marigold was faring.

Since Marigold was in no immediate danger, Malcolm felt comfortable leaving his sister at the boarding house but was mindful to leave her with some money. He wanted to ensure she had enough food, so she didn't have to decide between feeding Marigold or herself.

He had to admit that he had never seen his sister be so selfless before. It was a stark contrast to how she behaved growing up. It was evident that she loved her child above all else, and she took her role as a mother very seriously.

The coach came to a stop in front of his townhouse and a

footman promptly opened the door. He stepped out onto the pavement and adjusted his top hat. In a few strides, he came to the main door and headed into the entry hall.

Osborne stepped out from one of the rooms off the hall, and said, "My apologies, my lord, that I was not here to greet you."

"No harm done," he replied as he removed his top hat. "Is my father home?"

Osborne nodded. "Yes, he is in his study. He has been asking about you."

"Then I shall not keep him waiting." Malcolm extended his top hat to the butler and made his way to the rear of the townhouse. He knew this was going to be a most unpleasant conversation, but it had to be done. Enid and Marigold couldn't live at the boarding house indefinitely, and it would be best if they returned home.

Malcolm walked into the study and saw his father was sitting on the settee, a drink in his hand. If his bloodshot eyes were any indication, he had started drinking hours ago.

His father raised his glass and grumbled, "I see that you finally decided to grace us with your presence."

"I am honored that you would even notice my absence."

His father lowered his glass to his lap. "You missed dinner."

"I usually do."

"I was forced to dine with your mother alone and it was uncomfortable," his father said before he took a sip of his drink.

Malcolm came and sat down across from his father. "That is entirely of your own making. Did you even attempt a conversation with Mother?"

"We don't have much in common besides you."

"And Enid."

His father stiffened. "I believe I told you never to say that name in my presence again."

"You did, but you were wrong to do so," Malcolm said. "Enid is still your daughter."

"I have no daughter, not anymore."

Malcolm frowned. This was precisely how he had expected the conversation to go, but he refused to give up. He wouldn't go on letting his father pretend that he had no daughter.

"What Enid did was wrong," he started, "but her circumstances have turned dire, and she needs our help."

His father scoffed. "I do not care what her circumstances are. She betrayed this family when she eloped with..." he tossed his arm up, "that man."

"She has a child."

For a moment, his father's hard face softened, but then the hardness returned as quickly as it had gone. "That means little to me."

"It should mean everything to you," Malcolm asserted. "She has a one-year-old girl and her name is Marigold."

His father tossed back his drink before saying, "Of course it is a useless female. Enid couldn't even do something right and bear a son."

Malcolm resisted the urge to smile since he had correctly predicted how their father would respond to the news of Enid having a daughter. "Regardless, Enid needs our help," he pressed. "Her husband died, and she was left with nothing, forcing her to go live at a workhouse."

Leaning forward, his father placed the empty glass down onto the table. "She made her choice when she eloped with that blasted Longbourn fellow."

Could his father be so callous that he felt nothing at all that his daughter and granddaughter were residing at a workhouse? He knew his father was a pigheaded man, but surely he had some softening of his heart at discovering the dire state of his granddaughter?

His father continued. "Quite frankly, it serves her right

after making us weather the scandal that she caused for our family."

"Father…"

He held his hand up, stilling his words. "Perhaps her time at the workhouse will serve her well."

"How can you say that?" Malcolm asked, feeling his anger surge. "You want to abandon her to a fate worse than death."

"Enid abandoned us first or did you forget that!" his father shouted. "She is no longer my daughter."

Malcolm rose. "You are wrong," he said. "You have a daughter and a granddaughter, but you would rather pretend they don't exist."

His father scowled up at him. "Enid embarrassed this family, and I will not stand for it."

"You may carry on as you are, but I am not going to forsake Enid, not when she needs our help."

"I forbid you from doing so."

Malcolm lifted his brow. "You forbid me?" he asked with a dry chuckle. "Do you think that would stop me from helping my own sister?"

"It should. What Enid did was unforgiveable, and you just want to brush her mistakes under the rug."

"I do believe she has suffered enough," he said with conviction.

His father picked up the decanter. "You are soft, much like your mother," he said. "How would it look for us if we accepted Enid back into our family?"

"I do not care how it looks for us," Malcolm said.

As he poured himself a drink, his father remarked, "You should since a hint of a scandal could scare Miss Hendre off and where would that leave us? Our creditors are about to barge through our doors, and unless you marry that chit, we will be left destitute."

"I know my duty," Malcolm stated.

His father put the decanter down. "Have you convinced Miss Hendre to marry you yet?"

Malcolm shifted uncomfortably in his stance. "Not yet, but these things take time."

"We don't have the luxury of time, Son."

"I am aware," he responded. "I am taking Miss Hendre on a carriage ride through Hyde Park tomorrow during the fashionable hour."

His father picked up his glass. "That is promising."

As his father returned to his seat, his mother stepped into the room and asked, "Did I hear Enid's name mentioned?"

"Not now, Diane," his father grumbled.

Malcolm shot his father a look that implied he should behave. Then, he turned towards his mother. "We were discussing Enid."

His mother walked further into the room. "Is it true?" she asked. "Does she have a child?"

"She does," Malcolm confirmed. "A one-year-old girl named Marigold."

A bright smile came to her mother's face, which was something he hadn't seen in quite some time. "That is wonderful news. Have you met this child?" she asked.

"I have," he confirmed.

His mother turned her hopeful expression towards her husband. "May I go meet my granddaughter?"

"You may not," his father scoffed. "We want nothing to do with Enid or her child."

"But I—"

His father spoke over her. "You will not defy me on this!" He pointed his finger at Malcolm. "And you won't speak of Enid or of her child in our presence again."

"I cannot promise that," Malcolm said as he noted the crestfallen look on his mother's face. "Furthermore, if I had my way, I would welcome Enid home with open arms."

With narrowed eyes, his father responded, "She is not welcome in my home, nor that insipid daughter of hers."

"You don't even know Marigold," Malcolm contested. How could his father take a stand when he hadn't even met Enid's child?

"If she is anything like her mother, she will be a grand disappointment," his father spat out.

Malcolm had just about enough of his father. They weren't getting anywhere, and his father was just getting more riled up. It might be best if they continued this conversation when he wasn't so into his cups.

"Goodnight, Father," Malcolm said with an exaggerated bow.

His father waved his hand in front of him dismissively. "Be off with you before I choose to disown you, as well."

Malcolm put his hand over his heart. "Say it isn't so. The thought of never seeing you and your pleasant disposition again is disheartening," he mocked.

His mother put a hand up to her lips to hide a small smile. "That is awful of you to say, Malcolm," she chided lightly.

He approached his mother and offered his arm. "Let's leave Father to his brandy," he suggested.

She accepted his arm, and he led her out of the study. After a long moment, his mother looked over her shoulder and lowered her voice. "What does Marigold look like?" she asked in an eager voice.

"Well, she looks like a baby," he attempted. "She has ten fingers and ten toes."

His mother looked unimpressed at his feeble attempt. "You are terrible at offering up a description."

"Would you care to meet her?" Malcolm asked.

A sad, forlorn look came to her eyes. "I shouldn't. Your father would be so upset with me if he found out that I defied him."

"As opposed to how he normally is with you?" Malcolm questioned.

His mother came to a stop and dropped her hand to her side. "I know there is still good inside of George. I just need to be patient and hope the man that I love will return to me."

"I do believe that man has gone."

She patted his cheek. "You will understand one day when you are in love," she said. "Love is patient and long-suffering."

"I just hate seeing you constantly disappointed by Father."

She lowered her hand. "I will worry about George, and you need to see to Enid. I do not want her to suffer at that workhouse."

Malcolm gave her an amused look. "You were eavesdropping, I see."

Unabashed, she said, "Of course I was. This is my home, after all."

"Well, I have removed Enid and Marigold from the workhouse, and she is residing at a boarding house until we can convince Father to let them come home."

"That will be a tough feat," his mother said.

"I am well aware."

"But it is a fight worth fighting."

Malcolm bobbed his head. "I agree," he said. "If we both work together, we can wear him down until he has no choice but to let Enid return home."

His mother's eyes looked tired, and he couldn't help but wonder if her heart was tired, as well. He knew her well enough to know she rarely asked for help, and she held her worries close to her chest. Why did she have to pretend to be brave all the time?

"I know when Enid left us, I do believe it about broke your father. Perhaps her returning will change all of that," she said.

"One can only hope."

"Without hope, what else do we have?"

He placed a hand on her sleeve. "Go get some sleep, Mother," he encouraged. "I promise you that all will be well."

With a grateful smile, she turned to walk up the stairs.

Malcolm watched his mother's retreating figure and he hoped that his promise wasn't in vain. He knew his mother was hurting and he would do anything to see her smile as freely as she once did. He owed her that much.

Rosamond stared up at the canopy in her bed. She should be elated that she was going on her first carriage ride through Hyde Park but she found her heart was not in it. She couldn't seem to abide Lord Brentwood and she would be forced to endure his company for an extended period of time. What would they even discuss? She was quite sure that she had nothing in common with that infuriating man.

The men were different in the countryside. They were hard workers, mainly because their lives depended on it. They did not have excess time to go to a gentlemen's club or attend endless social events. Quite frankly, she was starting to miss the quiet life of the countryside. It was much simpler there.

But she didn't dare complain. For what she had been given was nothing less than extraordinary. She was given a chance to enter a world that she wasn't born into, but, in order to be accepted, she had to keep her past a secret. No sane man in high Society would ever be interested in a daughter of a seaman. If the truth about her ever got out, it could ruin everything that she had worked for.

This was her life now. This is what she wanted. She just needed to dismiss that nagging thought that she was a fraud, a phony.

A knock came at the door before it was opened, revealing Aunt Betsey.

"I am pleased to see that you are finally awake." Her aunt walked over to the drapes and threw them open, flooding the room with light. "Lord Ashington has requested that you join him for breakfast."

"Did he say why?"

Her aunt smiled. "I did not ask him. He stated his request to the butler and it was reiterated to me."

Rosamond sat up in bed. "I do hope everything is well."

Walking over to the wardrobe, her aunt retrieved a pale yellow gown with a square neckline and held it up for Rosamond's inspection. "Will this gown suit for your carriage ride with Lord Brentwood?"

She groaned. "Do not remind me."

With a confused look, her aunt asked, "Why is that?"

"Lord Brentwood is just awful," Rosamond replied. "His voice grates on my very nerves until I have no choice but to release my sharp tongue on him."

Her aunt laughed. "You poor child," she said. "If you think I feel sorry for you, then you would be sadly mistaken."

"No, but I just wish that I hadn't agreed to this carriage ride. What will we even talk about since we have nothing in common?"

"I am sure you can find something to discuss. The weather, perhaps?" her aunt joked.

Rosamond placed her feet over the side of the bed and rose. "I just hope I won't have to make use of my muff pistol."

"Why would you take a pistol with you?"

"I always carry a pistol on my person," Rosamond said. "I was raised in the countryside where it was perfectly acceptable to do so."

Her aunt draped the gown over the back of the settee. "But you are not in the countryside anymore. It is much more civil in Town."

"It doesn't matter to me. I do not like the feeling of being defenseless."

"Well, promise me that you won't threaten Lord Brentwood with the pistol."

Rosamond shrugged. "I can't. What if he becomes too familiar?"

Her aunt moved to stand behind the chair at the dressing table. "Let's style your hair before it grows too late."

As she sat down, Rosamond said, "I know what you are thinking."

"I doubt that."

"You think I am being silly since a handsome, rich viscount is showing interest in me."

Her aunt picked up the brush. "You think Lord Brentwood is handsome?" she asked innocently.

Drat. That had been a slip of the tongue. "He isn't unfortunate to look at," she admitted, "but then he opens his mouth and I find him unbearable."

"Just go on the carriage ride with an open mind," her aunt said. "First impressions are not always to be trusted."

Rosamond had to admit that her aunt had a point. She had fallen in love with George, and he turned out to be rather despicable. In the end, he chose greed over her. What if Lord Brentwood wasn't as awful as she thought him to be?

After her hair was tied into a chignon around the base of her neck, she rose and started getting dressed.

The door opened and Lady Anne slipped into the room. "Good, you are awake," she said. "We have much to do before your carriage ride with Lord Brentwood."

"What is there to do?" Rosamond asked.

Lady Anne gave her a knowing look. "We need to discuss the appropriate conversational topics that you must adhere to."

"Why can't I just have a frank conversation with Lord Brentwood?"

"No good would come from that," Lady Anne replied.

"You need to focus on controlling the conversation, so it does not control you."

Rosamond sucked in her breath as her aunt fastened the last of the buttons. These gowns were designed to look elegant, but the functionality of them was terrible.

As her aunt stepped back, Lady Anne waved her hand, encouraging Rosamond forward. "Come along, let's adjourn to the dining room. My father wishes to speak to you."

Rosamond followed Lady Anne out the door, and they walked down the hall together.

Lady Anne glanced over at her and asked, "What are the polite conversational topics that you should focus on with Lord Brentwood?"

"The weather, state of the gardens, music and appropriate books," Rosamond listed.

"Very good," Lady Anne murmured. "Now, what topics should you avoid?"

Rosamond held her finger up. "I can inquire about his family as long as I do not pry too deep." She held up another finger. "I must never discuss politics, religion, or anything that could spark a heated debate."

Lady Anne nodded her approval. "Gentlemen do not want to be preached to. They prefer women that are agreeable, especially as they first get to know them."

"How dull," Rosamond muttered as they started to descend the stairs.

"It won't always be that way, but you must play the game if you want to secure a husband of high social standing."

Rosamond grew quiet as they continued on to the dining room. Could she stand to marry a man that didn't truly know her thoughts and opinions? It sounded miserable not being able to express herself when the situation warranted it.

Lady Anne broke through her musings as they continued to descend the stairs. "You will not have a chaperone on this outing so you must be mindful to avoid saying anything that could reflect poorly on you or this family. Do avoid any snide comments since they are unbecoming."

"What if Lord Brentwood vexes me?"

"Then you grin and bear it," Lady Anne replied. "It is far preferable than hopping out of the carriage in the middle of Hyde Park during the fashionable hour. If you do so, you will be ruined, Child."

They stepped into the dining room and Lord Ashington rose from his seat at the head of the table. "Good morning, ladies," he said.

Rosamond murmured her greeting as she sat down at his right. A footman promptly placed a plate of food and a cup of tea down in front of her. She placed her napkin onto her lap and picked up her fork to begin eating.

Lord Ashington folded the newssheets and placed them down on the table. He met her gaze and said, "I do appreciate you joining me for breakfast since I have something important that I wish to discuss with you."

Now the aged marquess had her attention. She put her fork onto the plate and shifted to face him. She wasn't sure what he wished to discuss with her, but she found herself most curious.

With a glance at Lady Anne, he shared, "Lord Brentwood came to speak to me yesterday and we had an interesting conversation."

She wondered what that had to do with her. The less she knew about Lord Brentwood, the better.

Lord Ashington continued. "I thought you should know that he asked for your hand in marriage."

Rosamond's mouth dropped. It took her a moment to recover, but when she did, she blurted out, "Pray, say it isn't so."

He gave her a look of compassion. "I'm afraid it is, but I turned down his request," he said. "I told him that it was your decision as to who you will marry, and your decision alone." He paused. "Unless I was wrong in saying so?"

"Heavens, no," Rosamond rushed to respond. "I do not want to marry Lord Brentwood, not now, not ever. He may be a viscount, but I know we would not suit."

Lord Ashington reached for her hand and patted it. "Lord Brentwood was the first man to offer for you, but I am sure he won't be the last," he said. "But I will field their requests until I hear otherwise from you."

Why would Lord Brentwood wish to marry her? They had been at odds from the moment they had first met. To approach Lord Ashington instead of her was rather presumptuous on his part, proving her point that they would most definitely not suit.

Lady Anne's voice met her ears. "That is most encouraging," she said. "You haven't even been out for a few days, and you already received a marriage proposal."

"But Lord Brentwood didn't ask me. He asked Lord Ashington for my hand," Rosamond pointed out.

"That is not an entirely uncommon thing to do," Lady Anne remarked.

Rosamond reached for her teacup and took a long sip. A small part of her was flattered that she had received a marriage proposal but she didn't dare admit that. She couldn't. If she did, then they might wrongly assume that she considered Lord Brentwood a suitor.

Lord Ashington tossed the napkin from his lap onto the table. "If you will excuse me, I need to depart for the House of Lords."

"Must you?" Lady Anne asked. "We hardly see you anymore."

"I know I have been busy but there is much work that needs to be done," Lord Ashington said as he rose. "Besides, I know that I am leaving Rosamond in your capable hands, my dear."

Lady Anne smiled. "You are resorting to flattery now?" she asked. "My, you must be getting desperate."

Lord Ashington laughed. "I remember your mother saying that to me on more than one occasion."

"I remember," Lady Anne said.

With a parting glance at Rosamond, Lord Ashington departed from the dining room with a determined stride.

Lady Anne's eyes remained on the empty doorway. "My father is always fighting a cause or two, but sometimes I wish he would just slow down."

"He doesn't seem like a man that would enjoy a quieter life."

"No, he would not," Lady Anne agreed. "He is on a mission to give the poor access to clean water, but he has been met with plenty of opposition in Parliament."

"Sometimes doing what is right isn't always the easiest path."

Lady Anne brought her gaze back to meet hers. "Speaking of which, we still need to discuss what you will say about your past," she said. "It would be best if you spoke vaguely about your childhood or avoid it all together."

"I will try."

"There is no 'try'," Lady Anne asserted. "If someone discovered the truth about your past, it could be detrimental to your marriage prospects."

Rosamond frowned. "Do you suppose I will always have to live a lie?"

Lady Anne's face softened. "I know it may seem like an impossible feat now but it will be different when you have the protection of your husband's name."

"I know, but how can I get to know someone if I only converse in half-truths?" Rosamond asked.

"That is called a courtship," Lady Anne said. "No one reveals too much of themselves when they are trying to put their best foot forward."

Rosamond pressed her lips together as she tried to sort out her own thoughts. She didn't want to hide a part of herself when she was trying to determine if she would suit with a gentleman, but if she trusted the wrong person then it could ruin everything.

Lady Anne pushed back her chair and rose. "Shall we adjourn to the drawing room and wait for your callers to arrive?"

Mustering up a smile, Rosamond said, "I think that is a grand idea."

Chapter Seven

Malcolm pulled back on the reins of the open carriage and came to a stop in front of Lord Ashington's townhouse. He found that he was conflicted about spending time with Miss Hendre. He needed her to fall prey to his charms, but his heart was not in it. This would be a marriage of convenience, nothing more. At least Miss Hendre would look good on his arm at the social events they would be forced to attend as a couple.

A footman exited the townhouse and came to secure the carriage. Malcolm stepped down and adjusted his cravat. He needed to look his best to ensure Miss Hendre found no fault with him. This was a game that he was going to win. He had to. The stakes were too high not to.

He walked up the steps and his boots felt like lead. He should be pleased that he was spending time with Miss Hendre, but he dreaded their upcoming time together. He ignored the slight twinge of guilt that he felt for his intentions to deceive Miss Hendre, but it had to be done. He refused to be ruined and inherit a bankrupt title.

The door was promptly opened after he rapped the knocker against the door.

"Lord Brentwood," the butler greeted, opening the door wide. "Do come in. Miss Hendre is expecting you."

He stepped into the entry hall and removed his top hat.

"Follow me, my lord." The butler crossed the entry hall and stepped into the drawing room. "Lord Brentwood has arrived," he announced.

Malcolm took his cue and walked into the drawing room. He saw Lady Anne was standing next to the settee and Miss Hendre was by her side. She was dressed in an alluring yellow gown, her blonde hair elegantly styled, and she looked the epitome of perfection. He found no fault with her appearance. She was a beautiful young woman, there was no denying that, but she was far too opiniated for her own good.

He bowed. "Ladies," he murmured.

Miss Hendre dropped into a curtsy. "Lord Brentwood." Her words were cordial enough, but she didn't appear pleased to see him.

Lady Anne gestured towards the settee that was opposite of them. "Would you care to have a cup of tea?"

Malcolm's hands started fidgeting with his top hat. He was rather eager to leave for Hyde Park, but he knew it would be rude to refuse Lady Anne's offer. "I suppose one cup of tea wouldn't hurt before we depart."

The ladies returned to their seats and he sat down on the proffered settee, placing his hat down next to him. Miss Hendre reached for a teacup and poured. Then she extended the cup and saucer towards him.

"Thank you," he said.

Miss Hendre tipped her head in acknowledgement before she picked up her own teacup. She took a sip and lowered it to her lap. He tried to catch her gaze, but she managed to avoid it. This was not boding well for him.

Lady Anne spoke up. "Rosamond was just telling me how much she is looking forward to the carriage ride during the fashionable hour." She paused. "Weren't you, Dear?"

Miss Hendre smiled, but it appeared forced. "I was."

Malcolm waited for her to expand, but when she didn't, he said, "Wonderful. I have been counting down the moments since our last meeting." He smiled, hoping it might disarm Miss Hendre. But it appeared to have the opposite effect on her. Her back grew even more rigid, if that were even possible. He had never met someone with such perfect posture.

Lady Anne glanced between them before saying, "Rosamond is quite a talented singer. She intends to perform at Lady Haverton's soiree next week. Will you be in attendance?"

"I wouldn't miss it now that I know I will have the chance to hear Miss Hendre sing," Malcolm said.

"She even wrote her own song for the occasion," Lady Anne shared.

Malcolm shifted his gaze towards Miss Hendre. "That is an impressive feat. I had no idea you were so talented."

"But, alas, you haven't heard the song yet," Miss Hendre said. "Your opinion might change after the soiree."

"I doubt it. I admire a woman that pursues her passions."

Miss Hendre leaned forward and placed her teacup down onto the tray. "The song is about my mother. She was the one that encouraged me to write down the songs that came to my mind and I am so glad that she had the foresight to do so."

"I am a terrible singer," Malcolm admitted. "It is akin to the gurgling croak of a raven."

Lady Anne gave him an amused look. "Surely you jest."

"I assure you I do not. My mother is insistent that my talents lie elsewhere," Malcolm said.

Miss Hendre reached for a biscuit on the tray and asked, "May I be so bold as to ask where your interests do lie?"

Malcolm felt that this was a safe question and he knew he could answer honestly. "I engage in the usual trappings of gentlemen when I am in London."

"Which are?" Miss Hendre pressed.

"I enjoy boxing, spending time at the club, an occasional

lecture at the Royal Society, and I have even dabbled in fencing," he replied.

Miss Hendre did not seem impressed with his list of interests. She took a bite of her biscuit and shifted her gaze towards the windows. He would have given anything to know what she was thinking at that precise moment.

Lady Anne placed her hand on Rosamond's sleeve and said, "Rosamond has many interests that she would love to tell you all about. Go ahead, Dear. Tell Lord Brentwood what occupies your time."

"I enjoy reading..." Miss Hendre started.

Lady Anne interrupted her. "But she refrains from reading anything that is too controversial, such as politics or religion."

Miss Hendre nodded. "I also enjoy embroidery, paperwork, quilling and feather-work."

Malcolm resisted the urge to groan. Miss Hendre indulged in the same pastimes as nearly every genteel woman of his acquaintance. Why did they assume gentlemen would be interested in a woman that spent her time on boring pursuits?

He took a sip of his tea as he tried to take hold of this conversation. They were getting nowhere, and he couldn't help but wonder about the sudden transformation of Miss Hendre. Where was the passion that he had seen when they had argued before? She almost seemed as if she were uninterested or bored with him or this conversation.

Miss Hendre finished her biscuit and wiped the crumbs off her hand. She met his gaze and gave him a brief smile. Then she turned her attention towards Lady Anne.

In response, Lady Anne nudged her arm and gave her an expectant look.

Miss Hendre let out a sigh before addressing him. "It is a lovely day we are having, is it not?" she asked in a disengaging manner.

"It is." The last thing he wanted to discuss was the weather, but it was a safe topic. He placed his teacup down on the table and suggested, "Perhaps we should continue this riveting conversation on our carriage ride."

"What a fine idea," Lady Anne gushed.

Miss Hendre rose and said, "Allow me to retrieve my hat."

She didn't wait for his response before she hurried from the room. How odd! He almost preferred when they quarreled rather than her being indifferent towards him. Frankly, he didn't know where he stood with her and that was troublesome.

Botheration. Women usually were besotted with him and he had never had to work so hard at a conversation with a young woman before.

Lady Anne smiled up at him. "Rosamond has been looking forward to the carriage ride all morning."

He didn't believe that to be true, but he bobbed his head in response. "As have I."

Miss Hendre's voice came from the doorway. "I am ready to depart."

As he turned towards her, he tried to stop himself from staring at the ostentatious straw hat that she was wearing on her head. Bright peacock feathers fanned from the top, and they ran along one side. He had never seen anything quite like it.

Apparently, neither had Lady Anne because she asked, "Good gracious, where did you get that hat?"

"I made it for this special occasion," Miss Hendre said with a smile on her lips. "Do you like it, Lord Brentwood?"

He knew the only course of action here was to lie. He didn't dare tell her that it was hideous and it would garner far too much attention for the wrong reasons. But he had never understood women's fashion before.

"It is quite unique," he settled on saying.

Miss Hendre's smile grew. "I was hoping you would be pleased with it."

He approached her and held out his hand. "Shall we?"

She placed her hand on his and he led her out into the entry hall. As he turned to speak to her, he saw that the hat was tilted just at the right angle that he was unable to see her face. The peacock feathers made sure of that. Surely she hadn't planned that? But the more he dwelled on it, the more it seemed like she had done it on purpose.

Malcolm couldn't let on that it bothered him. He refused to give her that satisfaction. If she wanted to continue wearing that ridiculous hat, then so be it.

As they approached the main door, he asked, "May I ask where you found all of those peacock feathers?"

She turned her head quickly and the tips of the peacock feathers smacked him in the face. "A charming shop on Bond Street," she replied.

"How fortunate you were that they had them."

"It was an extravagance to purchase the feathers but I knew it would be worth it when I could see the look on your face when you first saw my hat," she said, her eyes sparking with mirth.

The minx. So she had planned this out. Why would she wear such an outrageous hat just to… what? Spite him? Annoy him? If she wanted a specific reaction, she was going to be disappointed.

"I must admit that I am impressed that you were able to create such a grand-looking hat," he said. "I have no doubt it will garner the attention of all that see it."

"Most likely," she replied as he led her out the door.

After he assisted her into the carriage, he went to sit next to her and reached for the reins. He urged the team forward and merged into traffic.

Malcolm glanced at her but her face was still concealed by that hat. How could he charm her if he couldn't even see her?

Miss Hendre kept her gaze straight ahead as she said, "I am sorry about Lady Anne's exuberance earlier. She is rather pleased this is to be my first carriage ride through Hyde Park."

"But you have been to Hyde Park before?"

"I have, but I normally go riding with my..." she hesitated, "cousin and her husband, Mr. Westcott," she replied. "We go in the morning hours so we can avoid the crowds."

"I am surprised I haven't seen you then. I prefer the morning hours as well."

"My horse isn't as grand as most horses in Town, but we have been together for a long time," Miss Hendre shared.

"I admire that."

"Lady Anne is insistent that I obtain a new horse, but I have refused. Why should I give up something that I love so dearly just so my horse isn't as ugly?"

"Your horse is ugly?"

"Terribly so, at least compared to the other horses in Lord Ashington's stable," she replied. "It has a large head and neck, making it appear quite ungainly."

Malcolm found himself chuckling. "I think I would very much like to see this horse."

"My mother said she saw something special in the horse when she bought it for me, and she was right," Miss Hendre said. "Bella has never let me down."

The way Miss Hendre said her words caused him to pause. Her last words were spoken softly as if she hadn't meant for him to hear. Who had let her down?

As he opened his mouth to press her, she pointed towards the entrance of Hyde Park and announced, "We are here."

Rosamond knew her hat was utterly ridiculous, but she did not care. She had been half-hoping that Lord Brentwood would have refused to take her on a carriage ride with her hat on, causing her to feign outrage. But, unexpectedly, he hadn't insulted the hat, but appeared to accept the fact that she would be wearing such a monstrosity on her head.

She held her head high as their carriage joined the others that had lined up along Rotten Row. As carriages passed by, she saw women blatantly staring at her hat and whispering behind their fans. Perhaps now Lord Brentwood would ask her to remove it when he saw the attention they were garnering.

She waited for his response.

And waited.

But he just stared straight ahead, his hands clutching the reins. He appeared deep in thought, which was something she didn't think he was capable of. Lord Brentwood was what she had imagined when she thought of a dandy in high Society. They did as they pleased, without regard for others. It was a shame, really. He was such a handsome man, but she didn't want someone that was vain and pretentious.

Lord Brentwood turned to face her, and she realized that she had been caught staring. She should have felt some embarrassment but that would imply she felt something for the man. Which she didn't. She just had to get through this carriage ride and hope he would never call upon her again.

His voice cut through her musings. "May I ask where you hail from?"

"Bracknell." She winced, knowing she shouldn't be so forthcoming with information about her past. She could practically hear Lady Anne's chiding voice.

"I am not familiar with that village."

"That is not a surprise since nothing of importance has happened there, but it is not terribly far from London."

Lord Brentwood nodded. "I can say the same of my village. It is up north in Liverpool."

"I would imagine you live in a grand country estate," Rosamond said.

"I do- Rosecliff Hall," he replied, puffing out his chest with pride. "It has been in my family for generations."

"How wonderful for you," she muttered.

He gave her an odd look. "Did you not grow up in a country home?"

"I did not." She frowned, wishing she could bite her tongue. If Lord Brentwood ever found out how she had lived in a modest manor, she had little doubt that he would find fault with her.

Lord Brentwood adjusted the reins in his hands, and he said, "The size of a home is not important, but it is the people that reside in it that count."

"I agree, wholeheartedly." Rosamond was surprised that such a deep thought came out of Lord Brentwood's mouth.

The surprise must have been evident on her features because he said, "You seem surprised by my remark."

"Quite frankly, I am," she responded. "You do not strike me as someone that overly cares about anyone but himself."

He smiled, flashing his white, straight teeth. "I know that we got off on the wrong foot, which was my fault entirely, but I am hoping we can start over."

Rosamond knew the polite thing to do would be to graciously accept his offer and begin anew with him. But she wasn't quite ready to concede, especially since she had a feeling that he always got his way.

She arched her eyebrow and asked, "Was there an apology somewhere in there?"

His smile remained intact. "I thought it was implied by my admission of fault."

"You must forgive me and my delicate constitution, but I need things spelled out for me to understand."

Now his smile dimmed. "I am beginning to question what kind of constitution you do have, Miss Hendre."

Rosamond brought her hand up to her chest, feigning

innocence. "I meant no offense, my lord. You must know that," she said, using his own words against him.

Lord Brentwood's jaw clenched. "You do not intend to make this easy on me, do you?"

"I do not." With any luck, Lord Brentwood would turn the carriage around and end this farce of an outing. It was going nowhere for either of them.

He studied her for a moment before saying, "You have my humblest apology for the way I have treated you up until now. It was terribly unfair of me to do so and it is not the proper representation of who I am."

Drats. His words appeared genuine, and she knew she would seem petty if she did not accept his apology. Why was he trying so hard to win her approval? They clearly did not suit, and she had no intention of ever accepting Lord Brentwood as a potential suitor.

As she opened her mouth to speak, she met his gaze and saw something she hadn't seen before- vulnerability. How could she turn him down now?

"I accept your apology," she said, "but I have no intention of marrying you." Why had she just said that? He had said nothing of marriage, but she felt inclined to inform him of that.

His eyes crinkled around the edges. "We shall see."

"We shall not see, my lord," she declared. "We are two fundamentally different people and I know my mind."

"So say you."

She pressed her lips together. "You are making me regret my decision to forgive you so easily."

One side of his lips quirked up. "That was you being easy on me?" he asked. "I would hate to see you being difficult."

Rosamond felt herself relax slightly at his words. "I will admit that I can be rather stubborn at times."

He reared back. "Say it isn't so."

Before she could stop herself, a soft laugh escaped her lips, causing her hand to fly up to her mouth.

Lord Brentwood looked rather pleased with himself. "I am hoping this means you are starting to enjoy my company."

"Can a person ever enjoy a thorn in one's boot?" she challenged.

"Why is it that you do not like me?" he asked. "Am I too charming for you?"

"No, that is most definitely not it."

"Then what is it?"

Rosamond thought it was best if she told a lie to appease Lord Brentwood since she wasn't quite sure what it was that vexed her the most about him. "I do not know you well enough to dislike you."

"Yet you are so adamant that we will not suit."

"That is true."

"And why is that?"

An errant peacock feather started drooping into her line of vision and she brushed it aside, only for it to return time and time again. Why had she thought it was a good idea to wear this hat? It was starting to become burdensome.

"Allow me," Lord Brentwood said as he moved to pluck the feather out of the hat. He extended it towards her. "I could see that it was bothering you."

"It was," she responded as she accepted the feather. "Thank you for that."

Lord Brentwood gave her an expectant look. "I believe you were about to tell me why we would not suit."

"Yes, I was." She paused. What could she say to him that would convince him? By him offering up an apology, it had caught her off guard, which was a rarity on her part. There was something about Lord Brentwood that she couldn't seem to put her finger on, causing her to be on edge.

Was it her own bias towards him? Or was he truly as cocky as she had led herself to believe? Knowing he was still waiting for a response, Rosamond said, "If you must know, I am looking for a love match."

"As am I."

Rosamond stared at him in utter disbelief. "Is that why you asked Lord Ashington permission to marry me with only limited interaction between us?" she asked, challenging him.

"I see that he told you."

"He did," she replied. "Would you have preferred he kept it a secret from me?"

He nodded his head. "Yes, but not for the reasons you are thinking."

"Please enlighten me."

The coach came to an abrupt halt as Lord Brentwood pulled back on the reins, maintaining a reasonable amount of distance from the coach in front of them. "It would appear we have come to a stop." He shifted towards her. "You may not think we suit, but I most assuredly do."

She opened up her mouth to object but he continued. "You are a beautiful young woman, but it isn't just your beauty that intrigues me. No, it is your intellect that holds me captive. You fascinate me, and I couldn't stand the thought of losing you to another."

"You can't lose what you don't have," she said.

"Precisely, which is why I went straightaway to speak to Lord Ashington about you, but he did the right thing by refusing me."

"You think so?"

"I know so," he replied. "It has forced me to prove to you that my intentions are real, and I promise you that I will convince you to marry me."

"That is mighty presumptuous of you," she huffed.

Lord Brentwood smirked. "I know what I want, and it is you, Miss Hendre."

Her back grew rigid as she declared, "I am not some prize to be won, my lord."

The carriage in front of them started moving again and Lord Brentwood flicked the reins to urge the team forward.

"Just wait," he encouraged. "I am sure that you will come to the same conclusion as I have."

Rosamond wasn't quite sure if she should be flattered by his advances or furious by his brazenness. He was being rather bold for a man in his circumstances.

"Regardless, you will find that I am not so easily won over by a handsome face and flattery," she said.

His lips twitched. "You think I am handsome?"

"I think you are entirely too cocky for your own good," she said as she attempted to save face after her unfortunate slip.

"But you do think I am handsome?" he said flirtatiously.

Rosamond rolled her eyes. "You are an intolerable man."

Lord Brentwood held her gaze before saying, "Come with me to the Royal Menagerie tomorrow."

"As tempting as that sounds, I'm afraid I am busy."

"I see," he said. "May I be so bold as to ask what it is that you are doing tomorrow?"

She bit her lower lip as she tried to come up with a believable lie. The only thing she knew for certain that she was doing tomorrow was waiting in the drawing room to receive her callers, if she had any. She had to admit that it might be preferable to go to the Royal Menagerie with Lord Brentwood.

"I may be able to move things around so I can accompany you to the Royal Menagerie," she said.

"Brilliant," Lord Brentwood responded.

"But this changes nothing between us," Rosamond rushed out. "I am not some love-struck maiden that wants to race to the altar with the first man that shows her favor."

"I never thought you were."

"Good," Rosamond said. "We are in agreement, then."

"That we are." Lord Brentwood extended her the reins. "Would you care to drive the team?" he asked.

She hesitated as she stared at the reins. "Are you in earnest?" she asked. No man had ever asked her to drive the carriage before.

"I am, assuming you know how to drive a coach."

"I do." Her eyes roamed over the other carriages in Hyde Park. "What will others think of us?"

"Does it matter?" he asked. "After all, you do not strike me as a young woman that cares what others think of her."

"My aunt would be furious."

"But your aunt isn't here, now is she?" he asked, encouraging her on.

A bright smile came to her lips as she accepted the reins. "Thank you," she said as she adjusted the reins in her hands. "This reminds me of when I used to drive our wagon to the village fair."

"Your wagon?" he asked. "You mean 'your coach'?"

"No, I spoke correctly."

Lord Brentwood eyed her curiously. "You are different, Miss Hendre."

"Is that a compliment or an insult?"

"It is most definitely a compliment."

Turning her attention towards the line of coaches, she wondered if perhaps she'd judged Lord Brentwood too harshly. He didn't seem as awful as she had made him out to be. But she was still sure of one thing- she would never marry him.

Although she was starting to believe it wouldn't be the worst thing to have him as a friend.

Chapter Eight

Rosamond gripped the leather reins in her hands as she drove the team down Rotten Row in Hyde Park. They had gotten a few bemused looks from people that passed by them, but she did not care. Her opinion of Lord Brentwood had grown immensely by this one thoughtful gesture. She was quite sure that most gentlemen of the *ton* would never have let her drive a carriage, but he had encouraged her to do so. It had been so unexpected, so out of character for him, that she decided it would be best to let bygones be bygones and not assume the worst in him anymore.

As the carriage started to pick up speed, she knew it was time to relinquish the reins to Lord Brentwood. It would be best if he drove the team on the busy streets of London.

"Thank you," she said as she extended the reins to Lord Brentwood.

He accepted the reins and asked, "Did you enjoy yourself?"

"I did, very much so," she admitted.

"Then it was well worth it," he said. "Although I was worried that your hat would be bothersome as you drove the team."

Rosamond reached up and adjusted the hat on her head. "I am beginning to think that this hat might have been a mistake."

"Pray tell, why do you believe that?"

"It is a bit much."

Lord Brentwood grinned. "But if you didn't wear the hat, then you would have been forced to look upon me more."

Rosamond laughed. "I'm beginning to believe that wouldn't be the worst thing."

"Careful, it almost sounds as if you are enjoying my company."

"I believe I am finding you to be much more tolerable than I once did."

Lord Brentwood drove the team out of Hyde Park and onto the cobblestone street. "If I had known this would have been your reaction to driving the coach, I would have handed you the reins much sooner."

"But then we would have missed out on a most informative conversation," Rosamond said.

"Yes, I do believe you were rather adamant that we would never suit."

"It is true, but at least I know that I do not need to make use of my muff pistol."

Lord Brentwood gave her an odd look. "You have a muff pistol on your person?"

"I do." Rosamond held up the reticule that was around her right wrist. "I do not leave my home without one."

"Why is that?"

"My mother always encouraged me to carry one," she said. "She thought it was best that I always had a means to protect myself."

Lord Brentwood leaned back on the bench. "It isn't the worst idea that I have heard, but I do hope you know how to properly handle a pistol."

"I do, my mother insisted that I learn to do so. We spent many hours perfecting my aim when I was younger."

"If you are not opposed, we could always practice our shooting together."

"I would like that."

"But you must promise me that you will not shoot me," he joked.

Rosamond cast him an amused look. "I won't, assuming you don't give me just cause to do so."

"I will strive not to." With a glance at her, Lord Brentwood said, "Your mother sounds like a formidable woman."

"That she was," Rosamond readily agreed. "She wished for nothing more than my happiness and I hope that I can live a life that would make her proud."

"You will."

"How can you be so sure, especially since we hardly know one another?" Rosamond asked.

Lord Brentwood grew solemn. "There is a fierceness about you that I find admirable. You are not some weak-willed young woman that I so frequently encounter in high Society."

Rosamond arched an eyebrow. "I see that you are resorting to flattery now."

"I am," Lord Brentwood said. "Is it working?"

"Perhaps."

"Good. That was my intention."

Rosamond's eyes left his and roamed over the congested street that was filled with carriages. At the rate they were moving, it would take quite some time before they arrived back at Lord Ashington's townhouse.

Lord Brentwood's voice drew her attention back to him. "Will you tell me about yourself?"

"That is rather a vague question," she replied. "What do you wish to know?"

"Let's start with what is most important," he replied. "Are you carrying any other weapons on your person?"

111

"I am not."

His eyes shone with mirth. "That is a relief."

"It is my turn to ask you a question."

"Fair enough."

Rosamond debated on asking him a myriad of things. She didn't want to ask anything too personal or that was considered taboo by Lady Anne. It might be best if she just focused on polite conversational topics, but how would she ever truly get to know Lord Brentwood if she did that? And she was starting to think it wouldn't be such a terrible thing to learn more about him.

Shifting on the bench, she asked, "Will you tell me about your family?"

Lord Brentwood visibly tensed. "There is not much to tell, I'm afraid. I have an overbearing father, a loving mother and a sister that brought shame down upon our family."

She could hear the terseness in his voice and knew it would be best if she swayed the conversation away from his family. Lady Anne had been right about avoiding such heavy subjects as family.

"The weather has been quite agreeable, has it not?" she attempted.

Lord Brentwood gave her a grateful look. "It has been, but I do not care to discuss the weather."

"Then what would you care to discuss?"

"You."

She looked over at him in surprise. "Me?" she asked.

He nodded. "I want to learn everything about you."

"That could take quite some time," she quipped.

"So be it."

Rosamond clasped her hands in her lap. "I don't know why you are interested in learning about me because I can assure you that I am not that interesting."

"Let me be the judge of that."

"All right, but I have the right to pass on questions that you ask," she said. "I am entitled to have some secrets."

Lord Brentwood furrowed his brow. "What kind of secrets could a lady possibly have?"

"You would be surprised."

"I doubt that, considering nothing seems to surprise me anymore." He paused. "You mentioned your mother, but you have said nothing of your father."

"That is because he died in the war before I was born."

"My condolences for your loss."

"Thank you, but I made peace with that long ago," Rosamond said. "My mother loved him dearly but it was too painful for her to speak about him. But she wore the gold band that he had given her on their wedding day until she took her last breath."

Lord Brentwood's eyes grew sad. "I grew up in a household where my parents loved one another, dearly, in fact. But it all changed when my sister eloped with a man that was below her station."

"I'm sorry," Rosamond said, unsure of what else she could say.

"There is no reason to apologize," he responded. "My father did not take my sister leaving well, and through his own selfish actions, he has ruined his once happy union with my mother."

"How is your mother faring?"

Lord Brentwood grew quiet. "I have never known a more remarkable woman. She loves my father, despite all that he has done, and hopes for a reconciliation."

"There is no love without hope and no hope without love," Rosamond said.

"My mother said something similar, but I believe she is just trying to convince herself that it will get better."

"Then don't take away her hope. That would be entirely unfair of you to do."

"She needs to be practical about it all or she will only continue to get hurt," he argued.

Rosamond shrugged one shoulder. "Love is not practical. True love doesn't always follow the rules and it is most assuredly not meant to be easy."

With a curious look, Lord Brentwood said, "It sounds as if you are speaking from experience."

"I am," she responded. "I was engaged once but I discovered I didn't know him as well as I thought I did. I could not condone his actions and it forced me to break the engagement."

"That is most unfortunate."

"When he died, I was heartbroken, wishing that things had been different. He had chosen to follow a path that would only benefit him, and not us."

Lord Brentwood shifted in his seat. "Was this before or after you became Lord Ashington's ward?"

"It was before."

"I couldn't imagine any circumstance where a man would willingly choose himself over a future with you."

Rosamond lowered her gaze as she blinked back the tears. Lord Brentwood's words touched her deeply. She still grieved George, despite all that he had done, but she was heartbroken that he had forsaken her. Why hadn't she been enough for him?

Lord Brentwood's voice broke through her musings. "You did nothing wrong."

Bringing her gaze up, she asked, "Why would you say such a thing?"

"Because when someone faces a terrible heartache, it is common for them to blame themselves," he explained. "I know I did when my sister eloped. The guilt nearly consumed me."

"How did you stop blaming yourself?"

"A part of me never has," he admitted. "I have just learned to deal with the nagging thoughts."

Against her better judgment, she revealed, "My betrothed tried to hurt someone that I care greatly about, and I was forced to take a stand against him."

"That must have been terribly hard on you."

"It was, but I would do it again, without hesitation," she replied.

Lord Brentwood looked at her as if he were seeing her for the first time. "You are an impressive woman."

Her lips twitched. "I see I have fooled you into believing so."

Lord Brentwood pulled back on the reins and it was only then that Rosamond realized they were in front of Lord Ashington's townhouse. She had been so engrossed in her conversation with Lord Brentwood that she had failed to notice they were approaching her home.

He stepped down from the carriage and came around to assist her. Once her feet were on the pavement, she removed her hand and created more distance between them.

"May I escort you inside?" he asked.

She shook her head. "That is not necessary, but I do thank you for the most enjoyable carriage ride."

"You are welcome," he said. "And I am looking forward to our tour of the Royal Menagerie tomorrow."

"As am I." Why had she just admitted that so freely?

Lord Brentwood smiled. "I am most pleased to hear you say that."

Taking a step back, she attempted to school her features. "Good day, Lord Brentwood."

He bowed. "Good day, Miss Hendre," he said. "Until tomorrow."

Rosamond swiftly turned on her heel and hurried up the stairs. Once she stepped inside, she let out a sigh. Good heavens, she thought. That was quite unexpected. Who would have thought that Lord Brentwood wasn't as awful as she had originally perceived him to be?

Brownell stepped out of the drawing room and asked, "How was your ride, Miss?"

Not wanting to reveal how much she had actually enjoyed herself, she decided to respond in a lackluster response. "It was tolerable."

But it had been so much more and that is what concerned her.

Malcolm sat in the back of White's with a drink in his hand. He had accomplished what he had set out to do. He was slowly turning Miss Hendre's heart towards him. At first, the contempt in her voice was undeniable but it all changed when he had offered to let her drive the carriage. It was a bold move, but it had been purely ingenious on his part. It had broken through Miss Hendre's defenses, and she had been much more open after that.

So why did he feel so uneasy about what he had done? But he already knew why. Miss Hendre wasn't the pompous and vain heiress that he had previously thought. She constantly deflected his attempts at flattery as if she didn't believe his words. Which was odd. Women always had responded to his flattery before. Yet Miss Hendre had proven time and time again that she was immune to it.

Regardless, his objective had not changed. He would marry Miss Hendre and use her dowry to save his family from ruination. Perhaps he might even grow to care for Miss Hendre, but he would never be foolish enough to fall in love with his wife. He had seen the heartache that useless emotion had caused for his parents, and he was determined not to make the same mistake. Furthermore, what had love done for

Enid? Her husband had died and left her penniless, forcing her to flee with her child to a workhouse, a most vile place, because the man's family refused to take her in. Love caused people to do the most illogical things and he was far too smart to fall prey to that. The only good thing that came out of Enid's marriage was Marigold.

Malcolm brought his glass up to his lips. He would be lying to himself if he didn't admit that he was looking forward to his trip to the Royal Menagerie tomorrow with Miss Hendre. She was proving herself to be quite different than the other women he had associated with. When she spoke, there was a genuineness in her words that he found fascinating. She didn't hide behind coy smiles or bat her eyelashes at an alarming rate, but she spoke from the heart.

He pushed down the familiar guilt that he felt for deceiving her. He had no choice in the matter and there was no point in bringing his conscience into this. With any luck, she would become so enamored with him that he could offer for her tomorrow, ending this farce of a courtship. But he suspected it would take much more effort on his part to win over Miss Hendre.

As he brought his glass down, he saw his two friends, Mr. Whitmore and Mr. Moore, approaching him with smiles on their faces. He had been friends with them since their days at Eton, where they bonded over their penchant for getting into trouble with their rowdy antics.

"Good evening," he greeted them as they reached for chairs.

They responded in kind as they sat down.

Mr. Whitmore leaned forward in his seat and his smile had not dimmed in the least. "How was your carriage ride with Miss Hendre?"

"It was pleasurable," Malcolm responded. "How did you know I went on a carriage ride?"

"The whole Town is abuzz with how you let Miss Hendre

drive the carriage," Mr. Whitmore said. "That was quite scandalous on your part."

Malcolm shrugged. "Miss Hendre seemed to appreciate the gesture, and I think it was quite brilliant on my part."

Mr. Moore interjected, "Was her hat really as unique as people are saying?"

"It was," Malcolm confirmed. "I have never seen anything like it before."

"Did she truly have a peacock killed just so she could use all of its feathers on the hat?" Mr. Moore asked.

Malcolm chuckled. "I doubt that."

Mr. Moore looked disappointed. "That would have been a tasty piece of gossip for sure."

"Since when did you care about what the gossips are saying?" Malcolm asked.

"I suppose it is because women always appreciate gossip and I am more than happy to oblige them," Mr. Moore said.

"Regardless, Miss Hendre designed the hat in an attempt to deter me from pursuing her," Malcolm shared.

He was met with blank stares.

"But you are a viscount and will one day be an earl," Mr. Whitmore remarked. "Does she not want to be a countess?"

"Apparently, she is looking for a love match," Malcolm said.

Mr. Whitmore let out a bark of laughter. "To be young and innocent," he mocked. "Every year, the wide-eyed debutantes are hoping to find their true love and the majority of them are disappointed to discover that love has nothing to do with marriage."

Mr. Moore nudged Mr. Whitmore with his elbow. "And you are more than happy to deprive them of their innocence."

"It is true," Mr. Whitmore said, bringing his hand to his chest. "Some would consider me a champion for the women."

"No one would consider you that," Malcolm remarked.

"You better be careful or else one of your liaisons could become disastrous for you."

Mr. Whitmore shook his head. "I am not marriage material, at least not in our circles," he said. "Being the younger son of a baron definitely has some perks."

"I would still be cautious," Malcolm urged. "It only takes one disgruntled brother or father to challenge you to a duel and I have seen you shoot. It isn't pretty."

"I can handle myself," Mr. Whitmore asserted.

Malcolm put his hands up in surrender. "Fair enough. I will not bring it up again."

A server placed three drinks onto the table and asked, "Will there be anything else?"

In response, Mr. Whitmore waved him off and reached for a glass. "I am far more interested in the fact that you have set your cap on Miss Hendre."

"Why is that?' Malcolm asked.

"You have told us, repeatedly, that you have no desire to ever marry," Mr. Whitmore replied. "Yet your actions are proving otherwise."

Malcolm tightened the hold on his glass. "My circumstances have recently changed and I am in need of a wife."

"A rich wife, apparently," Mr. Moore added.

"You are not wrong," Malcolm said. "Fortunately, Miss Hendre fits the bill."

Mr. Moore smirked. "What a romantic you are."

"Regardless, Miss Hendre is quite the catch this Season," Mr. Whitmore said. "Not only is she beautiful, but she is the ward of Lord Ashington."

"I am aware," Malcolm muttered.

"Then you must know that you aren't the only one that intends on pursuing Miss Hendre," Mr. Whitmore said.

Malcolm shrugged. "That means little to me."

Mr. Whitmore looked amused. "You have always been too

cocky for your own good, especially when it comes to the ladies."

"At least I draw the line at compromising them," Malcolm said.

"That is your mistake, not mine," Mr. Whitmore declared. "Besides, I have received no complaints from the ladies."

Malcolm huffed. "Yet! But there will be a day of reckoning for you."

"Perhaps, but until that time, I will enjoy myself immensely." Mr. Whitmore took a sip of his drink and eyed Malcolm curiously. "You seem more cantankerous than normal. Why is that?"

Mr. Moore bobbed his head. "I agree with Whitmore. What is bothering you?"

Malcolm didn't know why he was so annoyed, but he was. He just wanted to leave this blasted club and be alone with his thoughts.

He tossed back his drink before saying, "My apologies, but I'm afraid I won't be very good company tonight."

"You are never good company, but we welcome you anyways," Mr. Moore joked. "I can't help but wonder if Miss Hendre was the one that put you in a bad mood."

Mr. Whitmore gave him a knowing look. "I can't remember the last time a woman has had an effect on you like this."

"There is no effect. Have you considered I am just tired of being in your presence?" Malcolm asked.

"That is absurd!" Mr. Moore exclaimed, feigning outrage. "Whitmore and I are delightful and fun."

Malcolm reached for another glass. "Perhaps I will find you more enjoyable if I am drunk," he proposed.

Mr. Whitmore leaned back in his seat. "You protest too much, which makes me thinketh this is about Miss Hendre."

"Fine," Malcolm said. "I will admit that my thoughts have been preoccupied with Miss Hendre."

"You like her," Mr. Whitmore remarked knowingly.

"Good gads! Are you mad?" Malcolm asked. "I hardly know Miss Hendre."

Mr. Whitmore shifted in his seat to address Mr. Moore. "I can't recall a time when Malcolm has fallen for a lady. Can you?"

"I cannot," Mr. Moore said. "Quite frankly, I didn't think Malcolm would ever let anyone touch his fractured heart."

Malcolm looked heavenward. "Your time as a barrister is wasted. You should have written sonnets about love and relationships."

Mr. Moore tugged down on the lapels of his jacket. "I am quite gifted with the written word," he declared. "You have given me much to think about."

"I wish you luck with that." Malcolm shoved back his chair. "If you will excuse me, I have an errand I need to see to."

"At this hour?" Mr. Whitmore asked as he glanced at the darkened window.

Malcolm pulled out his pocket watch from his waistcoat pocket and saw the late hour. Where had the time gone? He had meant to leave earlier so he could go check in on Enid and her daughter. If he left now, there was a good chance that they would already be asleep when he arrived since it would take hours to go across town at this time.

He shoved the pocket watch back into his pocket and rose. "Regardless, it would be best if I retired for the evening."

Mr. Whitmore looked up at him in disbelief. "Who are you and what have you done with my friend?"

"You can stop with the theatrics," Malcolm said. "I have had a long day and I am tired."

"Too tired to drink away your woes?" Mr. Moore asked, holding his drink up.

"Not everything can be solved at the bottom of a glass," Malcolm pointed out as he pushed back in his chair.

Mr. Whitmore let out a dramatic sigh. "I don't even know you anymore, Brentwood." He waved his hand dismissively. "You may go."

Malcolm tipped his head at Mr. Moore. "Do tell our mutual friend that he is being an idiot this evening."

"I shall pass along the message," Mr. Moore said.

Once he took a step, Mr. Whitmore grabbed his arm and looked up at him. "Don't let this woman get into your head," he advised. "You must keep your wits about you."

"You can rest assured that I have no intention of letting Miss Hendre get into my head," Malcolm said.

Mr. Whitmore looked unsure. "Do not fall; stay strong. Just think of all the women you will disappoint once you settle on Miss Hendre."

"I told you that I have no choice," Malcolm responded. "I must marry Miss Hendre."

His friend released his arm. "It is a shame to see another man fall victim to the parson's mousetrap."

"Miss Hendre hasn't agreed to be my wife yet," Malcolm reminded him.

"But she will," Mr. Whitmore said. "She is a fool if she seeks a loftier title."

Malcolm shifted in his stance. "I'm not sure if she is looking for a title."

"Then she is a bigger fool than I thought," Mr. Whitmore responded as he turned back towards the table.

As he walked away, Malcolm couldn't help but wonder who the bigger fool was. Miss Hendre may be looking for a love match, which was laughable, but at least she was being true to herself. Whereas he was pursuing her with the intention of deceiving her into a courtship.

He needed to be mindful to remember what was at stake here. Nothing else mattered, at least to him. He just needed to stay strong and ignore these pesky feelings of guilt. No good would come from acknowledging them.

Chapter Nine

Rosamond was in the most pleasant mood as she descended the stairs. She had slept well, and she was eager to seize the day. Nothing would squash her growing excitement to see the Royal Menagerie with Lord Brentwood. She had heard rumors of the exotic animals that were housed at the Tower of London ever since she was a little girl. She couldn't wait to see for herself what the hype was all about.

Her eyes landed on a large bouquet of flowers that was placed on the table in the entry hall. It was an odd bunch since it was an assortment of every flower imaginable. There appeared to be no rhyme or reason to the mismatched bouquet, making it terribly ugly and out of place in the grand hall.

As she pondered why someone would send such a collection of flowers, her eyes landed on a card with her name on it. She reached for it and read:

I wasn't sure what your favorite flower was so I had them wrap up every flower that they had in the shop. I hope these flowers bring a smile to your face as the mere thought of you brings one to mine.

. . .

It was signed by Lord Brentwood and Rosamond found his kind gesture did, in fact, bring a smile to her lips. He could have just sent flowers, but he had been thoughtful in his approach. It was evident that he had remembered their previous conversation a few days prior when they had discussed flowers. And that made her feel heard.

Lady Anne's voice came from behind her. "What an unusual-looking bouquet," she declared in a critical voice.

"I think it is beautiful," Rosamond said as she turned to face Lady Anne.

"You would be wrong since it appears as if a child put together this assortment," Lady Anne remarked.

Rosamond laughed. "Lord Brentwood wasn't sure what my favorite flower was so he sent every flower he could get his hands on."

"That is one way to send flowers; the wrong way, mind you, but it was a nice gesture, nevertheless."

"I think it was sweet."

Lady Anne eyed her curiously. "Could it be that you are softening your stance towards Lord Brentwood?"

"I will admit that I find him to be much less vexing than I once did," she shared. "But I am still of the mind that we would not suit."

"Heaven forbid that you fall for a man that will inherit an earldom," Lady Anne said dramatically.

Lord Ashington's voice came from further down the hall. "Leave her be, Anne," he encouraged as he closed the distance between them. "Rosamond is the decider of her own fate, not you."

"I am merely providing encouragement where it is need-ed," Lady Anne defended, looking the epitome of innocence.

With a chuckle, Lord Ashington said, "I doubt that. I

know you, Child, and you like to insert yourself in other people's lives."

"To help them make the right choice," Lady Anne pressed. "If it wasn't for me, Lizette would have never married Tristan."

"I do believe I played a role in that, especially since it was my idea in the first place," Lord Ashington said.

"Yes, but I implemented your vision."

Lord Ashington turned his attention towards the flowers. "What an ugly bouquet," he acknowledged. "Who would dare to send such a thing?"

Rosamond spoke up. "Lord Brentwood sent them to me," she explained. "He wasn't sure what my favorite flower was so he had the shop send all of the flowers."

"That was a bold move on his part," Lord Ashington said.

With a glance at the flowers, Rosamond shared, "On a previous occasion we had discussed the importance of knowing a woman's favorite flower. Apparently, he took that conversation to heart."

"Apparently so," Lord Ashington agreed. "But enough of this, I need some coffee if I want to continue on. Shall we adjourn to the dining room?"

Lady Anne shook her head. "You and your coffee," she remarked.

As they walked towards the dining room, Lord Ashington said, "I do apologize for missing supper last night, but our meeting ran late at the House of Lords."

"It was a relatively quiet night," Lady Anne responded. "I retired early with a headache and Lizette and Tristan went to the opera."

"I never thought I would see the day that Tristan went to the opera, willingly," Lord Ashington said.

"It was Lizette's idea," Lady Anne shared.

Lord Ashington grinned. "The things men do for love," he said as they stepped into the dining room.

Rosamond went to sit down to the right of Lord Ashington and reached for a napkin. After she draped it onto her lap, she waited for the footman to place a cup of chocolate in front of her.

A footman handed the newssheets to Lord Ashington and he began reading as they all settled in.

After a long moment, Lady Anne spoke up from across the table, breaking the silence. "Rosamond will be visiting the Royal Menagerie with Lord Brentwood today," she informed Lord Ashington.

"Very good," Lord Ashington muttered as he continued to read the newssheets.

"There might be a chance that she will be mauled by a lion while she is there," Lady Anne said with a wink at her.

Lord Ashington bobbed his head. "It sounds most enjoyable."

Lady Anne exchanged a smile with Rosamond before she continued. "I did tell her that she could bring home a monkey as a pet."

"Wonderful idea," he said, his eyes roaming the articles.

A footman placed down a coffee cup in front of Lord Ashington and he promptly lowered the newssheets to the table. He reached for it and took a sip.

"Father, I do not think you were listening to me just now," Lady Anne said.

"I always listen to you," Lord Ashington attempted.

Lady Anne gave him a knowing look. "You gave permission for Rosamond to have a monkey as a pet."

Lord Ashington blanched. "Why would she want a monkey?"

"She doesn't, but you didn't know that when you agreed to it," Lady Anne replied. "I would encourage you to be more present over breakfast."

"Very well," Lord Ashington said as he put his coffee cup down. "Perhaps we can start with how Rosamond's carriage ride through Hyde Park with Lord Brentwood went."

Rosamond shrugged, not wanting to reveal too much. "It was uneventful."

"Interesting," Lord Ashington murmured as he reached for the newssheets. "Do you want to explain why there is a drawing in the Society pages of you wearing an interesting hat and driving a carriage?"

"I can explain," Rosamond rushed out as Lady Anne gasped.

Lord Ashington put the newssheets down. "By all means, go on," he encouraged.

"I wore the hat to try to discourage Lord Brentwood from taking me on a carriage ride through Hyde Park," Rosamond shared.

"But your plan failed," Lady Anne pointed out.

"It did, and I am most grateful for that," Rosamond said. "Once Lord Brentwood offered to let me drive the coach, I realized that he wasn't as awful as I had previously thought."

Lord Ashington lifted his brow. "He offered to let you drive?"

"He did," Rosamond replied.

"I have never heard of such a thing," Lady Anne huffed. "A woman does not drive a carriage, especially in Hyde Park. It would draw far too much attention."

Rosamond nodded. "I am aware, but I found it to be a thoughtful gesture."

"You should have refused him," Lady Anne asserted. "Now, you are depicted by a cartoon in the Society pages."

"That was not my intention," Rosamond said.

Lady Anne frowned. "Reputations have been ruined by much less," she admonished. "It is too early to know what effect this will have on you, but I would brace yourself for the repercussions."

"I understand," Rosamond murmured, lowering her gaze.

"It might be best if Lizette and Tristan accompanied you and Lord Brentwood to the Royal Menagerie," Lady Anne suggested.

"I am not opposed to that," Rosamond said. She always loved to spend time with her sister and brother-in-law.

Lord Ashington sighed. "Chin up, dear girl," he encouraged. "We have weathered through worse situations than this."

Bringing her gaze up, Rosamond said, "I never wished to bring scandal to your family."

"Scandal?" Lord Ashington chuckled. "This is hardly a scandal. I have no doubt that the gossips will move on once something more shocking comes along."

"Father, we should not downplay this," Lady Anne urged. "How else will Rosamond learn there are consequences to her actions?"

Lord Ashington's eyes crinkled around the edges. "There is a fine line between encouragement and criticism, and it's not always easy to know which side of that line you are on."

"I am not trying to criticize Rosamond, but I am worried for her," Lady Anne stated.

Lizette stepped into the room with Rosamond's peacock hat on her head. "Look what I found in Rosamond's room," she said, holding her hands up. "Isn't it extraordinary?"

"That is one word for it," Lady Anne muttered.

Lord Ashington stared at his granddaughter. "I daresay that the image in the newssheets did not do that hat justice."

Lizette laughed. "I think I could take out a few people with the number of feathers on this hat," she said before addressing Rosamond. "Where did you find such a hat?"

"I made it," Rosamond admitted.

"You are very talented," Lizette said. "Perhaps you can make me one, as well."

Lady Anne gave her a disapproving shake of her head.

"Please do not encourage this, Lizette," she insisted. "That hat should be burned, not celebrated."

"I think it is brilliant. The hat can act as a weapon of sorts," Lizette responded as she sat down next to Lady Anne. "Rosamond can remove the feathers and use the sharp edges as a way to protect herself."

"There is no need for Rosamond to protect herself since it is perfectly civilized here in Town," Lady Anne said.

"Yes, because it is unfathomable to think that someone might actually get abducted in London," Lizette joked.

The lines around Lady Anne's mouth deepened. "Do be serious," she stated. "What happened to you was an anomaly."

Lizette removed the hat from her head and placed it down onto the table. "When the hat isn't being worn it can also act as a decoration piece."

Lord Ashington looked amused as he pushed back his seat. "If you will excuse me, I need to depart at once for the House of Lords."

After the aged marquess departed from the room, Lady Anne reached for her teacup and addressed Lizette. "Do you have any objections to accompanying Rosamond and Lord Brentwood to the Royal Menagerie today?"

"I do not," Lizette replied.

"Good, then you can ensure that Rosamond will behave herself around Lord Brentwood," Lady Anne said before she took a sip.

Lizette's lips twitched. "It will take some effort on my part to ensure Tristan comes along, but I have no doubt I can convince him."

Lady Anne bobbed her head in approval. "Now, we should adjourn to the drawing room to receive Rosamond's callers, assuming she hasn't scared them all off due to her antics."

A line appeared in Lizette's brow as she gave Rosamond a questioning look.

"I drove Lord Brentwood's carriage through Hyde Park yesterday," Rosamond explained to her sister.

"Why would you do such a thing?" Lizette asked.

"It seemed like a good idea at the time," Rosamond replied.

"And now?" Lizette pressed.

Rosamond glanced at Lady Anne before saying, "I should have considered the repercussions of my actions."

Lizette grinned. "But do you regret it?" she asked knowingly.

"No," Rosamond replied.

Lady Anne tossed up her hands. "Have you learned nothing, Child?" she asked in an exasperated voice. "You will be the death of me. I am sure of it."

Rosamond attempted to hide her growing smile behind her fingers. She knew why Lady Anne was upset, and she was grateful for her concern, but she didn't regret what she had done. She couldn't change everything about herself to fit in to Society.

Malcolm adjusted his cravat as his valet went about organizing his bedchamber. He had a fitful night of sleep, mostly due to his thoughts continuously straying to Miss Hendre. It was maddening. Why couldn't he just banish her from his mind and be done with it? Yes, she was a beautiful young woman, but it wasn't just her beauty that caused him pause. And that is what infuriated him.

He didn't care that her eyes sparkled when she teased him or how two dimples would appear when she smiled. Those were things he shouldn't notice about her. How many times did he have to remind himself that no good would come from letting his guard down around Miss Hendre?

Regardless, because of her, he had given up on sleep and gotten out of bed at an ungodly hour. He hated being up at such an early hour, but he needed to travel across town to check on his sister and her child before he went to the Royal Menagerie with Miss Hendre.

A knock came at the door and his valet crossed the room to open it, revealing a young maid. She dropped into a curtsy and announced, "Lord Brentwood has a visitor."

"Well, who is it?" the valet asked.

"Mr. Osborne thought it would be best if he told Lord Brentwood himself," the young maid replied.

Now the young maid had Malcolm's attention and he turned towards the door. "Inform Osborne that I will be down shortly."

"Very good, my lord," the maid said before she left to do his bidding.

Once the door was closed, his valet asked, "Do you know who this visitor is?"

"I do not, but Osborne must have a good reason to conceal his identity," Malcolm replied as he walked over to the door. "I intend to go to Lady William Taylor's ball this evening."

"I shall see to the preparations, my lord."

Malcolm tipped his head before he departed from his bedchamber. As he walked down the hall, he wondered if his visitor was his sister. Would she have been foolish enough to have left the safety of the boarding house to visit him? Possibly, and that would explain Osborne's secrecy.

He descended the stairs and saw Osborne in the entry hall with an unusually solemn look on his face. The butler crossed the entry hall and waited for him at the base of the stairs.

Malcolm came to a stop on the last step and kept his voice low. "Is it my sister?"

"No, my lord, it is…" he hesitated, "Mr. Longbourn."

Stunned, he repeated, "Mr. Longbourn? Are you sure?"

Osborne held up a calling card. "I am," he replied as he extended it towards him. "He said the matter was most urgent."

Malcolm accepted the card and saw Mr. Longbourn's name for himself. Botheration. This didn't make any sense. Enid had told him that her husband was dead. So how was he here, acting very much alive?

"Where is he?" Malcolm asked.

"I showed him to the study," Osborne replied.

Malcolm nodded his approval. "Is my father home?"

"He left for the House of Lords about an hour ago and I don't expect him home until later this evening."

"Good," he muttered. He had no doubt that his father would be furious if he discovered Mr. Longbourn had been in their home. "Let's keep Mr. Longbourn's visit between us for now."

"That had been my thought as well."

He handed the calling card back to Osborne. "Ensure that we are not interrupted, for any reason."

"Yes, my lord," Osborne said.

Malcolm turned and headed down the hall towards the rear of the townhouse. He didn't know what was going on, but he was going to find out. The only thing he knew for certain was that Enid had lied to him, but for what purpose?

He stepped into the study and saw the tall, lanky Mr. Longbourn staring out the window, his hands clasped behind his back. He had a long face, straight nose, and neatly trimmed sideburns. Malcolm had never understood what his sister had seen in Mr. Longbourn, especially since he was poor and had no prospects.

Mr. Longbourn unclasped his hands and turned to face him. "Thank you for agreeing to see me, my lord."

He didn't have time for pleasantries, so he asked, "What is it that you want?"

If Mr. Longbourn appeared upset by his bluntness, he didn't show it. "I have come to see if you know of your sister's whereabouts."

Malcolm didn't owe this man anything and he felt compelled to protect his sister, at least until he discovered what she was about. "Why, did you lose her?" he mocked.

"Enid and I had a disagreement and she ran away with our child," Mr. Longbourn replied. "She has yet to return."

"When was this?"

"About two months ago," Mr. Longbourn said.

Malcolm lifted his brow. "She ran away two months ago, and I am only just hearing about this?" he demanded.

Mr. Longbourn frowned. "I am all too aware that I am no longer welcome in your home, but I am at my wit's end," he said. "I hired a Bow Street Runner to find her and he informed me that a young woman matching Enid's description was spotted here two days ago."

"He would be wrong."

"Are you sure?" Mr. Longbourn pressed.

It was Malcolm's turn to frown. "My father has disowned Enid and she wouldn't be foolish enough to return home. I can assure you that no aid would be rendered."

Mr. Longbourn ran a hand through his hair, appearing very much in distress. "I am utterly lost without my Enid," he said as he went to sit down on an upholstered armchair. "I can't fathom why she left."

Malcolm resisted the urge to groan. Why was Mr. Longbourn making himself comfortable? It was time for him to leave so he could go speak to his sister.

With crestfallen eyes, Mr. Longbourn asked, "Do you have any idea where your sister might be?"

He almost felt pity for the man... almost. But this was the man that had eloped with his sister, causing a scandal for their family. If he had truly cared for Enid, he would never have taken away her future.

"I do not," he lied. "Have you spoken to any of her friends?"

"Yes, all of them, but she didn't turn to any of them for help."

Malcolm went to sit across from Mr. Longbourn. "Enid will turn up," he encouraged. "Why don't you return home and wait for her?"

Mr. Longbourn didn't look convinced. "What if she doesn't come home?" he asked. "I can't help but wonder if she is dead in a ditch somewhere with our daughter."

"That is a morbid thought."

"What else am I supposed to think?" Mr. Longbourn questioned. "It has been two months and I have heard no word from her."

Malcolm needed to find out more about the Bow Street Runner. Leaning forward in his seat, he said, "You were wise to hire a Bow Street Runner. How long has he been on the case?"

"Just a little over two weeks," Mr. Longbourn replied.

"But Enid has been gone for two months," Malcolm said. "Why didn't you hire a Bow Street Runner sooner?"

Mr. Longbourn shrugged. "I thought Enid would grow tired of whatever game she is playing and return home to me."

"But you clearly underestimated how stubborn my sister is."

"I assure you that it won't happen again," Mr. Longbourn said with a slight clenching of his jaw.

Malcolm glanced at the long clock in the corner and knew it was time to rid himself of Mr. Longbourn. He had many questions for his sister and it would take quite some time to travel to her boarding house at this hour.

Rising, he said, "I will inform you at once if I hear from

Enid, but I would not be holding my breath. I daresay that we are the last people she would come to for help."

Mr. Longbourn bobbed his head. "I assumed as much, but I had to try." He heaved a sigh of frustration. "I am using funds that I can scarcely afford to pay the Bow Street Runner."

"It is for a good cause."

"Seeing as I am trying to find your sister, I was hoping you would consider helping me pay the Bow Street Runner's exorbitant fee."

Malcolm stared at Mr. Longbourn in disbelief. "You came here asking for money?"

"Just a small sum," Mr. Longbourn replied. "I haven't been able to work since I have been worried sick about Enid."

"Enid is your problem; not ours," Malcolm responded.

"But she is still your sister, and you don't want anything bad to happen to her. Do you?"

Malcolm narrowed his eyes slightly. "I do not respond kindly to being manipulated," he replied.

Mr. Longbourn put his hand up in front of him. "I have no intention of manipulating you, but it is imperative I find Enid before something bad befalls her."

"What if it already has?"

"I hope that isn't the case," Mr. Longbourn responded softly. "I just want a chance to apologize to her and make everything right again."

Malcolm didn't know why but he wasn't buying Mr. Longbourn's act. He claimed he desperately missed Enid, but he hadn't sought out a Bow Street Runner until she had been missing for almost six weeks. Something wasn't right here, but he couldn't put his finger on it. All he did know was that a Bow Street Runner would be a nuisance as he tried to sort out what he intended to do with Enid. Even if he brought her here, Mr. Longbourn had every right to force her to return home with him. That was his right as her husband.

"I will pay for the Bow Street Runner, but only on the condition that he will report to me," Malcolm said.

Mr. Longbourn shook his head. "Absolutely not!" he exclaimed. "Enid is my wife and I have a right to know what the Bow Street Runner discovers."

"That is understandable, and I will relay the information to you once the Bow Street Runner has discovered Enid's whereabouts."

"That hardly seems fair."

"Do you want me to pay for the Bow Street Runner or not?" Malcolm demanded.

"I do, but——"

Malcolm cut him off. "Those are my terms and they are not negotiable."

Mr. Longbourn pursed his lips. "Fine," he spat out, "but you will notify me at once when Enid is found."

"I would have it no other way," Malcolm said. "Inform the Bow Street Runner that I wish to speak to him at once."

"I will send word to him."

When Mr. Longbourn failed to get up from his seat, Malcolm gave him an expectant look. "Is there anything else you wish to discuss?"

"I was hoping to reopen the discussion about Enid's dowry," Mr. Longbourn said. "It is only fair that I receive it since I am entitled to it."

Malcolm couldn't believe Mr. Longbourn's audacity to ask for Enid's dowry when his father had made it clear that he would never see a farthing from it. "That is between you and my father, but I do believe he has made his stance known on it."

"I was hoping you would speak to him about it."

"And why would I do that?" he asked, uninterested.

Mr. Longbourn rose. "I'm afraid that I don't have the funds to care for Enid and my daughter in the way that I hoped to."

"That is a shame, but how does that concern me?"

"Seeing that Enid has a child now, I would think that you would show more compassion for your niece."

Malcolm held his gaze. "Enid made her decision when she eloped with you," he said. "I do not wish ill-will upon her or her child, but that is where my contribution stops."

Mr. Longbourn's eyes sparked with anger. "You are cold-hearted, my lord. It is of little wonder why Enid chose to leave you."

"Regardless, you are not welcome in our home," Malcolm declared. "If you by chance come when my father is here, I don't doubt he will make good on his promise to send for the constable."

"I will leave but I will be waiting for you to send word when the Bow Street Runner discovers Enid's whereabouts," Mr. Longbourn said before he walked over to the door.

Once Mr. Longbourn had departed, Malcolm waited only a moment before he walked over to the door and shouted, "Osborne."

The butler promptly appeared in the hall.

"Prepare my coach and have it brought out front," he ordered. "I have an errand that I need to see to at once."

"I assumed as much, and I had your coach prepared while you were speaking to Mr. Longbourn," Osborne said. "In addition, I took the liberty of securing three footmen to accompany you on your errand."

"That was most thoughtful of you," Malcolm responded. "I hope this particular errand won't take too long, but it is of the utmost importance."

"I wish you luck, my lord."

With a purposeful stride, Malcolm headed towards the main door. He had a lot of questions for Enid, and he hoped she would be forthcoming with the answers.

Chapter Ten

Malcolm exited his coach and headed into the modest boarding house on the outskirts of the fashionable part of town. As he passed through the narrow entry hall, the white-haired Mrs. Fleming stepped out of a room and moved to block his path.

"Lord Brentwood, what a pleasant surprise," she greeted as her critical gaze swept over him.

"Hello, Mrs. Fleming," he said. "How are you doing this fine day?" He didn't have time for pleasantries, but he couldn't bring himself to be rude.

"I am well, but my dear husband is not doing well. He has a cough that sounds like a pig choking on a bone."

"That is rather a specific sound."

"It is a sound that I will never forget." Mrs. Fleming glanced over her shoulder and lowered her voice. "I have taken it upon myself to watch over your sister and her child. She hardly leaves her room, and when she does, it has only been to get something to eat."

Malcolm nodded his approval. "I do appreciate your attentiveness to my sister."

"I won't always be so attentive because I do have other

tenants to care for," Mrs. Fleming remarked. "But I am sure I can be enticed to do so."

Knowing what this was about, he reached into his jacket pocket and removed a few coins. "I would appreciate your discretion," he said, extending the money to her.

Mrs. Fleming accepted the coins and slipped them into the pocket of her gown. "I am nothing but discreet, my lord." She stepped to the side to allow him to pass.

Malcolm brushed past Mrs. Fleming and headed towards Enid's room on the first level. He knocked on the door and he could hear movement coming from within.

A long moment later, his sister asked, "Who is there?"

"Malcolm," he replied.

The door was promptly opened, and Enid stepped back to allow him entrance. The room was small, but it was sufficient for his sister's needs. A bed was situated in the middle with a wardrobe on its right side and a desk sat near the lone window.

Marigold was sitting on the bed, and she let out a cry when she saw him. Enid went to pick her up and explained, "Marigold isn't always this fussy, but she still isn't feeling well."

"You don't need to worry about that. I have no doubt that Marigold will warm up to me, given time."

Enid propped Marigold onto her right hip and shared, "The doctor came by this morning and he said that Marigold's color is looking much better."

"That is good."

"I thought so," Enid said. "I can't thank you enough for everything that you have done for me and Marigold, but perhaps you might want to stop using Mrs. Fleming to spy on me."

"Duly noted." Malcolm went to sit on the bed and knew it would be best if he just said what needed to be said. "I had a visitor this morning."

Enid looked unconcerned as she glanced down at her daughter. "Did you now?"

"Yes, it was your husband- John Longbourn," Malcolm said. "Would you care to explain how that is possible when you told me that he was dead."

The color drained from Enid's face. "I can explain."

"Can you?" Malcolm asked. "Because I can't for the life of me think of why you lied to me."

Enid walked over to the window and peeked out from behind the drapes. "You didn't tell him where we were, did you?"

"Of course not. I wanted to give you a chance to explain why you ran away from him."

Enid started bouncing Marigold on her hip when she started getting fussy. "John is not a good man, but I didn't discover that until after I married him."

"You did elope with him. That does speak against his character."

"I know, but I thought we eloped because we were in love and it was our only chance to be together."

"There were other ways to go about it."

"How?" she asked. "Father refused to give him his blessing and I was young, naive and incredibly ignorant on the ways of men. John convinced me that Father was just trying to keep us apart and he would come around once we were wed."

"But Father is immensely pigheaded and never did come around."

She shook her head sadly. "It all changed when Father refused to give John my dowry. He became irate and irrational towards me. It wasn't long after that he started hurting me. I tried to hide the bruises on my face with powder but it was pointless. It got so bad that I stopped leaving the townhouse for fear of being stared at and pitied."

"Why didn't you come to me?" he asked.

Enid huffed. "What could you do? I belong to John, which

is something he reminds me of all the time. There was nothing you could do that would help me. The beatings grew more frequent and there were many times I passed out from them."

Malcolm clenched his jaw. "You still should have told me. I could—"

"Done what?" she asked, cutting him off. "Nothing could be done for me. I was in a prison of my own making and not even being pregnant got me a reprieve from John's heavy hand."

"What changed then?"

Enid went to place Marigold in the center of the bed and sat next to her. "John never struck Marigold and I took great comfort in that. But it changed two months ago when he started striking her for the tiniest infractions. That is when I knew I had to leave. I had to protect Marigold at all costs."

"So you went to a workhouse?"

She shrugged. "I had nowhere else to go and I knew that John would never find me there. We were safe and that is all that mattered."

"Why didn't you take some money with you?"

"What money?" she asked. "The part about losing the townhouse to creditors was the truth. John spent every farthing we had on gambling and his whores."

"What of Mother's pearls that you had been wearing on the night you eloped?" he asked.

Enid lowered her gaze as she admitted, "That went to feed us for many months."

Malcolm sighed as he rose from the bed. "Why did you suffer in silence for so long?" he asked.

"I told you—"

He spoke over her. "I would have gotten you away from him!"

"How?" she asked. "If you had, you could have been arrested for your involvement. The law is on John's side."

"Then we would have had Father petition Parliament for a divorce..."

Enid laughed. "Father would never have done such a thing for me, and you know it. The only way for me and Marigold to be free is to find a place that John will never find us."

Malcolm wracked his brain as he tried to find a solution to help Enid. "We will remove you far from London. You can stay at our country estate," he suggested.

"And what if John comes looking for me?"

"Then we would lie to protect you."

"You can't lie forever."

"For you, I would," Malcolm asserted. "I would do anything to keep you and Marigold away from John."

Enid ran her hand over Marigold's hair. "The best course of action is for me to disappear into the countryside. I could go from village to village until I find a job."

"What will you do with Marigold when you are at work?"

She sighed. "I don't know, but I can't risk John finding us. I do believe he would kill me if he ever got his hands on me again."

"Then we won't let that happen."

Enid gave him a sad smile. "I know you are trying to help, but I have to do this on my own."

"Why?" he asked. "Do you get a prize for being obstinate like Father?"

"Malcolm..."

He interrupted her. "I am not going to just let you disappear out of my life again. If you want to start over in some village, I will help you get settled."

"What if John discovers your involvement?" she asked. "He could go to the magistrate, and you could get into trouble."

"Let me worry about that." He sat back down on the bed and reached for Marigold's tiny hand. "You just focus on ensuring Marigold gets healthy."

Tears flooded Enid's eyes. "It has been so long since anyone has offered to help me."

"You and Marigold are safe now. I promise you that."

Enid swiped at the tears that rolled down her cheeks. "Thank you," she said on a sob. "I can't describe how wonderful it is to hear that."

Malcolm couldn't help but notice the dark circles under Enid's eyes. "Have you been sleeping?"

"I haven't," she admitted. "Every time I close my eyes, I have had the same reoccurring nightmare that John finds us."

"Why don't you rest now and I will watch over Marigold?"

Enid shook her head vehemently. "I couldn't possibly impose on you…"

"I assure you that it is no imposition." He reached down and picked up Marigold. "We won't even leave the room."

His sister looked as if she were going to refuse him but then she yawned. Her hand flew up to cover her mouth. "Perhaps I am more tired than I realized."

"Sleep, Sister," he encouraged.

Enid gave him a grateful smile before she laid her head on the pillow. It wasn't very long before her breathing deepened and she was asleep.

Malcolm turned his attention towards Marigold. "That was quick," he said in a hushed voice. "Your mother was tired."

Marigold stared at him for a long moment before she brought her hand up and stuck her fingers into his mouth.

He chuckled. "Let's keep our fingers to ourselves, shall we?" he chided lightly as he removed her hand. "It looks like it is just you and me for the next little bit. What do you do for fun?"

Marigold smiled up at him.

"Do you find me amusing, little one?" he asked.

A shadow went past the window, drawing his attention. He walked over and looked out towards the back of the boarding house but saw nothing amiss. Perhaps he had just imagined it. As he turned, he saw a burly man out of the corner of his eye and he was wearing a distinctive red waistcoat. *A Bow Street Runner.*

His heart dropped. But as quickly as he had seen the man, he was gone. Was this the Bow Street Runner that Mr. Longbourn had hired to find Enid? It was too much of a coincidence to dismiss. If this Runner reported back to Mr. Longbourn about Enid's location, the man no doubt would inform John of his involvement, making it much harder to help his sister.

Regardless, it was not safe for Enid to remain here any longer. He had to find a place that she would be safe until he could find a way to remove her from London.

A soft knock came at the door.

Malcolm had a good idea of who was on that other side of the door and he wasn't about to open it for the Runner. He approached the door and asked, "What is it that you want?"

"I just want to talk," a deep voice said. "I assure you that I mean you and your sister no harm."

"How do I know I can trust you?"

"You don't, Lord Brentwood," came his quick reply, "but time is of the essence."

Knowing he had little choice in the matter, he unlocked the door and opened it slightly. "I'm afraid I am at a disadvantage since I don't know your name."

The burly Bow Street Runner met his gaze, and his eyes had a determined gleam to them. "Let me in and I will be happy to disclose it."

Malcolm glanced over his shoulder at his sister and hoped he would not come to regret this. He opened the door wide and held his hand out.

The Bow Street Runner stepped into the room and closed the door behind him. With a glance at Enid sleeping on the bed, he kept his voice low, but it didn't take away from his commanding presence that filled the room. "My name is Greydon Campden," he revealed, "and I was hired by Mr. Longbourn to discover his wife's whereabouts."

"Yes, I am aware, but it is imperative that you do not reveal my sister's location. If you do, she could be in grave danger and..."

Mr. Campden put his hand up, stilling Malcolm's words. "I have been trying to find Lady Enid Longbourn for two weeks now and that led me to a workhouse. Which made me wonder why a lady would willingly choose a workhouse over residing with her husband."

Enid's voice came from behind him. "I had no choice," she said softly as she sat up in bed. "He would have killed me."

The Bow Street Runner held her gaze for a long moment, his expression giving nothing away. "I believe you. After all, I did do some investigating into your husband."

"Then you must know he is not a good man," Enid said.

"I do, my lady." Mr. Campden turned his attention towards Malcolm. "I'm not going to tell Mr. Longbourn where Lady Enid is on one condition."

"Anything," Malcolm responded.

"Get her as far away from London as quickly as you can," Mr. Campden advised. "I have a feeling that I am not the only one looking for Lady Enid."

Enid rose from the bed and went to collect Marigold from Malcolm. "Thank you, kind sir," she said as she held her child in her arms. "I don't know what I did to deserve your kindness, but I am most grateful for it."

The solemn look on Mr. Campden's face softened to a look that made him appear approachable- almost. "Three years ago, my sister spilled a drink on herself at a soiree and you most generously helped her, despite risking your own reputation along with hers. It is my turn to return the favor."

Realization dawned on Enid's expression. "You must be related to Lady Helena Campden."

"It is Lady Darlington now, and, yes, I am," Mr. Campden said.

Malcolm furrowed his brow at that revelation. It was evident that there was more than meets the eye with Mr. Campden. How was it possible that a gentleman from high Society was working as a Bow Street Runner without the gossips catching wind of it?

His eyes roamed over Mr. Campden's plain brown suit, giving no indication that he was a man of means, and his boots could use a good polish.

Unable to help himself, Malcolm asked, "You are a gentleman?"

Mr. Campden's jaw clenched. "Right now, I am a Bow Street Runner, and you should know that I don't take kindly to questions." His words held a warning.

As he went to apologize, Mr. Campden continued. "I'm afraid I must depart, but Lady Enid is safe here," he hesitated, "for now. Good day."

Mr. Campden departed from the room, being mindful to close the door behind him.

Enid's eyes remained fixed on the door. "I believe Mr. Campden."

"As do I," Malcolm said. "But in the meantime, I am not going anywhere."

Rosamond stared out the darkened window as she leaned her head against the windowsill. She had been looking forward to going to the Royal Menagerie but Lord Brentwood had never shown up to take her. She felt a myriad of conflicting emotions about the situation. She felt anger for the utter disrespect he had shown her, but she also couldn't help but be worried for his sake. What had happened to him that caused him to miss their date?

Lizette's voice came from behind her. "He isn't coming," she said, softly.

"I know," Rosamond responded as she turned to face her sister. "But I can't help but wonder if something terrible has befallen him."

"Let's hope not, but have you considered your initial assessment of Lord Brentwood was accurate?"

"I have considered that, but I thought Lord Brentwood was different, at least, I was starting to."

Lizette's eyes held compassion. "As did I, but he didn't even have the courtesy to send word that he would be delayed."

Rosamond knew that her sister was right. Lord Brentwood had servants at his disposal and he could have easily sent word. But, instead, he just left her wondering where he was all afternoon. If he had just been toying with her emotions, why had he sent flowers and a note earlier? It just didn't make sense.

Tristan stepped into the room and went to stand by his wife. "I see that Rosamond is no longer looking out the window for Lord Brentwood."

"I do believe she has given up for the day," Lizette said.

"That is good," Tristan acknowledged. "I was starting to wonder if she would leave her post to dine with us."

Rosamond tucked a piece of errant hair behind her ear. "I am sorry that you were forced to clear your schedule for no reason."

Tristan smiled. "Do not fret. There is always work to be done."

Lady Anne walked into the room and announced, "Brownell just informed me that dinner is ready to be served."

As they started walking towards the dining room, Lady Anne came to walk next to her. "How are you faring, Child?"

"I am well."

Lady Anne's eyes held concern. "Do not let Lord Brentwood's actions discourage you from your course," she encouraged. "There will be other suitors that won't be so inconsiderate of your time or feelings."

Rosamond did not like the position she found herself in. It appeared as if everyone around her felt only pity for her and her situation. She didn't need- or want- their pity. She was disappointed, but she wasn't devastated by Lord Brentwood's actions. Frankly, she didn't know him well enough for that kind of reaction. Yes, she was intrigued by Lord Brentwood, but it wasn't as if she had developed deep feelings for the man.

She couldn't wait to put today- and Lord Brentwood- behind her. As far as she was concerned, Lord Brentwood had displayed the type of man he truly was by his thoughtless actions. Now she just had to convince herself to stop dwelling on him. Which was proving to be an impossible feat. Her thoughts were continuously turning to him.

A footman pulled out a chair for her and waited until she sat down before pushing it back in. "Thank you," she murmured in response.

With a glance at the head of the table, Lizette asked, "Where is grandfather?"

"He is still at the House of Lords, but he sent word that he would be home shortly," Lady Anne replied.

"Should we wait for him?" Rosamond questioned.

Lady Anne shook her head. "Heavens, no," she replied. "If we do so, we risk our food being cold and that is something I cannot abide."

As if on cue, the footmen came to place bowls of soup in front of them.

Rosamond picked up a spoon and started eating. With any luck, no one else would bring up Lord Brentwood and they could all move on from this. Unfortunately, she wasn't so lucky.

"I am sorry that Lord Brentwood didn't take you to the Royal Menagerie today," Lizette said. "Perhaps we could go tomorrow."

Tristan bobbed his head. "I could move some things around and escort you ladies in the afternoon."

"That isn't necessary," Rosamond attempted.

"It is wholly necessary," Lizette responded. "The Royal Menagerie is not a sight to miss. The lions make me smile every time I lay my eyes on them."

Not wanting to feel like an interloper, Rosamond suggested, "Perhaps just you and Tristan should go and spend time together."

Tristan and Lizette exchanged a look filled with love before her sister said, "I know what you are trying to do and it won't work."

"What am I trying to do?" Rosamond asked innocently.

Lizette smiled. "You are trying to get out of going to the Royal Menagerie with us because you don't have an escort."

"Is it so obvious?"

"I promise that Tristan and I will behave," Lizette responded.

Lady Anne interjected, "I think it is a fine idea. Why should Lord Brentwood spoil all of your fun when you are in London?"

"He has hardly spoiled my fun," Rosamond argued.

"Will you come, then?" Lizette asked.

Rosamond knew what her sister was about. Lizette was trying to make her feel better, but it wasn't necessary. She had suffered disappointment before, and she had only grown stronger because of it. But Lizette was looking at her with a hopeful expression on her face and she didn't dare let her down.

"I will come," Rosamond agreed.

Lizette clasped her hands together. "We shall have such fun together."

Lord Ashington stepped into the dining room and Lord Brentwood trailed behind him. "Look who I found loitering outside our door," the marquess said, gesturing towards their guest. "I invited him to dine with us."

Lord Brentwood's eyes landed on her, and she saw the regret in his eyes. If she wasn't so angry that he was standing in front of her, clearly not in any form of distress, then she might have withheld her sharp tongue. But she was not inclined to do so.

"You are looking well, Lord Brentwood," Rosamond said in a dry tone. "I wonder if your pocket watch stopped working because you have arrived terribly late for our outing."

Lord Brentwood seemed to catch her words with no less regret than surprise. "Miss Hendre, I must offer my deepest apologies for not coming earlier, but I assure you that it couldn't be helped."

"I shall have to take your word for it," Rosamond responded briskly.

Lord Ashington sat down at the head of the table and addressed Lord Brentwood. "Please, take a seat so we may eat."

Lord Brentwood walked around the table and sat down next to Rosamond, much to her immense displeasure. Why did he insist on making himself a nuisance?

A footman promptly came to place a table setting in front of him. Once the bowl of soup was placed down, Lord Brentwood shifted in his seat towards her.

"Will you allow me to explain?" he asked in a hushed voice.

Rosamond kept her gaze straight ahead and her back rigid. "I don't want to hear your excuses," she said before she took a sip of her soup.

"I know you are angry, but if you will just listen…"

She spoke over him. "Now you are trying to dictate my emotions?"

He sighed. "I am doing no such thing."

"Good, because I do not believe we have anything more to say to one another," Rosamond asserted.

Lady Anne leaned closer to her and whispered, "Perhaps you should hear Lord Brentwood out."

"For what purpose?" she asked.

Lizette put her hand up close to her mouth and whispered from across the table, "I agree with my aunt. He might have a good reason for being ridiculously tardy."

Tristan cast Lord Brentwood a disapproving look. "I wouldn't trust the man if I were you," he advised her, not bothering to keep his voice low.

Lord Brentwood frowned. "I assume that everyone knows that I can hear all of you."

With an unapologetic shrug, Tristan said, "That changes nothing for me."

Lord Ashington glanced around the table with a furrowed brow before asking, "What did I miss?"

Lizette spoke up. "Lord Brentwood was supposed to escort Rosamond to the Royal Menagerie today, but he failed to show up."

"That is bad form on your part," Lord Ashington chided. "Do you have anything to say in your defense?"

Lord Brentwood looked unsure. "I was helping someone," he responded vaguely.

"You will have to do better than that if you want to be forgiven," Lord Ashington said.

A frown marred his lips as he admitted, "I was helping my sister."

Lady Anne let out a slight gasp. "Lady Enid?"

"Yes, my sister was in dire straits when she came to see me a few days ago, and I have been helping her," Lord Brentwood said.

Lizette lifted her brow. "Why would your sister be in dire straits?" she asked.

Lord Brentwood opened his mouth to explain, but Lady Anne spoke first. "Two Seasons ago, Lady Enid eloped with a man that was well below her station. It was quite the scandal in the day and it was never far from the gossips' lips."

Lady Anne continued as she waved her spoon in the air. "Lord Everton publicly disowned his daughter over the scandal and no one has heard from Lady Enid since then. It was quite tragic, in my humble opinion."

"That is all true," Lord Brentwood said, "hence why I don't want anyone to know I have been helping my sister."

Rosamond cocked her head. "Are you ashamed of helping her?"

"Quite the contrary, but I am doing so without my father's consent," Lord Brentwood replied. "There would be repercussions if he discovered what I was doing to help my sister. He isn't one to forgive so easily."

Rosamond had to admit that her respect for Lord Brentwood had gone up slightly. Not every man of his station would help someone that had brought scandal upon them, even if it was a member of their family. Lady Anne had taught her that members of high Society were only loyal to those that behaved properly within the bounds that had been established for hundreds of years.

"I applaud you for helping your sister," Rosamond admitted.

"You do?" Lord Brentwood asked, looking skeptical.

"I do," she replied. "I would imagine that it took a lot on your sister's part to come to you for help and I am glad that you didn't turn her away."

"I would have never done something so awful. I do not condone her actions, mind you, but I couldn't stand by and do nothing to help my sister in a time of need."

"I find that commendable."

Lord Brentwood held her gaze as he said, "I do not deserve your praise since I was only doing what my conscience dictated." His words held a sincerity to them that left her with little doubt that he was in earnest.

Rosamond felt her lips curve into a smile. "I do believe I have misjudged you… again."

"This misunderstanding was entirely of my own making. Had I not lost track of time then I would have arrived back in time for our outing." He leaned closer and whispered, "Which I was immensely looking forward to."

After he spoke his words, Rosamond could feel the warmth of a blush as it crawled up her neck. Good heavens, why had she reacted to him in such a fashion?

"I was looking forward to it, as well," she admitted as she tried to appear unaffected by his nearness.

"Then perhaps we could go tomorrow so I could rectify my most grievous error?" Lord Brentwood suggested.

Rosamond glanced over at Lady Anne, who promptly nodded her permission. "I would like that very much."

Lizette clasped her hands together and exclaimed, "What wonderful news! We shall have such fun."

Lord Brentwood gave her a baffled look. "We?"

"Lady Anne thought it would be best, given the circumstances, that my cousin and her husband accompany us," Rosamond explained.

"What a marvelous idea," Lord Brentwood said, his words lacking conviction.

As a silence descended over the table, Rosamond took advantage of it and started to eat her soup. She found she was rather eager to spend time with Lord Brentwood tomorrow, even if they were being chaperoned by her sister and brother-in-law. She was starting to get glimpses into the man that she suspected he truly was and not the person he wanted people to see.

Chapter Eleven

Malcolm sat in the darkened coach as it rolled down the cobblestone street. He had stayed later than he had intended at Lord Ashington's townhouse, but he was pleased with the progress that he was making with Miss Hendre.

After dinner, they had played card games and Lady Lizette had entertained them by playing the pianoforte. It had been a most pleasurable evening, but he had grown slightly nostalgic at the thought that his family used to interact similarly before Enid had eloped, driving a wedge between them.

Miss Hendre was proving to be quite the anomaly. When he had shared that he was helping his sister, he had expected judgment, but instead, he only received support. It was quite odd. Most women of the *ton* would try to distance themselves from any whiff of a scandal, especially the unmarried ones, and he was beginning to think he had spent time with the wrong ones.

He felt a sense of relief that he hadn't had to justify himself for wanting to help his sister. After all, it was the right thing to do. He refused to sit back and do nothing when he was in a position to help Enid.

But that was assuming he could convince Miss Hendre to

marry him. He needed her dowry to keep their estates afloat and to continue to live a lifestyle that he was accustomed to.

The coach came to a stop in front of his townhouse, and he waited for the footman to open the door. As he stepped onto the pavement, he saw a shadowed figure leaning against the wall that led towards the servants' entrance. A hat hung low on his head, concealing his face, but based upon the size of the man, he had an idea of who it was.

Malcolm approached the shadowed figure and was pleased when the moonlight hit his face, confirming his suspicions- Mr. Campden.

The Bow Street Runner straightened from the wall and gestured that he should follow him. They didn't speak until they passed the servants' entrance and arrived at the gate that led to the stables.

Mr. Campden turned to face him and asked, "What are your intentions towards Miss Hendre?" His tone was harsh, accusatory.

Taken aback, he asked, "Why do you wish to know that?"

"Let's say I have taken an active interest in ensuring Miss Hendre is happily settled," Mr. Campden replied.

Malcolm frowned. "Are you interested in courting Miss Hendre?"

"No, but your reputation does precede you, and I want to ensure your actions are honorable." The Bow Street Runner took a commanding step towards him. "Are they, or do we have a problem?"

He knew the only recourse he had right now was to lie. He couldn't tell Mr. Campden that the only reason he wished to marry Miss Hendre was for her dowry. But why did this man care so much to seek him out and threaten him?

Putting his hand up, Malcolm said, "I assure you that my intentions are honorable."

Mr. Campden didn't look convinced. "I do not believe you are telling me the truth so I will be watching you."

"For what purpose?"

"That is none of your concern."

"Does Miss Hendre know you are threatening me?"

A smirk came to Mr. Campden's lips. "I have not threatened you... yet. Consider yourself warned."

"It does sound an awful lot like a threat."

Taking a step back, Mr. Campden said, "Then you heard it wrong."

Malcolm wasn't sure how he should take Mr. Campden's interest in Miss Hendre, but he found it a bit perplexing.

A dog barking in the distance drew Mr. Campden's attention. "Be wary of Mr. Longbourn," he advised.

"I intend to."

"Good," Mr. Campden said before he started to walk away.

Malcolm called out to him. "Do you want to explain why that is?"

"Not at this time," the Bow Street Runner responded over his shoulder.

Unsure of what to make of Mr. Campden, Malcolm stared at his retreating figure until he disappeared from view. He was thankful for Campden's assistance when it came to Enid, but he didn't like that the Runner was acquainted with Miss Hendre. Why was he so protective of her? That was something he intended to find out.

He walked towards the front of the townhouse and entered the main door. No noise came from within, and the only light came from a few flickering candles in the entry hall. As he started up the stairs, he heard his father shout, "Absolutely not!"

Malcolm stopped on the step and let out a sigh. He had little doubt as to who his father was yelling at. He descended the stairs and headed towards his father's study.

As he stepped inside, he saw his father was standing near

the mantel over the fireplace and his mother was sitting on the settee, her back rigid.

His father's eyes landed on him and grumbled, "Wonderful, you have come to join us."

Undeterred by his father's lackluster response, Malcolm asked, "What is the commotion?"

"Nothing you need to concern yourself about." His father reached for his drink and took a sip. "You may run along now."

Malcolm wasn't in the mood to take orders from his father and walked over to his mother. "Are you all right?"

She smiled up at him, but it didn't quite meet her eyes. It never did. Not anymore. "I am," she replied. "We were just discussing Enid."

"No, *you* were discussing Enid and I am telling you that I don't want to hear that name in my presence again," his father countered.

"But she is our daughter…" his mother attempted.

His father swiped his hand in front of him and spoke over her. "I have no daughter. She lost that right when she eloped with that man."

"George…"

Tossing back his drink, his father slammed the glass onto the mantel with a loud clang. "I will not back down on this."

His mother pressed her lips together and turned her hopeful gaze towards Malcolm, indicating she wished for him to attempt to reason with his father.

Malcolm went to sit down next to his mother. "Enid is back in our lives, whether you want her to be or not."

His father scoffed. "As long as I am alive, she will never be welcomed in my home."

"You are being mulish, Father," Malcolm said.

"It is better than being made to look like a fool," his father declared. "Enid destroyed this family when she left."

"No, I think you did that all by yourself," Malcolm responded.

His father narrowed his eyes. "You know not what you speak of."

"Don't I?" Malcolm challenged. "Your drinking only got worse after Enid left and I hardly see you without a glass in your hand."

"You cannot possibly understand the pressure that I am under," his father said.

"I would, if only you would let me help you."

His father walked over to the desk and picked up a ledger. "While you are out with your friends, spending my money, I am the one doing all the work. I could use a little more gratitude from you."

"Then perhaps I should take over some of your responsibilities," Malcolm said.

His father dropped the ledger back onto the desk. "You have never taken an interest in it before. Why now?"

"It is time I take a more active role in my inheritance."

"You will fail."

Malcolm looked heavenward as he muttered, "Thank you for the vote of confidence."

"Managing our books is a difficult task and you spend all of your time at the club," his father said.

"People are capable of changing, Father."

"Not that much."

Malcolm gave him a knowing look. "Is that why you refuse to help Enid?" he asked. "You don't believe she has changed?"

His father visibly tensed, and he suspected he'd touched a nerve with him. "We are not discussing Enid. We are discussing *you*."

"Enid needs our help," Malcolm asserted.

"I have heard enough," he stated before he headed towards the door. "I am going to bed."

Rising, his mother pleaded, "Please, George, have a heart."

Stopping in the doorway, his father slowly turned around and said, "I told Enid not to marry that man, begged her, even. But she didn't listen to me. She thought she knew best."

"She was only seventeen and made a mistake," his mother attempted. "That mistake should not have to define her or her child."

"There are consequences to one's actions."

"I do believe she has suffered enough," his mother responded.

His father rested his arm against the door frame and leaned in. "If Enid had married Lord Cotswold as I told her to do, then none of this would have happened."

"But Enid didn't want to marry Lord Cotswold," his mother pressed.

His father fixed her with a level gaze, showing no signs of weakening. "If I recall, you didn't want to marry me at first either."

"Yes, but that was different."

"How?" his father demanded.

His mother's voice grew despondent as she replied, "Because we fell in love."

A sadness came to his father's eyes. The kind you sometimes see in those who want to change, but life won't let them. "That was long ago," he said.

"Not so long for me."

His father held his wife's gaze before saying, "I'm sorry. I can't give you what you seek." He dropped his arm. "Goodnight."

After his father departed from the study, his mother lowered herself down onto the settee. "I shouldn't have pushed him so hard," she said.

"You did nothing wrong," Malcolm assured her.

His mother blinked away her tears. "Tell me, what have you done to help Enid?"

"She is safe at the boarding house for now, but we need to move her to someplace where no one can find her," he said.

"Why is that?"

Malcolm hesitated before revealing, "Mr. Longbourn isn't dead."

She reared back. "He's not?" she asked. "Then why were Enid and Marigold at a workhouse?"

"Because Enid said it was preferable than being with her husband."

"How is that possible?"

Malcolm wondered how much he should reveal to his mother since she wore her heart on her sleeve. He didn't want to be responsible for distressing her, but there was a chance that she might have insight that might help the situation.

"Mr. Longbourn beat Enid relentlessly and she only left when he started hitting Marigold," he explained.

His mother closed her eyes but not before a tear slipped out and ran down her cheek. "My poor little girl," she whispered.

"Can you think of anywhere that Enid could go that she would be safe until we set up a new life for her far away from London?"

Her mother's eyes flew up. "What about the gatehouse at my cousin's manor in Brompton?" she asked.

"That is brilliant. But do you think Marjorie would allow that?"

"Marjorie is a little eccentric, but she has always had a soft spot for Enid, especially since she was also shunned by Society."

"But that hasn't stopped you from associating with her."

Her mother bobbed her head. "She is family, after all," she said. "I will go speak to her tomorrow and see if she would be willing to help Enid."

"I will feel much better when Enid and Marigold are far away from the boarding house."

"As will I," his mother said, rising. "I'm afraid it is past my bedtime. Goodnight, my dear."

Once he was left alone, Malcolm leaned his back against the settee and looked up at the ceiling. Why did he feel like such a failure? He had yet to secure Miss Hendre's hand in marriage and he was doing a terrible job at keeping his sister safe. Regardless, when stakes were this high, he had to keep going. He had no choice since he couldn't fail.

Rosamond sat in the drawing room as she waited, not so patiently, for Lord Brentwood to arrive for their outing to the Royal Menagerie. She was supposed to be working on her needlework, but her mind was on anything but. She wondered when he would arrive. She found that she was looking forward to spending more time with Lord Brentwood.

Lady Anne's voice broke through her musings. "He will come."

"I know, but…" Her voice stopped. "Who will come?" she asked innocently.

With a knowing look, Lady Anne replied, "I think we both know that you are waiting for Lord Brentwood to arrive."

Rosamond winced. "Is it so obvious?"

"It is to me," Lady Anne said. "I am glad that you are finally recognizing that Lord Brentwood would be an excellent choice for a suitor."

"I do find him somewhat interesting, but I am not ready to enter a courtship with him yet. There is still much that I need to know."

"Don't wait too long and risk having Lord Brentwood's interest wane."

"If his interest wanes so easily, then he is most assuredly not the man for me," Rosamond remarked.

Lizette stepped into the room and gave Lady Anne a disapproving shake of her head. "It would be best if you stopped trying to push Lord Brentwood upon Rosamond."

"I will not apologize for encouraging Rosamond to accept Lord Brentwood as a suitor. He would be a fine catch for Rosamond," Lady Anne asserted.

"Yes, but Rosamond doesn't just want to 'catch' a man. She wants to fall in love," Lizette said.

The butler stepped into the room and Rosamond perked up. She hoped this meant that Lord Brentwood had finally arrived.

Brownell met her gaze and announced, "Lord Brighton has come to call, Miss. Are you accepting callers at this time?"

Rosamond resisted the urge to groan. She had no desire to see Lord Brighton and hear all about his mother. But to turn him away would be rude and she knew Lady Anne would not approve of her doing so. With any luck, Lord Brentwood would arrive soon and she wouldn't have to spend too much time with Lord Brighton.

With gritted teeth, Rosamond said, "Send him in, please."

Brownell tipped his head before he went to do her bidding.

Lady Anne nodded her head in approval. "You did the right thing," she murmured.

A moment later, Lord Brighton stepped into the room. He wasn't an unattractive man with his straight nose and square jaw, but she took issue with the rest of his person. His personality was lacking in many regards, and he was much too eager to share useless facts about his mother.

Lord Brighton bowed. "Ladies," he greeted.

Rosamond smiled. "It is good to see you, my lord," she said.

"It is good to see you, as well," Lord Brighton responded. "You are looking lovely today, quite lovely, in fact."

"That is kind of you to say."

Lord Brighton shifted in his stance, appearing deucedly uncomfortable. "I was hoping for a moment of your time."

"You have it," Rosamond said.

He cleared his throat. "Privately, if you don't mind."

Rosamond didn't want to spend any time alone with Lord Brighton, but she also didn't dare turn down his request.

As she debated on what she should do, Lady Anne spoke up. "Why don't you two take a turn in the gardens and I will watch from the window?"

Lord Brighton looked eagerly upon her. "Do you have any objections?"

She had many objections, but she couldn't very well admit that to him. "I do not," she finally replied.

He approached her and offered his arm. "May I escort you to the gardens?" he asked.

Rising, Rosamond moved to accept his proffered arm. "Thank you," she murmured.

They didn't speak as they walked towards the rear of the townhouse and stepped outside. A footman had trailed behind them and took his post on the veranda. Once they were on the path, Rosamond withdrew her hand and clasped them in front of her.

Lord Brighton glanced up at the sky. "It is a lovely day we are having."

"It is," she agreed.

"My mother always tells me that 'the sun keeps the doctor away'," he said. "We take daily walks together."

"How fortunate you and your mother are so close."

Lord Brighton bobbed his head. "After my father died, it was just me and my mother for a long time. The only time I left was when I went to Harrow for a short spell."

"Did you enjoy your time at Harrow?"

"It was enjoyable, but my mother was lonely and requested that I come home," he replied. "She hired tutors to educate me at our country estate."

"I can relate. My mother was terribly lonely when I went to school, but I was fortunate that it was located just outside of our village, allowing me to return home once the day had ended."

Lord Brighton glanced over at her. "Are you close with your mother?"

"I was," she replied.

"My condolences for your loss."

She gave him a weak smile. "Thank you," she said. "I do miss my mother and I fear I will never truly get over her passing."

"My mother is quite healthy for her age, but I know there will be a time that won't always be the case."

"I wished I had enjoyed the little things more because they ended up being the big things that I miss the most about my mother," Rosamond revealed.

Lord Brighton came to a stop on the gravel path and turned to face her. "I am pleased that you understand how important it is to have a close bond with one's mother."

"I do," she said.

"I used to get teased relentlessly for my relationship with my mother, but it never bothered me. It only made my resolve stronger."

Rosamond went to resume walking down the path, but Lord Brighton placed his hand on her sleeve, stilling her. "Before we continue our tour of the gardens, I was hoping to ask you a question."

Drats. She had a sneaking suspicion of what that question would be and that was the last thing she wanted to hear from him.

Before she could respond, he dropped down to one knee

and reached for her gloved hand. "Miss Hendre, will you marry me?"

"I... um..."

He spoke over her. "I spoke to my mother, and she encouraged me to offer for you. She likes the fact that you have good childbearing hips."

Hoping that she had misheard him, she asked, "Pardon?"

"I am hoping for a large family," he said. "I need a young woman that is in robust health to accommodate my wish."

Rosamond worked to keep the frown off her lips as she thought of a way to politely turn him down.

"My offer is contingent on having my doctor examine you and determine that there are no issues for you to bear children," Lord Brighton said.

"You wish for a doctor to examine me?" she asked in disbelief.

"Yes, but my doctor has assured me the procedure won't take long or is too invasive."

Rosamond couldn't believe the audacity of this lord. He mentioned nothing of emotions but treated it more as a transaction. It was evident that he wanted children and it felt like any woman- with childbearing hips- would do. She removed her hand from his and took a step back. "I'm sorry, my lord, but I must refuse your offer."

Lord Brighton blinked. "You are refusing me?"

"I am."

"But why?" he asked.

Rosamond tilted her chin. "I want more from a marriage than just my ability to have children," she said.

He remained on one knee as he scooched forward. "I do believe I have blundered this offer. Will you give me another chance?"

"I'm afraid it won't make a difference."

"Just hear me out," he pleaded.

Against her better judgment, Rosamond nodded her consent.

Lord Brighton let out a sigh of relief. "Thank you." He was quiet for a long moment. "My income is ten thousand pounds a year and I can assure you won't lack for anything if you marry me." He smiled smugly as if he knew his admission would sway her decision.

She had no doubt that many women would be impressed by Lord Brighton's income, but she was not one of them. She wanted to fall in love and marry the one person she couldn't live without. She cared little of wealth since she could make do with a lot less.

"I'm sorry, but my position has not changed," she said.

His mouth dropped. "But I am rich."

"That may be true, but I am looking for a love match," she admitted.

"I could grow to love you."

"I don't want anyone to be forced to love me."

Rising, Lord Brighton dusted off his trousers before he said, "It wouldn't be too difficult. You are beautiful and have a pleasing disposition about you."

"That is kind of you to say, but we would not suit."

"My mother believes we would."

"I hesitate to contradict your mother, but I'm afraid I must do so in this case," Rosamond said.

Lord Brighton frowned. "I think you are making a terrible mistake, Miss Hendre."

"If that is the case, then I will have to live with the consequences," she responded. "And I would be remiss if I didn't tell you that I think it is quite distasteful that you placed a bet in the book at White's about me."

"There was no harm done," Lord Brighton responded with a slight shrug of his shoulder. "Every gentleman places bets in the book."

"It doesn't make it right, my lord."

With a glance at the back gate, Lord Brighton said, "I think it might be preferable if I excuse myself from here so as not to suffer any more embarrassment."

She dropped into a curtsy. "I wish you well, my lord."

Lord Brighton executed a stiff bow before he headed for the gate. Once he had departed from the gardens, Rosamond felt a profound sense of relief. She hadn't wished to dash his hopes, but she had no desire to marry him.

Rosamond headed towards the townhouse, and she dreaded the upcoming conversation that she no doubt would have with Lizette and Lady Anne. She was certain they had witnessed Lord Brighton's proposal out of the drawing room window.

As she stepped into the drawing room, she saw Lord Brentwood was sitting on an upholstered armchair and he was conversing politely with Lady Anne. He cut a dashing figure in his blue jacket and buff trousers.

When his eyes landed on her, she swore she couldn't breathe for a moment, causing her to wonder why she had such an unexpected reaction to him.

He promptly rose and bowed. "Miss Hendre," he greeted.

"Lord Brentwood," she responded with a slight curtsy.

His steady gaze held hers. His green eyes were very dark, uniquely so. She had known people before with green eyes, but none had held her captive as his did.

Lady Anne spoke up, drawing her attention. "Lady Lizette went in search of Tristan, but they should be back shortly."

"Wonderful," Rosamond murmured.

"How did your tour of the gardens go with Lord Brighton?" Lady Anne asked, reaching for her teacup.

Rosamond didn't dare reveal that he had offered for her, especially in front of Lord Brentwood, so she settled on, "It was pleasant enough."

Lady Anne seemed to accept her words as she took a sip of her tea.

Lord Brentwood's eyes roamed over her, and in them, she saw approval, making her feel beautiful. "You are looking lovely today," he acknowledged.

"Thank you," she said as she smoothed down her blue gown.

Lizette stepped into the room with Tristan following close behind. "We are ready to depart for the Royal Menagerie."

Tristan met Lord Brentwood's gaze. "It is good of you to show up today," he said gruffly.

Lizette placed a hand on Tristan's sleeve. "Remember we use kind words when we speak to others," she chided lightly.

Tristan smiled lovingly at his wife. "Yes, Dear," he said, offering his arm. "Let us depart now so I can return at a reasonable hour to finish my tasks at hand."

"While we are at the Royal Menagerie, you promised me that you wouldn't think about all the work you need to accomplish," Lizette reminded him.

"I will try," Tristan responded.

Lizette shook her head. "It is a good thing that I love you," she said before they departed from the drawing room.

Lord Brentwood approached Rosamond and offered his arm. "Shall we?"

Chapter Twelve

Malcolm was trying not to squirm under Mr. Westcott's relentless glare but it was proving to be nearly impossible to ignore the animosity that exuded from him. It was painfully obvious that Mr. Westcott did not approve of him, but the only opinion that mattered to him was Miss Hendre's. She was the one that he had to convince to marry him.

The ride to the Tower of London was taking much longer than expected due to the number of carriages that were on the streets. He was sitting next to Miss Hendre and their shoulders would occasionally brush up against one another as the coach jostled back and forth. No one seemed to be in a talkative mood, so little had been said since they left Lord Ashington's townhouse.

He glanced over at Miss Hendre as she stared out the window. Her beauty was evident, but it was only enhanced by the essence of her being. She continuously surprised him by the compassion she felt for others, and he knew it was not an act. She truly did care about others, and it put him to shame, knowing he was not worthy of her.

Mr. Westcott cleared his throat and he realized that he had been caught staring at Miss Hendre. He turned his gaze towards the window and saw that they were nearing their destination. He was counting down the moments until he could converse with Miss Hendre privately and be away from Mr. Westcott's prying gaze. Although he had a suspicion that Mr. Westcott would be a dutiful chaperone and wouldn't let them stray too far.

Lady Lizette's voice broke through the silence as she asked, "Have you been to the Royal Menagerie before, Lord Brentwood?"

"I have, many times, in fact," Malcolm said. He didn't dare admit that on his most recent visits he had always been accompanied by a different lady each time.

"Do you have a favorite animal on display?" Lady Lizette asked.

"I always look for the black leopardess known as Miss Peggy. Her skin is black, but she has deeper black spots that makes a most unusual combination," Malcolm replied. "She is known to hide out in the back of her den, making a sighting nearly impossible on most days."

"That would explain why I have yet to see Miss Peggy," Lady Lizette said.

"When I was younger, my favorite attraction was the Monkey Room. We were able to enter the room and interact with the monkeys," Malcolm shared.

Miss Hendre spoke up. "That sounds wonderful."

"It was, until one of the monkeys severely injured a boy's leg, causing the king to order their removal from the yard," Malcolm revealed.

"How awful," Miss Hendre murmured.

"I do believe that some people forget that these are wild animals that have been gifted to the royal family. They are not docile and should be shown the respect that they deserve," Malcolm said.

Mr. Westcott nodded. "I agree with Lord Brentwood.

These are not domesticated animals and they would just as easily kill you as run wild on the streets of London."

"What a morbid thought," Lady Lizette murmured.

"It is merely the truth," Mr. Westcott said with a slight shrug.

The coach came to a stop in front of the west entrance of the Tower of London and the coach dipped to the side as a footman exited his perch. The door opened and they all exited the coach.

Malcolm held out his arm to Miss Hendre and asked, "May I have the honor of escorting you inside?"

"Thank you," Miss Hendre responded as she placed her hand on his sleeve.

They approached the door, which had a figure of a lion over it, and he reached for the bell at the side to call for the keeper.

As they waited for the keeper to arrive, Malcolm heard the large cats roaring from within and he leaned closer to Miss Hendre and said, "I always love that sound. It brings back fond memories of when my mother would bring me here. I would beg her to bring me here the moment we arrived in Town and I wouldn't relent until she finally agreed."

"You seem like you are accustomed to getting your way," Miss Hendre said.

"I am, considering I can be rather persuasive," he replied.

Miss Hendre considered him for a moment before asking, "Have you ever not gotten your way?"

"It does happen, but only on rare occasions," he said with a slight smirk.

She didn't look impressed by his admission. "I do believe that our ability to handle challenges is a measure of our strength of character."

"I never said I didn't have challenges in my life."

"I meant no offense, but it just seems as if you are not inclined to struggle."

Malcolm frowned. "I have my struggles, just as everyone else does," he said. "No one is immune to problems."

"Perhaps, but one man's struggle is another man's opportunity."

"I will not apologize for the privilege I was born into," Malcolm said.

"Nor should you, but what good have you done with it?" Miss Hendre asked.

Malcolm wasn't quite sure how he could respond to Miss Hendre's question. She was right and it pained him to admit it. He had done very little with what he had been given, but what could he do? He was just one man.

Fortunately, their conversation came to a halt when a short, stocky man approached from the other side of the gate. He unlocked the door and asked, "Are you here for the tour?"

"We are," Malcolm replied, reaching into his jacket pocket. He removed four shillings and extended them to the keeper.

The man accepted the money and slipped it into his pocket. "Come along, then, and I will give you a tour," he encouraged, opening the gate up wide.

Once they had stepped inside, the keeper closed the gate and locked it. He turned back to them and smiled, but it appeared strained. "My name is Peter Wilkes, and I am a keeper here at the Royal Menagerie," he said. "To your right is the lion's tower, where the wild beasts are kept. They have been housed in a separate tower since the fourteenth century."

Mr. Wilkes headed towards the tower and spoke over his shoulder. "Please be cautious when approaching the dens and avoid any attempt to play with the beasts."

As Malcolm led Miss Hendre towards the tower, he said, "I am only one man."

A line between her brow appeared. "Pardon?"

"I am not in a position to help anyone, but it will be

different when I am an earl," he said. "I will be able to enact real change in Parliament."

"No matter what position someone is in, great or small, they can help alleviate another person's suffering."

"Forgive me for saying so, but what do you know about helping others?" he asked. "You are a lady and are the ward of one of the most powerful men in London."

Miss Hendre glanced over at him. "I wasn't raised wealthy," she said. "I had a very different beginning from most debutantes."

"Yet you are lecturing me on privilege, but you attend the same social events. That seems a little hypocritical to me."

She pressed her lips into a tight line. "You know very little about me, or about the challenges that I was forced to overcome to get right here."

"Surely it must not be too difficult," he mocked.

Miss Hendre removed her hand from his and responded, "Everyone has scars, but some are not visible. It doesn't mean they aren't there."

Malcolm didn't want to pick a fight with Miss Hendre, but he couldn't seem to help himself. What did she know about helping others in her grand townhouse? He was doing nothing wrong with his life. He was an heir to an earldom. His life was planned out, so why couldn't he enjoy himself until he had to succumb to a position that would consume him?

Before he could stop himself, Malcolm asked, "Do you want to know what your problem is?"

With a sigh, she replied, "I suppose you will tell me."

"You care too much about other people," he replied.

She furrowed her brow. "You consider that a problem?"

"I do, since you should be much more concerned about you and your future," Malcolm said. "If you do not marry well, then what do you have?"

Miss Hendre stopped and turned to face him. "I have my dignity."

"Dignity will not put food on one's table," Malcolm said. "You would eventually become a drain on Lord Ashington's finances if you do not wed."

"My entire existence is not determined by who I marry."

"Marriage brings forth security and you will have the protection of your husband's name."

Miss Hendre shook her head. "What if I choose poorly?" she asked. "Then what do I have, but a lifetime of misery."

"It is better than spinsterhood."

"So say you," Miss Hendre said. "A life where I am not valued by my husband is not a life I wish to have."

"But you would have standing amongst Society."

"That means very little to me when I am unhappy," she responded.

A clearing of a throat came from next to them. Malcolm turned to see Mr. Westcott and his wife staring at them with curious expressions.

"As fun as it is watching you two debate the practicality of marriage, it might be best if we caught up to the keeper so we can continue our tour," Mr. Westcott said.

"Yes, quite right," Malcolm responded, embarrassed that he had been caught in a spat with Miss Hendre.

As he was about to offer his arm to Miss Hendre, he noticed that she clasped her hands in front of her, clearly having no intention of allowing him to escort her any further. He resisted the urge to groan since this is not how he intended for the afternoon to go. He had planned to charm Miss Hendre, not fight with her.

Why was it so hard to win over Miss Hendre? He was beginning to think that she was looking for the impossible in a spouse. He was no different than most gentlemen of the *ton*, but she was trying to hold him to a different standard. How was that fair? After all, he wasn't a bad man but there was only so much he could do. He knew of the poor's plight from the newssheets, but it wasn't as if he mingled with them. Why did she expect more from him than any other woman he had ever associated with?

He followed behind Miss Hendre as he tried to think of something that he could say that wouldn't stir up a debate. He needed to woo her and it was becoming incredibly difficult to do so. Although, truth be told, he had never enjoyed sparring with someone as much as he had with Miss Hendre. But he would never admit that to her or anyone.

As the keeper talked about the history of the wild beasts, Miss Hendre came to a stop in front of a den where the lioness, Miss Fanny, was housed.

Malcolm came to stand next to her and revealed, "Miss Fanny is more ferocious than any other lion in the Tower."

"I wonder if she is unhappy because she is trapped in a den."

"The keepers take great care to keep the dens clean and they are very commodious," Malcolm assured her.

"Miss Fanny is still in a cage, no matter how gilded it is," Miss Hendre said.

"Yes, but it is for our benefit."

Miss Hendre seemed to accept his response as she moved on to the next den. She remained a good distance away from the iron gratings that enclosed the front of the dens but he could see her eyes roaming the structure.

Her eyes grew wide as she pointed at the den. "There is a dog in there with a tiger," she announced, her head turning towards the keeper.

Mr. Wilkes bobbed his head. "You need not worry. The dog has been with Harry since he arrived from Bengal. Those two are as thick as thieves and are often found playing with one another."

Lady Lizette interjected, "How is it possible that a tiger and a dog can be friends?"

"Harry is very tame, and has never shown any violence

towards the dog," Mr. Wilkes replied. "They complement one another, despite being very different."

Malcolm observed that the dog was curled up next to Harry and they were both resting. He could see how Miss Hendre was alarmed by such a sight, but the dog had been a regular visitor at the Royal Menagerie for as long as he could remember.

The keeper's words kept echoing in his mind. Was it possible for two very different people to complement one another? He knew Mr. Wilkes had been speaking about Harry and the dog, but his words still rang true. And the more he dwelled on it, the more he realized that it was entirely possible.

Rosamond didn't know why she grew so defensive around Lord Brentwood, but she did. She hadn't meant to argue with him about marriage, but he had just said the most ludicrous thing. For a woman, the hardest thing to do was get married. She was putting all her faith into that one person, hoping he would be a fair and loving husband. But what if he wasn't? What if she was stuck with someone that treated her horribly? She would have no way out, no recourse. She had come so close to marrying George but, fortunately, fate prevailed, and she had broken off the engagement.

Why couldn't Lord Brentwood understand that it was difficult to give your heart to someone and hope they didn't mistreat it?

Lizette's voice broke through her musing. "Have you seen enough of the leopardess?" she asked as she came to stand next to her.

Rosamond turned her head and saw her brother-in-law and Lord Brentwood were waiting for her at the end of the hall. "My apologies, I'm afraid I was woolgathering," she admitted.

Lowering her voice, her sister said, "I must assume you are woolgathering about Lord Brentwood."

"Perhaps I was briefly thinking of him," she attempted.

Lizette gave her an amused look. "What has you so concerned?"

"Lord Brentwood speaks of marriage as though it is impartial to the woman," Rosamond replied, "but it is not. It is a union that suppresses the woman."

"I had not taken you for such a naysayer."

"I wasn't always, but after I saw George for who he truly was, it made me hesitant to ever trust another with my heart."

"I see," Lizette said. "Have you told Lord Brentwood that yet?"

Rosamond shook her head. "Heavens, no," she replied. "Why would I reveal something so personal to a man that I hardly know."

"I think you know him better than you are letting on."

"Regardless, what if he dismisses my concerns."

"Then you will have your answer, but I do believe he may surprise you," Lizette said. "After all, the only way you can truly discover if you and Lord Brentwood will suit is by being vulnerable around him."

Rosamond bit her lower lip. "I don't know if I am ready to do that."

"Just be true to yourself, because the only person you have to answer to is you." Lizette glanced over at the men. "But you might want to hurry. I worry that Tristan might engage Lord Brentwood in a round of fisticuffs."

"Does Tristan not like Lord Brentwood?" Rosamond asked.

"Right now, he is taking his role of chaperone very seriously," Lizette replied as she started walking down the hall.

As they approached the men, Lord Brentwood gave her a questioning look and asked, "Are you all right?"

"I am," she replied, brushing off his concern.

They continued down the hall, admiring the wild beasts in their dens, and Rosamond found herself once again walking next to Lord Brentwood. Why was she constantly drawn to the man?

"I'm sorry if I upset you earlier," he said.

"It is of little consequence."

"To you, but I do not like knowing that I caused you any distress."

Rosamond took a moment to admire one of the many leopards as she worked up the courage to be honest with Lord Brentwood. She wanted to trust him but was afraid he wouldn't take her concerns seriously. Slowly, she admitted, "I'm afraid the thought of marriage terrifies me."

Lord Brentwood gave her a baffled look. "Why is that?"

"As I mentioned before, I was engaged once and it did not end well," she admitted. "I can only imagine the misery I would have endured if I had gone through with the wedding."

"Yes, you were most fortunate that you did not marry that man, but that doesn't mean you shut off your heart."

She met his gaze. "Have you been in love before, Lord Brentwood?"

"No, I have not."

"Love lingers, even when it is gone," Rosamond said.

Lord Brentwood's eyes held compassion. "A love worth taking a chance over is never a lost opportunity. Every person that we encounter can teach us something, whether it be for our benefit or our detriment."

Rosamond nodded. "You make a good argument."

Turning back towards the den, Lord Brentwood said, "It is only fair that I share something that I fear since you just did."

"What could you fear?"

A slight huff came out of his lips. "Very few people can

get through life without having fears." He paused. "Sometimes I feel like I'm living a meaningless life and I get frightened."

"Then you must do something about that."

"That is easier said than done," Lord Brentwood remarked. "I am expected to do my duty, no matter the costs."

Rosamond could hear the pain in Lord Brentwood's words, and she knew he believed his words deeply. "You are a good man, Lord Brentwood."

"No, I am not," he rushed to say.

"You speak of duty, yet you still risked your father's wrath to help your sister," Rosamond said. "I would say that speaks volumes to your character."

Lord Brentwood watched her, as if he couldn't quite believe the sincerity in her words. "Why is it that you are constantly trying to look for good in other people?" he asked. "Sometimes people are inherently bad."

"Are you one of these people?"

"I hope I'm not, but I cannot claim that all of my intentions are genuine."

Rosamond resumed down the hall as she said, "My mother was always encouraging me to look for good in people. She believed that if you greeted the world with kindness that you would receive it back tenfold."

"What foolish nonsense," Lord Brentwood said, his words light.

Rosamond smiled. "I didn't always agree with her, but now that she is gone, I wish I could turn back time and just have one more conversation with her."

"I think you would like my mother," Lord Brentwood remarked. "She is also an optimist that believes everything will eventually work out in the end."

"I look forward to meeting her."

"You should know that my mother is my greatest ally," he shared.

"As any good mother should be."

"She believes me to be quite perfect, despite my many flaws."

Rosamond's lips twitched. "And what flaws might those be?"

Lord Brentwood chuckled. "I am a smart enough man not to answer that question."

"Pity," she joked.

Lord Brentwood clasped his arms behind his back. "I hope I am not prying, but I did witness Lord Brighton offering for you," he said.

With a slight wince, she murmured, "Yes, that did happen."

"I must assume you turned him down since you are with me right now, at least I am hoping you did."

She nodded her head. "I did, but he was rather persistent."

"You can't fault the man for knowing what he wants."

"He did tell me that his mother approved of the union," she shared.

"Thank heavens for that," Lord Brentwood teased.

Rosamond found that she enjoyed this lighthearted side of Lord Brentwood. She didn't know why his words resonated so deeply with her, but they did. They seemed to speak to her very soul, for better or worse.

Lord Brentwood cleared his throat. "I met an acquaintance of yours," he started. "A Bow Street Runner to be exact."

"I presume you speak of Mr. Campden."

"I do," Lord Brentwood said. "How is it that you came to know him?"

Rosamond shrugged one shoulder, trying to appear indifferent on the matter. "He helped me with a delicate situation once."

"Which was?"

"I would prefer not to speak about it." And she didn't. How could she explain Mr. Campden without revealing her secrets?

Fortunately, as they rounded the corner, they saw Miss Bolingbroke and her brother standing in front of a den as a keeper stood nearby. Rosamond had been introduced to Miss Bolingbroke by her sister and she found her to be a delight.

Miss Bolingbroke turned her head, and a bright smile came to her lips at the sight of them. "What a pleasant surprise," she declared.

After they exchanged pleasantries, Lizette said, "Had we known you intended to come today, we would have invited you to join us."

"That is kind, but Caleb and I decided at the last minute to come. We both needed a reprieve from my mother," Miss Bolingbroke shared.

"Why is that?" Lizette asked.

Miss Bolingbroke let out an exaggerated sigh. "She was going on and on about how we are not married yet and how she is going to die without any grandchildren."

"Oh, dear," Lizette murmured.

Rosamond gestured towards Lord Brentwood and asked, "Have you been introduced to Lord Brentwood?"

Miss Bolingbroke shook her head. "I have not."

"Allow me to rectify that," Rosamond said. "Miss Boling-broke, allow me the privilege of introducing you to Lord Brentwood."

Lord Brentwood bowed. "Delighted."

Miss Bolingbroke dropped into a curtsy before turning her attention back to the ladies. "Are you enjoying yourselves on your tour?"

"We are," Lizette replied. "Tristan has taken me many times, but this is Rosamond's first time touring the Royal Menagerie."

"I remember my first time and it was most unfortunate," Miss Bolingbroke said with a slight shudder.

Her brother chuckled. "When we were children, we visited the Monkey Room, and they started throwing their excrement at her."

"It isn't funny," Miss Bolingbroke declared.

"It was, just a little," Mr. Bolingbroke teased.

Miss Bolingbroke did not appear amused. "I thought it was befitting that the Monkey Room was closed down shortly thereafter."

"That was because the monkeys attacked a boy, and it had nothing to do with them flinging poop at you," Mr. Bolingbroke said.

"Regardless, those nasty animals got what was coming to them in the end," Miss Bolingbroke stated.

"You will have to excuse my sister, but she is not fond of monkeys," Mr. Bolingbroke joked, "or hyenas."

Rosamond lifted her brow. "Hyenas?"

"Hyenas make the most unusual and eerie sound, making it seem like they are laughing at me," Miss Bolingbroke explained.

"Hyenas are not laughing at you," her brother said.

"That is what they want you to think, but they know what they are doing," Miss Bolingbroke declared. "It is all a game to them."

Her brother cast his eyes heavenward. "I do not think I can debate this one more time with you."

"That is because you know I am right," Miss Bolingbroke responded.

Lizette spoke up. "If you will excuse us, we are nearing the end of our tour and we must depart soon. I promised Tristan that we wouldn't stay too long here since he has his duties that he needs to tend to."

Miss Bolingbroke tipped her head in response. "If you are not opposed, I shall call upon you shortly."

"We will be looking forward to that," Lizette responded.

Once they had resumed walking down the hall, Lord Brentwood kept his voice low as he asked, "Miss Bolingbroke is rather odd, is she not?"

"I disagree," Rosamond said. "I find her to be quite delightful."

"Do you not find it strange that she thought a hyena was laughing at her?" he pressed.

"I find it refreshing that she speaks her mind," she replied. "Furthermore, if you expect me to say one disparaging word about her, you will be sorely disappointed. Miss Bolingbroke has been nothing but kind to me since I arrived in Town."

Lord Brentwood put his hand up in surrender. "Forgive me," he said. "I clearly misjudged Miss Bolingbroke."

"Yes, you did."

He leaned closer and asked, "Dare I hope that I stir up strong emotions within you, as well?"

Rosamond didn't dare turn her head to look at Lord Brentwood for fear of what he might see in her. She couldn't explain what he meant to her, but she knew he meant more to her than she was letting on. He was starting to occupy far too much of her thoughts. But that didn't mean she would admit that, at least not to him.

Knowing that he was still waiting on a response, she replied, "You are mistaken, Lord Brentwood, if you suppose I hold any emotions for you, and I would ask you to behave in a more gentlemanlike manner."

Lord Brentwood smirked. "I am rather fond of you, too."

"I said nothing about being fond of you."

"I know."

Rosamond pressed her lips together so she wouldn't engage Lord Brentwood in further conversation. He wasn't wrong; she was fond of him. But why did her heart have to be turning for him?

Chapter Thirteen

Malcolm watched as Marigold leaned her head against Enid's chest as they drove in the coach to Brompton. They didn't have much further to go but he was growing restless. He wanted to ensure that Enid was safe so he could return home and get some much-needed rest. He'd had a fitful night of sleep because he couldn't stop thinking about Miss Hendre.

Every moment he was with Miss Hendre caused him to question his resolve. Her smile, her laugh were what his dreams consisted of. But he couldn't falter now. What would become of his family? Could he stand by and let his father be thrown in debtor's prison? Although he doubted it would come to that, but they would have to sell off the entailed properties, leaving him with nothing but a title to inherit.

Why did Miss Hendre have to be so blasted beautiful, on the inside and out? She made him question everything, forcing him to look inward. He wanted to be a better man because of her.

Botheration. This would not do. He was trying to convince Miss Hendre to marry him, but he was doing a terrible job at it. Rather than just being agreeable, he had discovered he wanted to know more about her, her thoughts and feelings. She was like a breath of fresh air in his stale life.

His sister's voice broke through the silence. "What has you so quiet, Brother?"

"Nothing of importance," he replied dismissively.

"I doubt that," Enid said. "You have hardly said a word to me since we left the boarding house and I am growing concerned."

"Why would you be concerned?"

Her eyes flashed with mirth as she replied, "Because by now, you would have chided me for something I have done, whether it would have been in the past, present or future."

Malcolm huffed. "I daresay that you are exaggerating."

"Perhaps, but I can't help but wonder what has you so quiet."

With a glance out of the window, he said, "I have a lot on my mind."

"Anything I can help you with?"

"No." The last thing he needed was his sister's help. He just needed to suppress his feelings and hope they would go away on their own.

Enid shifted Marigold in her arms as the child's eyes grew heavy. "I am here if you want to talk."

"Well, I don't," he said, his words coming out much harsher than he intended. "Forgive me, that was uncalled for."

"There is nothing to forgive."

Malcolm adjusted his cravat before asking, "Have you prepared yourself to see Marjorie?"

"That is not something that one can prepare for," Enid replied. "Although I am most grateful for her allowing me to stay in the gatehouse."

"You must remember that no one can know you are there."

Enid arched an eyebrow. "Who would I tell?" she asked.

"All my friends turned their backs on me when I eloped with John."

"That wasn't unexpected."

"No, but it still hurt, nonetheless."

Malcolm cocked his head. "Do you regret marrying John?"

"No, because it gave me Marigold," she replied. "Nothing is as rewarding as holding your child in your arms."

"I can only imagine."

"You will experience that one day."

Malcolm grew quiet. "I would quite like that, but I am not sure if it is in the cards for me."

Enid gave him a curious look. "I thought you had settled on marrying Miss Hendre?"

"I did, but it is proving to be rather difficult to convince her of that," he admitted.

Enid let out a laugh before saying, "That must be awful for you, especially since you have always gotten your way."

"That isn't true."

"It is," Enid responded. "You are the heir, the golden child. I was just a mere afterthought."

"Is that how you perceive yourself?"

"No, that is how Father treated me," Enid replied. "He found fault with everything I did and never relented."

Malcolm leaned forward. "Why didn't you say anything to me?"

"When would I have done that?" she asked. "You were always off with your friends, leaving me behind to deal with Father."

"What about Mother?"

Lowering her gaze, Enid replied, "Mother always tried to stand up for me, but I could see the disappointment in her eyes, as well."

"Mother loves you and misses you."

"I know, and I hope one day I can introduce her to Marigold."

Malcolm placed his hand on Marigold's back as she slept. "It will happen. I promise you that."

The coach drove past Marjorie's gatehouse and continued on to a rounded courtyard that was flanked by a large townhouse. The gold trim around the windows contrasted nicely with the red brick and white portico.

Enid's eyes remained fixed on the window as she said, "I forgot how enormous Marjorie's townhouse is."

As the coach came to a stop, a line of servants exited the townhouse and stood in line to greet them. A footman exited his perch, placed the steps down and opened the door.

Malcolm exited first and held his hand out to assist Enid out of the coach. Her feet had just stepped onto the cobblestones when Marjorie, the Dowager Countess of Sherborne, appeared on the top step. Her once vibrant black hair was fading, and the wrinkles on her face were starting to deepen. She was wearing a maroon gown and brightly colored feathers protruded from her straw hat.

Enid leaned closer to him and whispered, "I have never seen so many feathers on a hat before."

A smile came to his lips at the thought of Rosamond's peacock hat that she had worn in a vain attempt to scare him off. "I have," he said, "and it was a sight to behold."

Marjorie held her arms out wide. "Enid!" she exclaimed. "I am so pleased that you are here."

As her words left her mouth, Marigold lifted her head off Enid's chest and turned her sleepy eyes to look at Marjorie.

Marjorie gasped. "What an adorable baby," she gushed. "It is refreshing to see a handsome baby. I do not care for ugly ones and there are far too many in Town for my liking."

Enid giggled. "That is terrible of you to say."

"But you can't tell someone that their baby is ugly,"

Marjorie said with a wave of her hand. "Trust me, I have tried and it did not end well."

Enid started walking up the steps and Malcolm followed behind. Once they stopped in front of Marjorie, her eyes perused the length of Enid, and she asked, "Dear heavens, what are you wearing, Child?"

"I'm afraid it is all that I have," Enid admitted.

Marjorie frowned. "I will have my lady's maid retrieve my old gowns and see if they can be altered for you."

"I do not wish to be a burden."

"Nonsense," Marjorie declared. "You could never be a burden, but Malcolm could."

Malcolm blinked. "I beg your pardon?" What had he done to earn her ire?

Marjorie placed a hand on her hip. "You would let your sister and her child wear these rags without rectifying the situation?"

"I... hadn't thought of that," Malcolm said.

"That is the problem with men; they do not think," Marjorie whispered to Enid. "It is up to us women to solve all the problems."

Enid brought her hand up to cover her growing smile.

Marjorie gestured towards the entry hall of her town-house. "Shall we go inside and have some tea?" she encouraged.

"I do not wish to dirty your furniture with my clothing," Enid said as she ran a hand down her soiled garment.

"Hush, you don't need to worry about that," Marjorie encouraged. "I am just pleased that you will be staying with me for the foreseeable future."

Enid furrowed her brows. "I thought I was staying in the gatehouse."

"You may or you can reside in the main house with me," Marjorie said. "I have seen to a nursery being prepared for Marigold's stay on the second level."

"That is most generous of you," Enid responded.

Marjorie placed her hand on Enid's sleeve but promptly removed it and looked down at her glove with disapproval. "It might be best if we get you out of those clothes at once and into a bath."

Enid's eyes lit up. "I would love a nice soak."

Turning towards a footman, Marjorie snapped her fingers. "Inform Mrs. Bates that Lady Enid would like a bath and send for Sarah to tend to the child."

The footman tipped his head before he went to do her bidding.

Marjorie headed inside and they followed her into the grand entry hall. Black and white tiles ran the length of the floor, the ceiling held a painted mural, and the walls were painted a dark blue that contrasted nicely with the woodwork.

"I hope you do not mind, but your mother shared some of what you have endured these past couple of years," Marjorie said in a hushed voice. "I assure you that you are safe here. My household staff is known for their discretion, and they will keep your presence a secret here."

Enid let out a sigh of relief. "Thank you."

Marjorie turned her head and shouted, "Britt!"

A tall, elderly man walked out from one of the rooms that were adjacent to the entry hall. "Yes, my lady."

"This is Britt," Marjorie introduced. "He has been my butler for many years and he will ensure you are well taken care of."

Enid smiled at the butler. "Thank you."

Britt's kind eyes met hers. "Anything you desire, all you but need to do is ask."

Marjorie clapped her hands together. "Britt, I have no doubt that Lady Enid and Miss Marigold are famished. Will you see to a tray being brought up?"

"As you wish, my lady," Britt said.

As the butler walked off, Marjorie's eyes followed him and

revealed, "His body has slowed down over the years, but his mind is still sharp."

A young maid with blonde hair descended the stairs and came to a stop next to Enid. She dropped into a curtsy. "My name is Sarah, and I will be caring for Miss Marigold," she said as she held her hands out to receive the child.

Enid briefly tightened her hold on Marigold before she reluctantly handed her over to the maid. "She just woke up from a nap and will be ready to eat."

Sarah bobbed her head. "I promise I will take good care of her, my lady."

"Thank you," Enid murmured as she looked longingly at her child.

Marjorie waved the maid off. "Good heavens, you will see Marigold again," she declared. "And you must stop thanking the servants, it is not very becoming of you."

Enid's eyes remained on Marigold as the maid carried her up the stairs. "I do hope Marigold won't fuss too much for Sarah."

"She will be fine. Children are resilient," Marjorie assured her. "I am more concerned about your state."

"I am much better now that I am here," Enid said.

Marjorie didn't look convinced. "We shall see." She turned her attention to him. "You may run along now, Malcolm. I shall see to Enid."

Malcolm was a smart enough man to know when to bow out, especially when he was not needed. "Very well, but I shall return shortly to call upon Enid."

"I would expect no less from you," Marjorie said.

Enid placed a hand on his sleeve. "Thank you, Brother," she hesitated, "for everything."

"You are welcome," he responded.

After he said his goodbyes, he exited the main door of the townhouse and stepped into the coach. He felt much better about leaving Enid and Marigold here and he had no doubt that Marjorie would shower them with kindness. It was no less than Enid deserved.

Now that Enid was safe, Malcolm decided a ride through Hyde Park would clear his mind.

Rosamond raced her horse down a path in Hyde Park as she tried to catch up to Lizette, but it was doing little good. Her horse was no competition for Lizette's prized mare, and she always ended up losing.

Lizette reined in her horse near the Serpentine River and graciously accepted the win without saying a word.

Rosamond came up alongside of Lizette and said, "I don't know why I let you talk me into racing."

"Because it is fun," Lizette said with a smile.

"No, it is fun for you because you always win," Rosamond countered.

"I do not see a difference," Lizette joked.

Rosamond shook her head. "I am surprised that Tristan let us ride through Hyde Park without him."

"I'm not, considering he insisted that we bring along four grooms," Lizette said, glancing over her shoulder.

Rosamond followed her gaze and saw the grooms standing guard as they sat on their horses a short distance away. "I will admit that it does seem rather excessive, but I think it is sweet that Tristan is so protective of you."

Her words seemed to brighten Lizette's smile even more. "That he is," she admitted. "He is a good husband to me."

"I have no doubt that Mother would have enjoyed knowing that you found such a happy union with Tristan," Rosamond shared.

Lizette grew quiet. "I wish I'd had the opportunity to meet our mother, just once."

"As much as she would have loved that, she would have never allowed it," Rosamond said. "She didn't want to disrupt your life, in any way."

"I know, and I understand the reasons why she felt that way, but it doesn't mean I can't wish that things had been different."

Rosamond adjusted the reins in her hand. "I can't imagine what my life would have been like if our mother hadn't told me about you," she said. "I would have been living a quiet life in the countryside, none the wiser."

"And I would have never known I had a sister," Lizette said. "No, I think everything turned out precisely how it was supposed to."

"That is a wonderful thought."

Lizette gave her a curious look. "Are you happy?"

"I am," she rushed to reply. "Why wouldn't I be? I have more than I ever thought possible."

With a reflective look in her eyes, Lizette said, "I have learned that it is not *what* you have in your life, but *who*."

"I agree, and I have been blessed to have been so completely embraced by Lord Ashington and Lady Anne. I couldn't ask for a better guardian. He has given me a life that I could have only dreamed of before."

"You deserve every good thing that has happened to you," Lizette said.

Rosamond cocked her head. "Are you happy?" she asked, turning the question back onto her sister.

"Yes, but I do miss the simple life of living in the country," Lizette said. "Sometimes, I feel as if I don't belong in London."

"I understand that feeling, wholeheartedly, but one day you will be a marchioness. You most assuredly do belong here, whereas I am just a country bumpkin."

"You are no such thing!" Lizette exclaimed.

"Living here in London, being immersed in high Society,

it is different than what I thought," Rosamond said. "I have to hide a part of me just to fit in."

"As do I."

"But Tristan knows the truth about you," Rosamond insisted. "Am I to keep my past hidden until after I am wed or do I just continue to live a lie?"

"I can't answer that," Lizette replied. "But our secrets could ruin not only us, but the people we love."

Rosamond sighed. "It is a heavy burden to carry these secrets alone."

"You have me."

"For which I am most grateful," Rosamond said. "I just hope I am fortunate enough to find love like you did."

"You can't force love. You will love who you love but it is something that is most unexpected," Lizette advised.

Lord Brentwood sprung to her mind, and she wondered how he would respond to her humble past. Would he accept her for who she truly was or would he cast her aside once he learned the truth? The thought of him rejecting her caused her heart to ache.

With a knowing look, Lizette asked, "Are you thinking about Lord Brentwood?"

"I am," Rosamond replied, seeing no reason to deny it.

"I would have to be blind to not notice how close you two have become," Lizette said.

Rosamond bit her lower lip. "He will be an earl one day. He will need a wife that is above reproach, not someone that has a sordid past."

"You hardly have a sordid past," Lizette argued.

"I would have killed George if Lord Roswell hadn't already taken the shot," Rosamond admitted. "That is hardly an action becoming a countess."

"George was unhinged, and he would have killed me. Your actions that day helped save me."

"I know, for which I am most grateful, but the image of George lying dead on the ground will forever haunt me."

Lizette gave her a sad smile. "I can't imagine how difficult that must be for you."

"He wasn't always a bad man," Rosamond assured her.

"I believe you."

The sound of a horse whinnying in the distance drew her attention. Rosamond turned her head and saw Lord Brentwood approaching.

"Speak of the devil," Lizette said with amusement in her voice.

Lord Brentwood held his hand up in greeting as he grew closer. "Good morning," he said, reining in his horse.

Rosamond tipped her head. "Good morning," she responded as she tried to ignore her heart beating faster in her chest. Why did his mere presence cause her to respond in such a fashion?

"It is a fine morning for a ride, is it not?" Lord Brentwood asked.

"It is," Rosamond agreed.

Lord Brentwood smiled, and her eyes dropped to his lips. What would it be like to kiss him? Good heavens, where had that thought even come from? The last thing she needed was to have these wayward thoughts about him.

Appearing oblivious to her discomfort, Lord Brentwood's eyes roamed over her horse. "So this is your infamous horse?"

"Yes, this is Bella."

"I had expected a much uglier horse based on your description," Lord Brentwood said.

Rosamond leaned forward and ran a hand down her horse's neck. "We get along just fine, but I'm afraid Bella doesn't realize she is a horse. She always wants to be a part of the conversation."

"That is an odd trait for a horse to have," Lord Brentwood remarked.

"Perhaps, but I find it endearing," she said. "When I was younger, I would often read to Bella in the mornings. I was convinced that she understood what I was reading."

"You used to read to a horse?" Lord Brentwood asked in disbelief.

Rosamond grinned. "I did, and I can tell you that Bella does not appreciate Shakespeare."

Lord Brentwood shifted in the saddle before asking, "Would it be too presumptuous to speak privately with you for a moment?"

Rosamond glanced over at Lizette for permission, who promptly nodded her head. "I would enjoy that," she said.

Lord Brentwood dismounted and handed the reins off to a groom who had stepped forward. Then he walked around her horse and went to assist her. She leaned forward, positioning her hands on his broad shoulders, and he placed his hands on her waist. Gently, he lowered her down until her feet were on the ground but his hands lingered for a moment longer than what would be considered proper. Not that she minded. She always felt lost in his touch since he held her in a way no one had in all her life.

After he took a step back, he offered his arm, and he began to lead her away.

Not wanting the silence to stretch into becoming awkward, Rosamond asked, "How is your sister faring?"

"She is well," Lord Brentwood replied. "I removed her from the boarding house and she is now residing with a family member that has sympathy for her plight."

"That is good."

"It is, but I do hope that my father will let her return home soon enough," Lord Brentwood said. "I have yet to discuss it with him again."

"Why is that?"

"My father is not one to forgive easily, especially when it is a matter of pride. Enid besmirched our family name and he takes his legacy very seriously."

Rosamond glanced over at him. "Over his own daughter?"

"I never said it was right, but that is the way it is in my family," Lord Brentwood replied. "I have no doubt that he will be furious when he discovers who Enid is residing with."

"Why should that matter to him?"

Lord Brentwood huffed. "My mother's cousin was the third daughter of gentry and she managed to attract the eye of an earl. My father considers her an upstart and refuses to have anything to do with her."

"I see," Rosamond said, even though she didn't see.

"It is rather remarkable that someone that came from such humble circumstances was able to secure such an advantageous marriage."

"You think being a daughter of a gentry is a 'humble beginning'?" Rosamond asked.

"Don't you?"

Rosamond frowned. She could only imagine what Lord Brentwood would think of her if she admitted to being a daughter of a seaman. She was a commoner, a nobody. Would he stop pursuing her if he knew the truth? She may have an impressive dowry, but that didn't change her past.

Knowing that Lord Brentwood was still waiting for a response, she replied, "I do not think it is fair to judge someone solely based upon their lineage."

"I'm afraid in our circles that is nearly impossible," he said. "A daughter of gentry will always struggle to find her place within high Society."

"Why?" she demanded.

"Because everyone knows that she doesn't belong, no matter the fancy gowns or the jewels she wears."

Rosamond removed her hand from his arm. "I think that is rather pompous of you to say," she said.

Lord Brentwood looked puzzled by her response. "I meant no offense."

"But you did offend me, my lord," Rosamond stated. "In one breath, you condemn your father for his treatment of her, but in the next breath, you admit that she will never be accepted. I fail to see the difference between the two of you."

"My father and I are hardly the same," Lord Brentwood said in a firm tone.

"Aren't you?" she asked. "Both of you refuse to accept someone based upon their merit."

Lord Brentwood ran a hand through his hair. "I am not saying that it is right, but that is the way it has always been."

"Then you should change that."

"How?" Lord Brentwood asked. "Members of high Society are not exactly known for their acceptance of others that are different than them."

Rosamond wanted to tell him the truth. It was on the tip of her tongue to do so, but she knew that her secret could ruin others that had been nothing but kind to her. She couldn't do that to them.

Spinning on her heel, she started walking back towards her sister but was stopped by Lord Brentwood's hand on her arm.

"What did I do wrong?" he asked as he gently turned her to face him. The sincerity in his voice caused some of her anger to dissipate.

"You did nothing wrong," she replied.

"I don't understand then," he said. "What has you so upset?"

Rosamond sighed. The only person that she could be disappointed in was herself. Lord Brentwood thought the way that he did because he was raised to do so and it was unfair of her to think that she could change him. "You are exactly what I would expect from someone in your position," she said, resigned.

He furrowed his brow. "Is that an insult or a compliment?"

"It is neither. It is merely a fact."

Lord Brentwood took a step closer to her. "I am not standing in front of you as a viscount, but as a man that doesn't want to lose you over something as trivial as what I said wrong."

"It isn't trivial, at least to me."

"Explain it to me, please," he said.

Rosamond knew she owed him that much, but she knew that she needed to choose her next words carefully. "If Lord Ashington hadn't made me his ward, you would have never given me any notice."

Lord Brentwood grew solemn. "I cannot say with certainty that is true, but I am glad that fate intervened, and we have gotten to know one another."

Finding strength inside of her that she didn't know she had, she asked, "Why are you pursuing me?"

His lips curled into a smile. "I have never met someone quite like you," he admitted. "You make me want to be a better man, not just because I want to win your favor but because I want to one day be worthy of you."

Rosamond felt herself smiling as he looked at her in a way that made her feel beautiful. It was then, as he held her unwavering gaze, that she knew she was starting to fall in love with him.

Chapter Fourteen

Malcolm sat in an upholstered armchair as he sipped his drink. He had retired to his club shortly after riding through Hyde Park as he tried to harbor the gnawing guilt that he felt for pursuing Miss Hendre. She didn't deserve his false advances, but he was beginning to wonder if they were false. He had set out to convince Miss Hendre to marry him, at any cost, but now he wondered if the cost was too high.

He had done something intolerably stupid and had let his defenses down when it came to Miss Hendre. He had grown to care for her and didn't want to subject her to a loveless marriage. She deserved better. But what was he to do? If he didn't marry her, then his family would be subjected to ruination. He couldn't stand by and let that happen.

"Botheration," he muttered under his breath. Since when did he care about other people's feelings? He had only ever cared about himself. It was much simpler that way. So why did he now feel as if he needed to take Miss Hendre's feelings into account?

This is precisely why he never wanted to fall in love. There are consequences to caring for another so deeply that you put them before yourself. He had seen too many people make the same mistake and they evidently lived to regret it.

Malcolm said what needed to be said, and did what needed to be done, in order to convince Miss Hendre that he was the man for her.

Malcolm turned his attention towards the fire that was in the hearth and let out a sigh. Since when did courting a woman grow so complicated?

A familiar voice came from next to him. "Why so gloomy?" Mr. Whitmore asked as he held a glass in his hand.

"You are drunk," Malcolm stated, not bothering to look up.

"Not yet, but I am trying." Mr. Whitmore took a sip of his drink. "I tend to think better with a drink or two inside of me."

"Or three?" Malcolm joked.

"Life is too short to be sober, my friend," Mr. Whitmore said as he sat down.

Malcolm leaned forward and placed his nearly full glass down onto the table. "I need a clear head right now."

With a knowing look, Mr. Whitmore said, "There is only one thing that would cause someone to become so despondent- a woman."

"You know not what you speak of," Malcolm remarked.

Mr. Whitmore gripped the lapels of his jacket and declared, "Perhaps, but I am widely considered to be an expert on women."

"That is not the least bit true."

Mr. Whitmore smirked. "I have never gotten a complaint before."

"That is because you are associating with the wrong type of women," Malcolm pressed.

"I would be careful since you used to have no objections mingling with those women."

"I have changed my ways."

"So I have noticed, but you do not appear any happier as a result of it," Mr. Whitmore remarked.

Malcolm grimaced. "I don't know what I am."

"That is the problem, then."

Mr. Moore appeared by Mr. Whitmore's side and announced, "I ordered a round of drinks for us."

"Lovely," Mr. Whitmore said before he tossed back the rest of his drink.

Mr. Moore sat down across from Malcolm. "It is good to have you back at the club, Brentwood. Your absence has been noticed by many of the patrons."

"I have been busy," Malcolm said.

Mr. Moore bobbed his head. "I am aware. It would appear that your courtship of Miss Hendre is going off without a hitch."

"Why do you say that?"

"The Society page has reported on your comings and goings with Miss Hendre," Mr. Moore shared. "It even made mention that you appeared rather close to her at the Royal Menagerie."

"Nothing untoward happened," Malcolm assured him.

"I wish it had, then you could marry the chit and move on," Mr. Whitmore declared. "It has been awfully lonely without you these past couple of days."

Malcolm glanced over his shoulder at the other men in the room and asked, "Do you ever get tired of just sitting around and drinking?"

Mr. Whitmore gave him a blank stare. "What else would we do with our time?"

"I don't know, but surely there must be more to life," Malcolm replied.

Eyeing him curiously, Mr. Moore asked, "What more do you want?"

Malcolm frowned. "Forget I said anything," he said. He

wasn't even quite sure what he was looking for so how could he explain that to his friends.

Mr. Moore sat back in his seat. "I know what the problem is," he stated. "It happened to my older brother as well."

"Is it a rash?" Mr. Whitmore asked.

Mr. Moore chuckled. "Why would you think it was a rash?"

"We could put some salve on it and fix up Malcolm, good as new," Mr. Whitmore said. "Then we can go on as we have been."

"This problem is much worse," Mr. Moore said as he placed a hand over his heart. "Our dear friend has fallen in love."

Mr. Whitmore let out a groan. "Say it isn't so."

Malcolm put his hand up. "I am not in love with Miss Hendre," he asserted. "I just need to marry her."

"There is no shame in loving one's wife," Mr. Moore pointed out.

"She hasn't agreed to be my wife yet," Malcolm said.

"And, why not?" Mr. Moore asked. "You could have convinced a handful of women to marry you by now. What is the hold up?"

"There isn't one. These things take time," Malcolm remarked.

Mr. Moore didn't look convinced. "My brother fell for his wife, too," he said. "It was quite disappointing to watch but they are very happy."

Mr. Whitmore interjected, "No one who settles on one woman could truly be happy."

"That is because you haven't found the right woman to tempt you," Mr. Moore argued.

"The right woman is the one that I am currently with," Mr. Whitmore said.

Mr. Moore shook his head. "You are past hope." He

turned back to face Malcolm. "You are someone that I can still work with."

A server came and placed three drinks on the table before he collected the empty glasses and walked off.

Mr. Whitmore promptly reached for a glass and asked, "What are your symptoms?"

"Symptoms?" Malcolm asked.

Mr. Moore looked heavenward. "Being in love is not a disease."

"Pity. At least a disease can be treated with the right medicine," Mr. Whitmore said. "But falling in love can ruin one's life."

"It might be best if you just sit there and don't say anything," Mr. Moore remarked.

Mr. Whitmore held up his glass in acknowledgement.

Mr. Moore met Malcolm's gaze and asked, "I know that every fiber of your being is against falling in love, but would it be so bad if you did?"

"Yes!" Malcolm exclaimed. "I have seen firsthand what love does to people and I refuse to go down that path."

"I assume you speak of your parents?" Mr. Moore asked.

"I am."

Mr. Moore grew quiet. "My parents loathe one another, and they can hardly be in the same room," he shared. "But that hasn't stopped me from searching for a woman that I won't be able to live without."

"I am not you," Malcolm stated. "I just need a rich wife and Miss Hendre fits the bill."

"So you have said, but I think you have fallen for her," Mr. Moore said.

"Why would I have done something so foolish?" Malcolm asked.

Mr. Moore smiled. "Because you have finally met your match."

"No, no, no…" Malcolm's voice trailed off. "You know not

what you speak of." He could deny it all he wanted but he knew he cared for Miss Hendre, more than he should. But that was a far cry from falling in love with her.

"I am a barrister so I deal in facts," Mr. Moore said as he moved to sit on the edge of his seat. "You changed the moment you started pursuing Miss Hendre, some would even argue for the better."

Mr. Whitmore huffed. "I wouldn't."

"You stopped wasting your time at the club and you now spend your days with Miss Hendre," Mr. Moore continued. "Furthermore, and the most telling sign, you can't help but smile when you say her name."

"I do not." Malcolm paused. "Do I?"

"You do," Mr. Whitmore replied. "What am I going to do now? I can't lose another friend to the parson's mousetrap."

Mr. Moore shifted to face Mr. Whitmore. "This isn't about you, you know?"

"I feel as if it is," Mr. Whitmore said. "You spend your time doing barrister stuff and Malcolm would always be up for anything."

"It is not as if I am dead," Malcolm remarked.

"You might as well be," Mr. Whitmore stated. "Once you fall in love, you are of no further use to me."

"Will you stop with the theatrics?" Malcolm asked. "I will admit that I enjoy Miss Hendre's company…"

Mr. Whitmore groaned.

"… but I can't possibly be in love with her," Malcolm said. "I wouldn't be foolish enough to make that mistake."

"Why would it be so bad if you did?" Mr. Moore pressed.

Malcolm pressed his lips together as he delayed his response. He never wanted to give someone the power to hurt him. He would rather protect himself- and his heart- than be vulnerable with Miss Hendre.

"A wise man does not fall in love with his wife," Malcolm said.

"Hear, hear," Mr. Whitmore agreed.

Mr. Moore dropped his head. "Why do I bother? I might as well be talking to a brick wall."

"Thank you," Mr. Whitmore said as he took a sip of his drink.

"That was not a compliment," Mr. Moore stated, rising. "If you will excuse me, I have work that I need to see to."

"Don't go. Stay and have a drink with us," Mr. Whitmore encouraged.

Mr. Moore slid his glass over to Mr. Whitmore. "You can stay and indulge in mine," he said. "I have had my fill of nonsense for today."

Malcolm rose. "I think it is best if I return home, as well."

"I will walk you out," Mr. Moore said as he gestured towards the door.

As they exited the club, Malcolm felt compelled to say something to his friend. He didn't want him to think that his advice wasn't appreciated. "I know you are trying to help, but I assure you that I know what I am doing."

Mr. Moore stopped and turned on the pavement. "You are better than this."

"Than what?"

Gesturing towards White's, Mr. Moore replied, "Whitmore is content to carry on the way he has been, but it is time for you to decide what you really want out of life. You have a real chance at happiness with Miss Hendre."

Malcolm opened his mouth but Mr. Moore continued. "I have known you for a long time, and I have seen the way the demise of your parents' relationship has affected you. But that doesn't mean you should give up on love."

With a clenched jaw, Malcolm said, "I don't love her."

Mr. Moore placed a hand on his shoulder. "Then don't marry her."

"I have to."

"You are fortunate," Mr. Moore said as he withdrew his hand. "Not everyone has the opportunity to fall in love."

"I told you, I don't—"

Mr. Moore spoke over him. "You are wasting your breath. You can deny it all you want but we both know that you do."

Malcolm crossed his arms over his chest. "Why are you so insistent that I am?"

"Because, my friend, if you are fortunate enough to find love, you must have the courage to take it. You should shout it from the rooftops or sing a song," Mr. Moore advised.

"I don't sing."

Mr. Moore offered him a weak smile. "Then you don't deserve her," he said before walking off.

Malcolm watched his friend's retreating figure and wondered who the bigger fool was. Was it him, who believed that love was a weakness? Or was it Mr. Moore, who seemed to believe that love could conquer all?

Either way, despite his feelings for Miss Hendre, he couldn't make the mistake of ever revealing the truth. To do so would leave him exposed.

"Then you don't deserve her," kept echoing through Malcolm's mind as he reviewed the ledgers that sat in front of him on the desk. He had spent hours going over the accounts as he tried to become familiar with them. He was hoping to find a solution that would get them out of their volatile financial situation without having him marry Miss Hendre.

He knew in his heart that he didn't deserve Miss Hendre and he never would. If he went through with this marriage, he would grow to hate himself for tricking Miss Hendre into marrying him. And, if she ever discovered the true reason for his courtship, then she would grow to hate him. He couldn't do that to her or himself. No, he needed to give her a chance at finding true happiness- with another. It had to be this way.

His father walked over to the desk with a drink in his hand. "I'm surprised you have lasted as long as you have."

"Thank you, Father," Malcolm said dryly.

"As you can see, the coffers are empty and we are in desperate need for an influx of cash."

Sitting back in his seat, Malcolm responded, "I agree, but I can't help but notice all the money that you wasted on gambling."

"It was merely a trite sum."

"By my estimation, you spent almost ten thousand pounds," Malcolm said. "That is not a 'trite sum'."

"You don't need to concern yourself with that. It is in the past and we need to look forward," his father said dismissively.

"How am I supposed to overlook that?"

His father took a sip of his drink. "You have no right to judge me," he growled. "It is my money, after all."

"It was, and you did a good job of squandering it all."

"I don't answer to you, Son."

Malcolm sighed. No good would come from fighting with his father, especially when he got this way. He was stubborn and he would never admit fault. "Regardless, I have found a few ways to raise some funds."

"For what purpose?" his father asked. "Once you marry Miss Hendre, we will have her dowry and be out of the red."

"About that," he hesitated, knowing he was about to stoke his father's anger even more, "I don't think I can go along with the plan to marry Miss Hendre anymore."

Malcolm watched his father visibly stiffen and the man's nostrils flared slightly. "Pray tell, why is that?" he asked.

"I do not think it is fair to marry Miss Hendre since we hardly know one another."

"You know enough," his father responded. "She has a

large dowry, and you are in need of it. What more is there to know?"

Rising, Malcolm reached for a piece of paper. "If we sell the Dowager House at our country estate, we could have enough money to buy farmland equipment."

"Or you could marry Miss Hendre and we could buy all the equipment we need and then some."

Ignoring his father's comment, Malcolm pressed forward. "We could sell off the land to the north of our estate."

"Where would I hunt?"

"We would still retain plenty of woodland that would sustain hunting," Malcolm assured him.

His father slammed his empty glass down onto the desk. "I don't understand where this is coming from. You said that you would marry Miss Hendre."

"At the time, I thought it was our only option, but there are other ways we can survive this."

"The creditors are practically knocking at our door," his father said. "We do not have time to wait. We could lose everything."

Malcolm placed the paper down onto the table. "If we show them that we have a plan—"

"They don't give a whit if we have a plan, they only care if we have the money. And we don't." His father shook his head. "You had one job."

"You are willing to have me throw away my future to save you from financial ruin."

His father advanced towards him. "Save *us!*" he exclaimed. "You are my heir and this will all be yours one day, assuming you don't blow this."

Malcolm stared at his father in disbelief. Was his father so self-absorbed that he didn't realize it was he who had blown it? "It was you that got us into this situation, or do I need to remind you of that?" he shouted. "Your poor investments and incessant gambling have toppled us. You, not me, have ruined us!"

His father matched his tone. "Yes, and a marriage to Miss Hendre would solve all our problems."

"I can't marry Miss Hendre," Malcolm said, standing his ground. "There must be another way."

"There is no other way! We have already been through this."

"I can't accept that."

His father tossed his hands up in the air as he walked over to the hearth. "What is so wrong with Miss Hendre that you can't marry her?" he asked.

"There is nothing wrong with her."

"Then what is it?"

Malcolm knew his father would mock his reasonings, but he decided to tell him, nonetheless. Not that he owed him an explanation. "I want Miss Hendre to marry the man of her choosing; a man that loves her for her and not what she can give him."

To his surprise, his father let out a bark of laughter. "I see what this is about," he said. "You care for her."

"I do," he admitted.

His father did not look amused, despite his loud laughter. "I did not raise you to be a simpleton," he snapped. "Your duty is to this family, not to some misguided notions about emotions. Or did you forget that?"

Malcolm was tired and he had just about enough of his father. "How could I forget?" he asked. "You remind me constantly of it."

"Yet you still stand before me, wifeless." His father paused. "What do you think will happen to your lovely Miss Hendre if you withdraw your suit?" he mocked. "Do you think she will go on to find love?"

"I hope so."

His father shook his head. "No, another fortune hunter

will scoop in and claim her for himself, leaving you with nothing but regret," he said. "Is that what you want for Miss Hendre?"

Malcolm knew his father was baiting him but he refused to back down. Not now. "I want Miss Hendre to be happily settled."

His father scoffed. "Happily settled?" he repeated. "There is no such thing. For a while, you can pretend that all is well but then the tides change, leaving you more miserable than you ever thought possible."

"That won't happen to Miss Hendre."

"How do you know that?" his father asked. "You are throwing her to the wolves. Fortune hunters and rakes will prey on her. She will be helpless, and for what? Because you suddenly decided to grow a conscience?"

He knew his father was exaggerating to prove his point, but there was some truth to it. He had no doubt that despicable men would pounce on the opportunity to marry a ward of a marquess. It wasn't a matter of if, but when.

His father stared at him with his wrinkled brow furrowed. "If you care for Miss Hendre, you must marry her to protect her," he asserted.

Malcolm was many things but being stupid was not one of them. He knew that his father was trying to manipulate him. It was his usual tactic when he was trying to get his way. However, he didn't want to play his father's game anymore. He was going to do right by Miss Hendre, regardless of the consequences.

Miss Hendre was clever, and he hoped that she would be able to navigate the marriage mart. There were still some good, honorable gentlemen that would give her the love match that she so desperately wanted and deserved.

Malcolm met his father's gaze and said, "I am protecting her in my own way."

"You are a fool!" his father shouted. "You have brought ruination upon us. No heiress will want to marry you now."

"So be it."

His father turned back towards the mantel and placed his hands against it, his face flushed with anger. He didn't speak for a long moment and the only noise was the crackling of the fire. Finally, he spoke. "You will regret this one day," he said. "One day, you will discover that love is not enough."

"I said nothing about love."

His father faced him. "You didn't need to. There is only one reason why a man would turn his back on his family."

"I am hardly turning my back on you," Malcolm argued. "I have found ways that will save us from financial ruin."

"Yes, but for how long?"

As Malcolm went to respond, a knock came at the door.

"Enter," his father ordered.

The door opened and Osborne stepped into the room. "A Mr. Davidson has requested a moment of your time, my lords."

"Who the blazes is Mr. Davidson and why does he think he is so important to meet with me at this late hour?" his father asked.

"He is a Bow Street Runner and he said he had a few questions about Lady Enid," Osborne replied.

His father's face grew hard. "Inform this Runner that I do not want to talk about her."

A man's voice came from behind the butler. "If you would prefer, we can talk down at my office and it will be much less comfortable for you."

Osborne stepped back, and a stocky man appeared in the doorway. His hair was red and it was brushed to the side. "As you were previously told, my name is Mr. Davidson, and I am here to ask about Lady Enid's whereabouts."

His father waved his hand dismissively in front of him.

"Why would I know where she is?" he asked. "I disowned her once I discovered she'd eloped."

"Yes, with a Mr. Longbourn," Mr. Davidson said, walking further into the room. "But he is under the impression that you know where his wife is."

"He would be wrong," his father snapped back.

Mr. Davidson shifted his gaze towards Malcolm. "Mr. Longbourn said that he spoke to you earlier, but he felt you weren't being truthful with him," he said. "Do you know where Lady Enid is?"

Malcolm knew he had no choice but to lie. He didn't want to reveal his sister's location and have her returned to her husband. He would do whatever it took to protect his sister, even if there were repercussions to his actions.

"I do not know where my sister is," Malcolm lied.

"But if you did, would you tell Mr. Longbourn?" Mr. Davidson pressed.

"No," came his prompt response.

Mr. Davidson didn't look impressed by his admission. "Lady Enid is in a lot of trouble," he said. "She ran away from her husband and took their child with her. It would be in your best interest to cooperate with me."

"That is a shame, but it has nothing to do with me," Malcolm stated.

The Bow Street Runner took a step closer to him, no doubt in a misguided effort to intimidate him. "It is my opinion that Lady Enid is not of sane mind and needs to be found before she hurts herself or her child."

Malcolm walked over to the door and held it. "It is late, and I believe I have already answered your questions to your satisfaction."

Mr. Davidson approached him and came to a stop in front of him. "You will find that I am rarely satisfied."

"I pity your wife, then," Malcolm remarked.

In a low, menacing voice, Mr. Davidson said, "I will find Lady Enid, with or without your help."

"I wish you luck."

Mr. Davidson held his gaze for a long moment before he brushed past him. Malcolm turned and watched him walking away until he turned a corner, disappearing from view.

His father's voice broke through the silence. "Where is she?" he asked.

"Somewhere safe."

"Do you intend to tell me?"

"I do not," Malcolm replied as he departed from the study. He was not in the mood to continue conversing with his father, especially at this late hour. He was tired and wanted to sleep. With any luck, his thoughts wouldn't be consumed by Miss Hendre but he feared that was inevitable.

Chapter Fifteen

Rosamond was conflicted. She wanted to trust her heart, but she had been fooled before. Yet, somehow, Lord Brentwood had managed to break through her carefully constructed defenses and claim her heart. How could she have done something so careless?

Her desire was to secure a love match this Season but why did it have to be with Lord Brentwood? He was undeniably handsome, but it was the way he had touched her soul that caused her to question everything. He spoke to her with such care and consideration that she knew she had found her match. However, it could all change once he discovered that she wasn't the person he thought she was. And that thought terrified her.

Reaching for a cup of tea, she took a sip before she placed it back onto the table. She was sitting in the dining room and she was grateful for the chance to be alone with her thoughts, giving her the reprieve she needed. How she missed the idyllic life of the countryside. She would spend hours in the garden as she carefully tilled the ground, and no one would disturb her solitude.

Not that she had any reason to complain. Every one of

her needs were met here and she never wanted for anything. Her life had turned out better than she could have ever imagined. So why couldn't she convince herself that she belonged here? No matter how hard she tried, she knew that she was a fraud. This was never supposed to be her life.

But she desperately wanted it to be true.

Lady Anne stepped into the dining room with Lord Ashington trailing close behind. "Good morning, Rosamond," she greeted. "I hope you slept well."

She didn't. Every time she closed her eyes, she thought of Lord Brentwood and she couldn't seem to banish him long enough from her thoughts to fall asleep. But Lady Anne didn't need to know that. "I did sleep well," she lied.

Lord Ashington came to sit at the head of the table and a footman handed him the newssheets. "Would you care to read the Society page?" he asked her.

Before she could respond, Lady Anne spoke up. "A woman does not read the newssheets in front of a gentleman."

"Yes, but we are family," Lord Ashington responded.

"Regardless, it is simply not done," Lady Anne insisted as she placed a white linen napkin onto her lap. "You mustn't encourage Rosamond to break the rules of propriety."

Lord Ashington opened the newssheets and his eyes roamed over the pages. "I just thought Rosamond would want to read the Society page since she is mentioned."

Rosamond perked up. "What does it say?"

Lady Anne gave her a chiding look. "A lady must not appear overeager to hear a tasty piece of gossip, even when it is about her."

The marquess chuckled. "Leave her be," he encouraged. "It is not every day when one has an article written about them."

"I am just trying to ensure that Rosamond knows what is expected of her when she runs her own household," Lady Anne said.

"And you are doing a splendid job. But you must let Rosamond be free to make her own choices," Lord Ashington argued.

Lady Anne looked as if she hadn't considered that possibility. "I agree," she conceded in a tone that lacked conviction.

Lord Ashington grinned as he folded the newssheets and placed them onto the table. "According to the Society page, our Rosamond is on course to have the match of the Season."

"I should say so," Lady Anne huffed. "A match between her and Lord Brentwood would be most advantageous."

"This is assuming that Rosamond is interested in making a match with Lord Brentwood," Lord Ashington said.

"Of course she is interested." Lady Anne gave her a pointed look. "Aren't you?"

Rosamond bit her lower lip as she delayed her response. She didn't dare tell them that she was in love with Lord Brentwood. If she did, she had little doubt that Lady Anne would start planning her wedding and she wasn't there yet. She needed more time to sort through her thoughts.

In a reserved voice, she replied, "I am not as opposed to him as I once was." There. That was the truth. Hopefully, it would appease Lady Anne and Lord Ashington.

Lady Anne smiled. "That is wonderful news."

Rosamond thought it might just be best to reveal her concerns and hope they could offer words of wisdom to her. "I just worry that Lord Brentwood might not approve of how I was brought up in a small village," she said.

With a blank look, Lady Anne asked, "Why would you need to tell him that?"

"I feel that I am hiding a part of myself from him."

Lady Anne considered her for a moment before saying, "You may speak of your past but do avoid mentioning you were poor."

"We were hardly poor," Rosamond argued.

"That is what poor people would say," Lady Anne remarked.

Lord Ashington frowned. "That is rather insensitive of you to say, Dear," he said. "Rosamond's upbringing may have been different from ours but that doesn't mean we should pass judgment."

Lady Anne gave her a weak smile. "I do apologize. I merely believe it is unwise to reveal too much of your past to Lord Brentwood. If you do, it could open up a Pandora's box, so to speak."

Rosamond blew out a puff of air. "That is my concern, as well," she responded.

"Regardless of your past, you are still my ward," Lord Ashington said.

"I mean no disrespect, but I am more than just your ward," Rosamond remarked. "I had a whole other life before I came to live with you."

Lord Ashington's eyes held compassion as he said, "You did, and I do not want you to discount that. It makes you have a unique perspective that most people of high Society do not have."

Brownell stepped into the room and announced, "Lord Brentwood has come to call upon Miss Hendre." He met her gaze. "Are you available, Miss?"

Rosamond felt a smile come to her lips. "I am," she rushed to reply. "Please show him to the drawing room."

"Very good," Brownell said before he departed from the room.

Lady Anne pushed back her seat. "We mustn't keep Lord Brentwood waiting for too long."

Lord Ashington gave her an encouraging smile. "If you do not think Lord Brentwood will accept you for who you truly are, then it is his loss, not yours," he said. "Trust yourself, and do not think you have to settle."

Touched by his words, Rosamond murmured, "Thank you."

She followed Lady Anne out of the dining room and through the entry hall. As she stepped into the drawing room, she saw Lord Brentwood, standing in the center of the room. He met her gaze and smiled, causing her heart to take flight. She loved the way she felt around Lord Brentwood. The way he looked at her, made her feel like she was the most beautiful woman in the room.

Lord Brentwood bowed. "My ladies," he greeted.

Rosamond lowered herself down into a curtsy. "My lord," she murmured.

"I hope I did not call too early," Lord Brentwood said.

Lady Anne waved her hand dismissively in front of her. "You did no such thing," she responded. "We were just finishing breakfast."

Lord Brentwood shifted his gaze to Rosamond and asked, "If you have no objections, I was hoping to speak privately to you for a moment."

Rosamond glanced at Lady Anne first for permission, who nodded in the affirmative. "We can speak in the gardens," she suggested.

He approached her and offered his arm. As he led her out of the drawing room, Rosamond felt herself growing increasingly nervous. She had a suspicion of what he wished to discuss with her, but she still wasn't sure how she would respond. Could she accept his offer of courtship, despite him not knowing the truth about her?

Once they had stepped outside, a footman went to stand watch by the door, and they continued down one of the paths. Neither of them spoke and Rosamond feared the stretch of silence was growing awkward, propelling her to ask, "It is a lovely day, is it not?" Good heavens, did she just ask that? Could she think of nothing clever to say?

"It is." Lord Brentwood dropped his arm and turned to

face her, his boots grinding on the gravel. "I... um... do not wish to take too much of your time, but I... um... feared if I did not speak to you at once then I would lose my nerve."

Rosamond found his stammering to be oddly charming and she realized that she could see herself having a future with this man. They had a lot to work out, but he was a good, honorable man. He would treat her with the same kindness he had always bestowed upon her. She just needed to trust herself, as Lord Ashington had told her to do. She wanted to be with Lord Brentwood.

She saw Lord Brentwood wipe the sweat off his brow with the back of his hand and he kept shifting back and forth in his stance. She found it endearing how nervous he was and she wanted to remember everything about this moment.

Lord Brentwood cleared his throat. "Miss Hendre..." he started.

"Rosamond," she corrected. "I think it is only appropriate if you start using my given name."

His face softened. "Rosamond," he said in an intimate voice. "I... um..." His voice stopped.

Feeling compassion well up inside of her, she placed her hand on his sleeve and said, "I think I know what you are going to say."

"I doubt it."

"It is all right," she assured him. "Whenever you are ready, I am here to listen."

Lord Brentwood glanced down at her hand on his sleeve. "I have enjoyed getting to know you and I find you to be extraordinary," he said. "You have changed my life, for the better."

Rosamond smiled, hoping it provided him the encouragement he needed to say his next words. She yearned to hear them.

"But," he hesitated, "I have decided that I must withdraw my suit."

Her smile vanished as she removed her hand. Had she misheard him? "Pardon?"

"I know this is sudden, but I do believe your reputation won't suffer if we cut ties now." He ran a hand through his hair, and his eyes held a sadness she hadn't seen before. "I would even be willing to assist you in finding a new suitor."

Rosamond's eyes widened in disbelief. Was he in earnest? "You wish to help me find a suitor?"

"I would, not that you need assistance, but if you did…" His words trailed off. It sounded as if his admission had cost him greatly.

She could feel the tears well up in her eyes and she didn't dare cry in front of Lord Brentwood. If she did, he would know how badly he had hurt her, and she couldn't let that happen. He may not care for her, but she loved him.

Blinking back her tears, she spun on her heel and hurried towards the townhouse.

"Rosamond," Lord Brentwood called out after her.

She didn't dare turn around and hear what he had to say. She was sure that her heart couldn't take that.

Lord Brentwood caught up to her and placed his hand on her arm, turning her to face him. His face was etched with sorrow, or was it regret? She couldn't tell but he looked utterly beside himself. "Please, Rosamond, you must know how sorry I am." His words sounded sincere, which caused them to cut her deeper.

Keeping her gaze firmly on the lapels of his jacket, Rosamond attempted to keep her voice steady as she said, "Please unhand me."

He dropped his hand and took a step back, looking contrite. "I do not want to lose you over this," he pleaded.

Stunned, she met his gaze. "You never had me to begin with." She turned away from him and addressed the footman. "Please escort Lord Brentwood out of the townhouse. He is no longer welcome here."

The footman tipped his head as he went to open the door. Keeping her head held high, Rosamond stepped into the townhouse and waited until she was out of sight before she let the tears fall from her eyes. How had she been so foolish to fall in love with a man that didn't truly care for her? She had been so swept up in the fairy tale that she must have missed the signs.

Rosamond swiped at the tears that were streaming down her face as she rushed to her bedchamber. The sooner she could be alone, the better. She felt her heart breaking and there was no one to blame but herself. Fool her once, shame on him, but fool her twice… it was shame on her.

She opened her bedchamber door and slipped inside. Then she closed it and slid her back down the wall until she sat on the floor, her knees tucked up against her chest.

A knock came at the door. "Rosamond," Lady Anne said. "May I come in?"

As much as she wanted to be alone, she knew it would only be a matter of time before she had to confess her shame. "Yes," she said.

Lady Anne opened the door and stepped inside. With one look at her, she let out a soft sigh and sat down next to her. "Do you want to talk about it?"

She shook her head.

With kindness in her voice, Lady Anne said, "Then I will just sit with you."

Rosamond let out a sob and leaned into Lady Anne, who wrapped her arm around her shoulders and kissed the top of her head.

"It will be all right, Child," Lady Anne murmured.

She knew she would eventually need to pick herself up off this floor and move on, but for now… she would cry.

Malcolm was an idiot. Perhaps the biggest idiot that had ever lived, he surmised. He had done the honorable thing by withdrawing his suit with Rosamond, so why did he feel like he had just made a terrible mistake?

He kept replaying the conversation, over and over again, wondering what he could have done- or said- differently. Why didn't Rosamond see that it was for the best? He had only been using her for her dowry, and she deserved so much more. But the hurt that had been evident on her face had been his undoing. His inability to comfort her when she needed it the most pulled at his heartstrings. He felt lost and alone.

It wasn't supposed to be this way. Emotions were not supposed to be a part of his plan, but he had never intended to fall in love with Rosamond. Yes, he was in love with her, and he could deny it no longer. Not that he planned to tell anyone. He had just let Rosamond walk out of his life because he couldn't trick her into marriage. He was the cad in all of this.

Malcolm leaned forward in his seat and reached for his glass. He had been at White's since he had properly ruined his life earlier today, but he wasn't drunk enough to ignore the pain in his heart. How he wished that he could slink away and pretend that he hadn't done something so intolerably stupid.

Lord Roswell's voice came from next to him. "You look like death, Brentwood."

"Thank you for that," Malcolm muttered, not bothering to look up. "If you don't mind, I wish to be alone."

To his great annoyance, Lord Roswell sat across from him in an upholstered armchair. "What happened?"

"Nothing," Malcolm responded as he brought the glass up to his lips.

Lord Roswell didn't look convinced. "Your answer won't come from the bottom of that glass."

"No, but it might help."

A server approached them but Lord Roswell waved him

off, no doubt in an attempt to get Malcolm to stop drinking. Not that it mattered. He could always order another drink when he was ready. If he had his way, he wouldn't be able to remember today.

He could do without the pity that was reflecting in Lord Roswell's eyes. He doubted that his friend had ever experienced the pain associated with unrequited love.

Lord Roswell leaned back in his chair and asked, "Now, what has you so upset?"

"It is none of your concern," he replied in a harsher tone than he had intended. Why couldn't his friend see that he was not in the mood for company?

"I must assume this has to do with Miss Hendre."

Malcolm's hand tightened around his glass. "Why do you assume that?"

"Only a woman could cause a man such grief," Lord Roswell replied. "Am I wrong to assume so?"

He shook his head. "You are not wrong."

"Did she reject your offer of courtship?"

Again, he shook his head. "No."

"Then I am at a loss as to why you are so upset."

Malcolm took a sip of his drink, then admitted, "I withdrew my suit."

Surprise registered on Lord Roswell's face. "Why would you do such a thing?" he asked, baffled.

"I realized that we wouldn't suit so there was no reason to keep stringing her along," he lied.

Lord Roswell didn't speak for a long moment before saying, "Then you did the right thing."

"I know." Malcolm tossed back the rest of his drink and slammed the glass down on the table. He caught the eye of a passing server and indicated he wished for another drink.

"That doesn't explain why you are so distraught," Lord Roswell said.

Malcolm frowned. "Does it matter?" he asked, hoping his friend would drop this inquest.

"It makes me wonder if you care about Miss Hendre, more than you are letting on."

"You don't know what you are talking about," Malcolm grumbled. "Miss Hendre was a nice distraction, but it is time that I move on."

Lord Roswell crossed his arms over his chest as he studied Malcolm. It made Malcolm wonder what he saw. "I don't believe you."

"Well, it is the truth," Malcolm asserted. When had his friend become so blasted observant? And why did he care so much?

"Convince me."

Malcolm looked heavenward. "Why would I do that?" he asked.

"My thought on the matter is that you are afraid of the feelings that Miss Hendre evokes inside of you, causing you to run away," Lord Roswell replied.

Malcolm stared at his friend in disbelief. How had his friend so accurately interpreted the situation?

Lord Roswell continued. "You don't have to answer, Malcolm, but I think you should really think about what it is that you want."

"I know what I want," Malcolm said.

"What is that?"

Malcolm smirked. "I do not want to be tied down to one woman for the remainder of my days. I wouldn't wish to deny all the other ladies the pleasure of my company." Even he couldn't stomach that lie, but he hoped that Lord Roswell bought it.

But he wasn't so lucky.

"Brentwood…" Lord Roswell started.

He put his hand up. "I do not want to discuss this any longer. I made my decision and I want you to respect it."

A server approached the table and placed down a glass before retrieving his empty one. "Will there be anything else, my lord?"

"Yes, keep the drinks coming," Malcolm replied.

As the server walked off, Lord Roswell looked at the glass in his hand and asked, "Are you sure you haven't had enough?"

Malcolm huffed. "You are not my keeper."

"No, but I am your friend."

Holding up his glass, Malcolm said, "A friend would help me celebrate that I have not fallen prey to the parson's mousetrap."

Lord Roswell pressed his lips together, appearing as if he had much to say on the subject. But Malcolm didn't need a speech or words of wisdom. He just wanted to drink away his sorrows and hope that tomorrow would be better.

Mr. Campden came to sit across from him, but he was dressed as a gentleman. Where was the red waistcoat marking him as a Bow Street Runner?

"I heard your insistent babbling from across the room so I thought I would encourage you to lower your voice if you don't want everyone to know what ails you," Mr. Campden advised.

Lord Roswell tipped his head at Mr. Campden. "Greydon," he acknowledged.

"Roswell," Mr. Campden responded. "May I ask why you are playing nursemaid to Lord Brentwood?"

"He's not," Malcolm interjected. "He chose to join me, against my wishes, I might add."

Mr. Campden met his gaze. "I take it this has to do with Miss Hendre."

Malcolm tossed up his hands. "Good gads, there must be something else that we can discuss," he asserted.

"Yes, it most definitely has to do with Miss Hendre," Mr. Campden stated.

Rising, Malcolm said, "I do not have to take this, especially from you." He pointed at Mr. Campden, his finger swaying. "You don't get to have a say in my life."

Mr. Campden's eyes roamed over the room. "Sit down, Brentwood," he ordered.

"Why should I do anything that you say?" Malcolm demanded.

"Because you are attracting unwanted attention," Mr. Campden explained. "All eyes are on you."

Malcolm turned his head and saw that Mr. Campden was speaking the truth. A few gentlemen had the decency to avert their eyes, but most were watching him with mild curiosity. He decided to take the Bow Street Runner's advice and sit down, but he did so begrudgingly.

As he slouched in his chair, he couldn't help but wonder if Lord Roswell knew that Mr. Campden acted the part of a gentleman, but he masqueraded as a Bow Street Runner. Not that it was his place to reveal such a secret. He would never do such a thing, considering Mr. Campden had assisted him with his sister.

Mr. Campden grew solemn as he addressed Malcolm. "I need to speak to you."

Rising, Lord Roswell said, "That is my cue to leave." He gave Malcolm a pointed look. "Do put the glass down and get some sleep."

After Lord Roswell walked away, Mr. Campden moved to sit on the edge of his seat and lowered his voice. "Is Lady Enid somewhere safe?"

"She is," Malcolm confirmed.

"Good," Mr. Campden responded.

Malcolm matched Mr. Campden's low tone as he said, "I received a visit from another Bow Street Runner about Lady Enid."

Mr. Campden gave him a blank look. "Who?"

"A Mr. Davidson," Malcolm replied. "Did you not know another Bow Street Runner was assigned to find Lady Enid?"

"Can you describe this man?" Mr. Campden asked.

Malcolm brought his hand up to his temple as he recalled, "He was stocky with red hair and he had a terrible temperament. He threatened to find Lady Enid, with or without me."

Mr. Campden's jaw clenched. "You weren't speaking to a Bow Street Runner."

"Then who was I speaking to?"

"A man that generally finds what- or who- he is seeking," Mr. Campden said. "And the methods he uses are typically unsavory."

Panic welled up inside of Malcolm. "Is my sister safe?"

"I hope so."

"That isn't good enough for me," Malcolm said.

Mr. Campden abruptly rose and tugged down on the ends of his blue jacket. "I will send someone to guard Lady Enid, at least until we can find this imposter."

"Do you want me to tell you where my sister is?"

"There is no need," Mr. Campden said. "I already know."

Malcolm furrowed his brow. "How is that possible?"

Mr. Campden looked amused. "You might want to become more observant of your surroundings."

"You followed me?" he asked. "For what purpose?"

A look came into Mr. Campden's eyes that he couldn't quite discern. "My reasons are my own," he said gruffly. "Just don't go anywhere near Lady Enid, at least for now. You are being followed."

"How do you know that?"

"You must trust me." Mr. Campden's alert eyes left his and darted over the room. "You must go on as if everything is normal. Do not give any indication that you know you are being followed. It is imperative that you do so," he advised. "Do you understand?"

"I do."

Mr. Campden nodded his head in approval. "I will be in touch," he said before he walked off.

Malcolm went to take a sip of his drink but stopped. It might be best if he stopped now and attempted to have a clear head. But then the image of Rosamond came to his mind, and he tossed back his drink. He just needed to forget about her-even if it was just for a moment.

Chapter Sixteen

Rosamond was done crying. She had spent far too much time dwelling on Lord Brentwood and it was time that she moved on. That was easier said than done but she was determined to do so. He would occupy her thoughts no longer. She would prove to him- and herself- that she didn't need him in her life. She was doing just fine without him.

The afternoon sun streamed through the windows as she worked on her needlework. She pulled the needle through her fabric and paused. She had been working on placing her initials onto the delicate fabric but she had made a mistake. She had done Lord Brentwood's initials instead. Perhaps she couldn't banish him from her thoughts so easily.

Lady Anne's voice came from next to her on the settee. "You are slouching, Dear," she chided lightly.

Rosamond straightened in her seat because she was afraid Lady Anne would make her balance a book on top of her head. That was her usual punishment, but she was in no mood to do so today.

Lizette spoke up from her seat near the window. "I think we should let her slouch, just this once," she said as she worked on a painting.

"A broken heart is hardly a reason to slouch," Lady Anne admonished. "We wouldn't want her suitors to think she is uncivilized."

"I have no suitors," Rosamond pointed out.

"That is only because you started to show favor to Lord Brentwood. I have no doubt that they will return once word gets out," Lady Anne said.

Rosamond sobered at the mention of Lord Brentwood's name. She hoped her heart would stop aching at the mere thought of him. Why had she let him in? She should have known better. Had her past experiences taught her nothing?

Lizette placed her paintbrush down and said, "I think we should stop speaking of Lord Brentwood."

"I agree," Rosamond said. "Surely there must be something else we can talk about."

Brownell stepped into the room and announced, "Miss Bolingbroke and Lady Esther Harington have come to call."

"Please send them in," Lady Anne ordered.

Rosamond placed the needlework onto the table, knowing she would need to fix her error before anyone else noticed it.

Miss Bolingbroke stepped into the room with Lady Esther following close behind. When her eyes landed on Rosamond, she declared, "I just heard the news. Lord Brentwood is a cad."

"Pardon?" Rosamond asked. How had she heard the news so soon?

Miss Bolingbroke came to sit down on an upholstered armchair. "My brother, Caleb, was at the club and he overheard Lord Brentwood talking about how he is no longer pursuing you."

Rosamond pressed her lips together. "He was?"

"Yes, but Caleb said that he was deep into his cups," Miss Bolingbroke replied. "When Caleb told me the news, I knew I needed to come over here straightaway and see how you are faring."

"I am fine," Rosamond said, hoping her words sounded convincing enough.

"It is all right if you are not okay," Miss Bolingbroke assured her. "I know that I wouldn't be, especially since Lord Brentwood had seemed to be taken by you."

Lizette interjected, "We decided we wouldn't speak of Lord Brentwood. He isn't worthy of Rosamond's time or notice."

Miss Bolingbroke nodded. "I agree. I shall not mention his name again."

Rosamond turned her attention to Lady Esther and smiled. "It is good to see you again," she said.

Lady Esther was much more reserved than Miss Bolingbroke but there was a fierceness about her that she found admirable.

"Likewise, but I wish it was under better circumstances," Lady Esther responded.

Miss Bolingbroke rose and approached Lizette. "I wish I could paint like you," she remarked, her eyes roaming over the painting. "My attempts are awful, and I end up just wasting the paint."

"I told you that I would be happy to help you," Lizette said.

"I am not sure even that will help," Miss Bolingbroke admitted. "I must accept there are some things that I am not good at."

Lady Anne addressed Lady Esther. "How is Lady Mather feeling?"

At the mention of her stepmother, Lady Esther visibly tensed. "She is well," she replied cordially, but there was a terseness to her words.

Lady Anne continued, not appearing to notice Lady Esther's discomfort. "I spoke to Lady Mather at Lady Daniel's soiree, and she was a delight."

"Yes, she can certainly act the part," Lady Esther muttered.

Rosamond knew from previous conversations that Lady Esther was not close to her stepmother, at least not anymore. Knowing that it was a sore subject for her, she decided to change the subject by asking, "Would anyone care for tea?"

Lady Esther offered her a grateful look. "I would," she said.

Leaning forward, Rosamond picked up the teapot and poured a cup of tea for her guest. Then she extended the cup towards Lady Esther.

"Thank you," Lady Esther acknowledged.

Miss Bolingbroke returned to her seat. "I do not think I could drink another cup of tea. My mother was insistent that we entertain callers all morning and I drank entirely too much tea as I tried to ignore them."

"Why would you wish to ignore your guests?" Lady Anne asked.

"Because they weren't there for me," Miss Bolingbroke replied. "Besides, my mother has given me a list of topics that I must adhere to when speaking to guests."

Lizette placed her paintbrush down and questioned, "A list?"

"Quite frankly, I embarrass my mother with some of the things I talk about and she is determined to rein me in," Miss Bolingbroke replied.

"I doubt your mother is embarrassed by you," Lady Anne attempted.

Miss Bolingbroke sighed. "It is true," she replied. "A few days ago, I was telling Lady Corby about the mating rituals of elephants."

"Good heavens, why would you feel the need to discuss that?" Lady Anne asked, aghast.

"I read about it in a book and I was trying to make conversation," Miss Bolingbroke explained with a slight shrug of her shoulder. "Lady Corby only seemed to speak to me about my marriage prospects, which are very limited at the moment."

"May I ask why you are even reading about the mating rituals of elephants?" Lady Anne pressed.

"For research," Miss Bolingbroke replied.

As Lizette removed her apron, she asked, "How is your book going?"

That had evidently been the right thing to say because Miss Bolingbroke perked up. "Very well," she replied. "I intend to start writing it soon."

"I think it is brilliant that you are going to write a book," Rosamond said. "I wish more women had the courage to do so."

Miss Bolingbroke's hands grew animated. "Every time I am about ready to start writing the book, my mind starts whirling and I think of ways to make it even better."

"And how do elephants tie into it?" Lizette asked as she closed the lids to her paints.

"I don't know... yet," Miss Bolingbroke replied. "But I love nothing more than reading and learning new things."

"A lady should not read such vulgar things," Lady Anne advised.

"That is precisely what my mother says," Miss Bolingbroke said, "but I have come to accept that I am a grand disappointment to her."

"Surely that is not true," Rosamond insisted.

Miss Bolingbroke's shoulders slumped slightly. "My mother was a diamond of the first water in her day, and I am just awkward."

"You are perfect, just the way you are," Lizette asserted.

Brownell walked into the room and said, "Pardon the interruption, but Lord Roswell Westlake would like a moment of Miss Hendre's time."

"Send him in," Lady Anne ordered.

Rosamond noticed that Miss Bolingbroke sat straighter in her seat and even smoothed out her gown. She had often wondered if her friend held Lord Roswell in high regard. Miss Bolingbroke had never said anything but she seemed to come more alive when he was around.

Lord Roswell stepped into the room and his eyes roamed over them, pausing for one silent moment on Miss Bolingbroke. An added warmth came to his eyes which had not been there before, but he blinked, and it was gone. Perhaps she had just imagined it, she wondered.

He bowed. "Ladies," he greeted.

Rosamond tipped her head. "What a pleasant surprise, my lord," she said. "Would you care for a cup of tea?"

"I would, thank you," he said as he went to sit down near Lady Esther.

After Rosamond poured a cup of tea, she extended it towards him.

Lord Roswell accepted it and took a sip before lowering it to his lap. "I wanted to ensure you are all right."

So that is what this visit was about. Lord Roswell must have heard about Lord Brentwood withdrawing his suit and he was here to offer his sympathies.

In a voice that was far more convincing than she felt, she replied, "I am well."

Lord Roswell didn't look convinced. "There is nothing wrong if you aren't," he said. "I do believe you and Lord Brentwood were well suited for one another."

"He made his choice," Rosamond responded.

"I know, but..." he started.

Rising abruptly, Rosamond said, "If you will excuse me, I need a moment." She didn't bother to wait for anyone to reply before she rushed out of the room. The last thing she wanted to talk about was Lord Brentwood.

She felt tears well up in her eyes as she stepped into the

entry hall, and she wiped away the ones that had begun to slide down her cheeks. Why couldn't she stop crying over Lord Brentwood? He had cast her aside and she needed to accept that.

Lord Ashington stepped into the hall and approached her. His eyes held compassion as he came to a stop in front of her. "I must assume these tears are over Lord Brentwood." His words held no judgment, just understanding.

"They are, but I wish they would stop," she murmured.

"A broken heart will heal, and the scars will fade," Lord Ashington said. "But you must give yourself time."

"I should have never let Lord Brentwood in."

Lord Ashington's face softened. "To love someone with your whole heart is one of life's greatest gifts."

"It doesn't feel like a gift," Rosamond said.

He placed a comforting hand on her sleeve. "Right now, you are in the midst of it, but I assure you that it is worth it. Keep going, and don't try to safeguard your heart."

Rosamond bit her lower lip as she admitted, "I don't think I can do it again. My heart is irrevocably broken."

Lord Ashington's eyes grew reflective. "The right person will put it back together for you," he said. "My late wife still holds my heart, and I don't dare take it back." He paused. "Even when she forgot who I was, I knew. She was the love of my life."

Brownell's voice came from behind her, startling her. "Your coach is ready, my lord."

"Tell the driver I will be just a moment," Lord Ashington ordered, dropping his arm. "I am talking to my ward."

"I do not wish to make you late," Rosamond said.

Lord Ashington smiled. "There are some things that are far more important than arriving on time," he assured her. "You are one of those things."

Rosamond felt tears come to her eyes, but these were

happy tears. "Thank you," she murmured, hoping her words properly expressed her gratitude.

"I have learned that the hardest times often lead to the greatest moments of my life. It is important that you keep going, hoping for the best," Lord Ashington said. "And when in doubt, drink chocolate. That is what my wife used to say."

Rosamond felt a smile come to her lips. "Your wife sounds very wise."

"She was," Lord Ashington replied in a soft, reflective voice. "I couldn't have asked for a better woman to be my wife. She was my whole world."

The sound of a clock chiming in the distance could be heard and Rosamond encouraged, "You should go. I don't wish to keep you from your duties."

"Did my old man ramblings help you?" he asked with mirth in his eyes.

"They did," she replied.

He leaned forward and kissed her on the cheek. "Be patient with yourself... and Lord Brentwood," he said as he took a step back.

"I want nothing to do with Lord Brentwood," she declared.

"We shall see," Lord Ashington responded before he walked over to the door.

Rosamond watched as Lord Ashington departed from the townhouse and she couldn't believe he encouraged her to be patient with Lord Brentwood. As far as she was concerned, she wanted nothing to do with that infuriating man ever again.

So why didn't her heart agree with her?

Malcolm staggered through the main door of his townhouse. He found that no matter how hard he tried, he couldn't drink away his woes. The look of betrayal on Rosamond's face when he told her he was withdrawing his suit was permanently etched into his mind. Would he ever be able to reconcile what he had done to her or to himself?

He wondered where he went from here. He had no desire to go back to the person he was before Rosamond came into his life because he was a better man now.

He noticed a light coming from the drawing room and he was curious as to who was up at this late hour. He stepped into the doorway and saw his mother sitting in a chair by the hearth. She was staring at the fire with a vacant expression and her shoulders were slumped. She looked defeated and sad.

Not wanting to startle her, he said in a low voice, "Mother."

Her eyes snapped towards him. "Malcolm, you are home late."

"I am, but I am wondering why you haven't retired to bed yet," he remarked as he walked further into the room.

She tried to smile, but her eyes expressed her sadness. Why did his mother always have to act so strong around him? "I'm afraid I just got caught up in my thoughts," she said.

"Anything you wish to share?"

"I wouldn't wish to burden you."

Malcolm went to sit across from her in an upholstered armchair. He was regretting how much he drank this evening, but he at least had enough sense left to know that his mother needed him. Although he wasn't sure he was in the right mind to offer any advice.

As he stretched out his legs in front of him, he asked, "What has you so upset?" He assumed it was about his father, as it usually was, but he didn't want to be so direct.

His mother glanced down at her hands in her lap. "Your

father is being rather stubborn about letting Enid return home."

"I assumed as much."

"I know she can't come home until we resolve the issue with her husband, but I just miss her so much," his mother admitted. "And now, she has a child. I do not think my heart can go on without seeing them."

"You must for the time being. We can't have anyone discover where Enid is staying, for her sake."

His mother nodded slowly. "I just fear that I am a terrible mother."

"You are the best of mothers."

With a glance at the empty doorway, his mother said, "George is stubborn to a fault, but I thought he would yield on this."

"Father is pigheaded."

"He wasn't always this way," his mother remarked. "I don't know why he took Enid eloping so hard. It was as if he became a different person afterwards."

"We all took Enid leaving rather hard."

"But she is still my daughter, and I love her, regardless."

"I know."

His mother sighed as she turned her attention back towards the fire. The light danced in her eyes, reflecting the anguish in them.

He considered if this was what love did to a person. His mother was willing to stand by her husband, no matter what. But at what point would she accept the fact that her husband was a different person now?

His mother shifted her gaze back towards him. "I understand that you broke off your suit with Miss Hendre."

"Did Father tell you that?"

A sheepish smile came to her lips. "I will admit that I was shamelessly eavesdropping."

"I am not surprised," he said. "But, yes, I did break things off with Miss Hendre."

"I thought we were ruined if you do not marry her."

He gave his mother an amused look. "It would appear that you didn't eavesdrop on the entire conversation," he said. "If you had, you would have heard my plan to keep our estate afloat. We will have to sell the Dowager House and some land, but it should give us enough money to buy the required farming equipment."

"Wouldn't it be easier if you just married Miss Hendre?"

"It would be," he admitted, "but I decided that we would not suit."

"Why is that?"

Malcolm wasn't quite sure what to say. He didn't want to lie to his mother, but he didn't dare tell her the truth. If he did, she would see right through him and know that he had fallen in love with Rosamond. That was something he couldn't risk.

He shrugged his shoulder. "It is just a feeling that I have." He knew he was being vague but he hoped that his mother didn't press him.

But he wasn't so lucky.

"Can you give me one reason why you wouldn't suit?" his mother pressed.

Drats. What could he say that would appease his mother? He couldn't think of one thing that bothered him about Miss Hendre. She was perfect, at least to him. Her smile warmed up his heart in a way that the sun never could.

Knowing his mother was still waiting for a response, he said, "She is…" he paused, "too cheery."

His mother furrowed her brow. "You find fault with her because she is 'too cheery'?"

"Yes, it is infuriating," he lied.

"I see," his mother murmured. "After all, who would want

to be with someone that has a pleasant disposition?" There was a teasing tilt in her voice.

His mother leaned her back against her seat and watched him. Malcolm was afraid that his mother could see right through him and his ridiculous lie. But he needed to stay strong. It might be best if he retired for the evening and put an end to this conversation.

As he went to rise, his mother asked, "You love her, don't you?"

He stilled. "How can I love her?" he asked. "I hardly know her."

"That didn't answer my question."

Malcolm rose and stepped closer to the mantel. "Love is a useless emotion," he declared.

"No," his mother said with a shake of her head, "love is the greatest gift of all."

"How can you say that?" he asked. "Father has turned on you and you spend all of your days pining for what you used to have." The moment his words left his mouth, he realized that he had been entirely too harsh.

As he went to apologize, his mother spoke first. "I never said that being in love was easy. It is messy, complicated, and there are times that you don't want to go on. But love is being willing to ruin your good, comfortable life for a chance at a great one."

Malcolm knew his mother would understand once he explained his situation. He took a deep breath before admitting, "I only intended to marry Miss Hendre for her dowry and then I was going to send her away."

"That would have been rather harsh of you."

"At first, I thought Miss Hendre was pretentious and we couldn't seem to speak without fighting," he shared.

"And now?"

He sighed. "And now... I would do anything to hear her voice one more time."

Rising, his mother came to stand next to him. "You must tell her the truth," she encouraged.

"What good would that do?" he asked. "She will hate me when I tell her that I only pursued her for her dowry."

"Yes, but perhaps she loves you, too."

"I never said that I loved Miss Hendre."

With a knowing look, his mother said, "You didn't have to."

"It is pointless," he declared. "She will never forgive me."

"You are not the first man to pursue a woman for her dowry," his mother said, "and I doubt you will be the last."

"Yes, but I don't want her to know that I was a fortune hunter."

His mother placed a hand on his sleeve. "What is done is done, but now you have your future you must consider."

"I am, and I do not see Miss Hendre in it. She deserves a man that loves her for her, and not what she can bring into a marriage."

"You can't be that man?" his mother asked.

Malcolm turned his attention towards the fire as it crackled. "It is better if I let her find a love match. That is what she wants; that is what she deserves."

His mother dropped her hand. "You are stubborn, just like your father," she said. "You love her, she loves you…"

"I don't presume to know that she loves me," he said, speaking over her.

"… but you don't know for certainty."

He shook his head. "No, I don't know."

"Don't you owe it to yourself to ask her?" she asked.

"What good will that do?"

His mother gave him a pointed look. "A life without love is a lonely existence, especially if you had it within your grasp but let it slip away."

Malcolm knew his mother was speaking true, but he was afraid. What if he confessed his feelings to Rosamond and she still turned him down? Could his heart take such a rejection?

"Trust what your heart is telling you to do rather than your head," his mother encouraged.

"I don't know if I can," he admitted.

His mother smiled. "Just imagine what your life would be like without Miss Hendre in it, and I think that will be your answer."

Malcolm had always surrounded himself with women, but none of them had captivated him as Rosamond had. She had brought a breath of fresh air to his life. He wanted all of her, forever, just him and her, every day.

He looked heavenward as he admitted, "I love her."

"I know," she said. "What are you going to do about it?"

"I don't deserve her, though."

"Perhaps, but will that stop you?"

Malcolm met his mother's gaze and felt determined. "I am going to tell her the truth and hope that she can find it in her heart to forgive me."

"I am glad to hear that."

With a glance at the darkened window, he said, "I will call upon her tomorrow and hope that she will receive me."

"Good, because that will give you time to take a bath." His mother scrunched her nose. "You stink."

"I do not," he attempted.

"You do," his mother asserted. "I just didn't want to say anything until we finished our conversation."

Malcolm leaned forward and kissed his mother on the cheek. "Thank you, Mother, not for saying I stink, but for helping me see reason," he said.

"You are welcome."

"I think it might be best if I retire for the evening and I will take a long soak in the morning."

His mother returned to her seat. "Goodnight, Son."

"Are you not tired?"

Looking up at him, she replied, "I don't think I could sleep right now."

"Would you like me to stay to keep you company?"

"No, go sleep," she encouraged.

Malcolm placed a loving hand on her shoulder. "I love you, Mother."

"I love you, too."

As he walked out of the drawing room, he felt buoyed by the conversation that he'd had with his mother. It was time he was brave or else he might lose Rosamond forever.

Chapter Seventeen

Rosamond was jostled back and forth as the coach traveled down the uneven cobblestone street towards Lady Stafford's soiree. She was in no mood to pretend that all was well when she just wanted to crawl back into bed and wake up when her heart didn't ache so badly.

She had been determined to not cry one more tear over Lord Brentwood but it had been a vain attempt. Why was she acting like a simpering miss? She was stronger than this. But she didn't feel strong at the moment. Despite all of this, she still loved him.

She had every reason to be happy. She was dressed in an exquisite gown, pearls were woven through her elaborate hairstyle and she was surrounded by loved ones. But she shouldn't have to convince herself that she was happy. She had been given so much, but there was one thing that Lord Ashington couldn't give her- a love match. That, she had to obtain on her own, and she had failed spectacularly.

Lizette's voice broke through her musings. "Are you with us, Rosamond?"

She brought her gaze up. "I am."

"We were just discussing how beautiful your gown is," Lizette said.

"It is, isn't it?" Rosamond responded as she turned her head towards the window.

Lady Anne spoke up. "Dear heavens, I think we lost her again." She patted Rosamond's sleeve. "You must be more present this evening or else you will get the gossips' tongues wagging."

"I don't know why you insisted I come," Rosamond said. "I am not in the mood to be jovial."

"If you didn't come, then people might speculate that you were at home, pining over Lord Brentwood."

Rosamond tensed. "I am most assuredly not pining after him."

"I know, but when something like this happens, it is important for you to be seen in high Society," Lady Anne advised. "It proves that his rejection means little to you."

"He didn't reject me; he just withdrew his suit," Rosamond clarified. She felt it was important to point out that distinction.

Tristan reached for his wife's hand as he said, "Regardless, he is your past. Now you must look forward to your future."

"I am well aware," Rosamond said.

Lady Anne shifted sightly on the bench to face her. "We should discuss what you will need to do if Lord Brentwood is at the soiree."

Rosamond felt a pit in her stomach at the thought of seeing Lord Brentwood. "You don't think he will be here tonight, do you?"

"There is a chance, and you will need to be prepared," Lady Anne said. "I can assure you that all eyes will be on you."

She let out an unladylike groan. "That sounds awful."

Lizette gave her an encouraging smile. "Do not fret. We will be with you and Tristan is great at lip reading."

"I am," Tristan stated, puffing out his chest. "It is a skill that I developed over time."

"Why have I never heard of this unusual talent before now?" Rosamond asked.

"I didn't wish to give away my advantage," Tristan said with a smile.

Rosamond knew what Tristan and Lizette were trying to do and she appreciated it, nonetheless. They were trying to cheer her up, but her heart wasn't in it. It was too weighed down.

The coach came to a stop in front of a whitewashed town-house and it dipped to the side as the footman exited his perch. The door opened and a footman placed his hand in to assist them out of the coach.

Once her feet were on the pavement, Rosamond withdrew her hand and clasped her hands in front of her. She saw the line of patrons that were making their way through the main door and she resisted the urge to run away. She needed to do this to prove to herself- and Lord Brentwood- that she didn't need him in her life.

They proceeded to the back of the line and it wasn't long before they stepped into the entry hall. The tall, thin Lady Stafford and her heavy-set husband were receiving their guests by the main door.

Lady Anne approached Lady Stafford and kissed her on the cheek. "Elizabeth, it is good to see you looking so well," she said as she leaned back.

Lady Stafford reached up and touched her fading black hair. "It is amazing what a trip to Bath can do for the skin."

"I shall have to try that." Lady Anne gestured towards Rosamond. "Allow me to introduce you to my father's ward, Miss Rosamond Hendre."

Rosamond knew what was expected of her and dropped into a curtsy. "My lady," she murmured respectfully.

Lady Stafford watched her with a mixture of kindness and curiosity. "You are an enchanting young woman."

"Thank you," Rosamond responded.

The countess leaned closer to her and said, "Keep your head held high. You have nothing to be embarrassed about."

Unsure of what to say, Rosamond just nodded.

Lady Stafford leaned back and turned to address Lizette. "Dear child, how are you enjoying marriage?" she asked.

Rosamond took that opportunity to step back and take a deep breath. She knew that Lady Stafford's words were meant to be encouraging but she felt only dread as her eyes roamed over the room. Women and gentlemen were glancing her way with curious looks on their faces. Some of the women were even blatantly staring at her as they had fans in front of their faces.

Lady Anne appeared by her side. "Just keep smiling," she advised. "Don't give them the satisfaction of knowing they are getting to you."

"Am I just to pretend that everyone isn't staring at me?" Rosamond asked.

"Yes, because it will only be a matter of time before they move on to something else," Lady Anne said.

Lord Roswell broke through the crowd and she was pleased to see a familiar face. He came to a stop next to her and bowed. "Miss Hendre," he greeted. "Lady Anne."

Lady Anne tipped her head. "Lord Roswell."

He turned his attention towards her. "Would you care to take a turn around the room?"

"Are you sure?" Rosamond asked.

Lord Roswell looked amused by her response. "I am; hence why I asked."

"I don't know if it is a good idea," Rosamond admitted. "I wouldn't want your reputation to suffer by being associated with me."

Holding out his hand, Lord Roswell said, "I dare anyone to say anything disparaging about you in my presence."

"But…" she started.

Lady Anne nudged her shoulder. "Go on, then."

Rosamond hesitantly accepted Lord Roswell's outstretched hand and let him lead her around the room.

Lord Roswell glanced over at her. "How are you faring?"

"I am well," she attempted. She hoped the more she said those words, the more she would come to believe them.

He didn't look convinced by her quick reply. "I would prefer the truth, if you don't mind."

Rosamond pressed her lips together as she delayed her response. She wasn't quite sure how she was feeling so how could she adequately express her thoughts? One thing she did know was that it was a mistake for her to come this evening. She wasn't ready, despite what Lady Anne thought.

She slipped her hand out of his and said, "I shouldn't have come this evening."

"I must assume that Lady Anne thought it was the right thing to do," Lord Roswell said, keeping his gaze straight ahead.

"It was," Rosamond admitted.

Lord Roswell tsked. "No doubt you would have remained in bed all evening. Perhaps even indulged in a cup of chocolate?" he asked.

Rosamond looked at him in surprise. "That is precisely what I would have done. How did you know?"

"That is my sister's usual response when she is tired of behaving like a proper lady."

"I think I would like your sister very much."

Lord Roswell chuckled. "Octavia is a very lively young woman, but she tries so hard, for my mother's sake."

"Lady Anne did tell me that your mother is ill," Rosamond said. "I am sorry to hear that."

His smile slipped. "We are not sure how much time we have left with her, but we intend to make the time count."

"It was not easy to watch my mother's health decline," Rosamond admitted. "I keep having dreams that I run into my mother in the most random places. I wake up with a smile on my face, only to remember that I am alone."

"You are hardly alone," Lord Roswell said. "You have Lizette, Lady Anne and, for what it is worth, Tristan."

"I adore Tristan."

"That is only because Lizette has turned him into a tolerable person," Lord Roswell joked. "You should have met him before. With one look, he would scare chickens."

"That is hardly fair since chickens scare easily."

"Children, then."

Rosamond laughed. "Thank you," she said. "It feels good to laugh, even for a moment."

Lord Roswell placed his hand over his heart. "What good am I if not for comedic relief?" he teased.

"You are quite amusing."

He lowered his hand and his eyes roamed over the room. "Not to put a damper on this conversation, but I did speak to Lord Brentwood today."

Rosamond sobered. "I do not wish to talk about him," she stated, her words curt.

"I know, and you have every good reason not to, but I think you should hear him out," Lord Roswell said.

"How can you ask that of me?"

"I have known Lord Brentwood for a long time and I have never known him to be so distraught over a woman before," Lord Roswell replied.

Rosamond let out a slight, disbelieving huff. "He was the one that withdrew his suit. No one forced him to do so."

"Yes, but I do believe he regrets doing so."

"Is that so?" she asked, uninterested. She refused to run to Lord Brentwood and let him hurt her all over again.

Lord Roswell came to a stop by the French doors that led to the veranda. "Lord Brentwood is on the other side of these doors, and he is hoping to speak to you," he shared.

Her eyes grew wide. "You tricked me."

"No, it is entirely up to you if you go outside," Lord Roswell said, putting his hand up. "But I think you should hear what he has to say."

"Why should I do that?" she asked.

"Because, deep down, you know that you two belong together."

Rosamond glanced towards the veranda. "Even if that were true, how can I trust Lord Brentwood ever again?"

"That is for you to decide," he said. "I only promised Lord Brentwood that I would get you to the door."

"Traitor," she muttered.

Lord Roswell grinned. "I promise I won't ever do anything so devious again, but desperate times call for desperate measures."

"This is hardly a desperate time."

"Lord Brentwood tried to call upon you today, multiple times, in fact, but he was turned away," Lord Roswell shared. "Aren't you the least bit curious as to what he has to say?"

She was, but she didn't dare admit that to Lord Roswell. But could she find the strength to go confront Lord Brentwood?

Lord Roswell kept his voice low as he said, "You have stared down the barrel of a pistol before and didn't flinch. I daresay you are brave enough to go speak to Lord Brentwood." He paused. "I will be close by to ensure you are properly chaperoned."

Rosamond couldn't seem to come up with any feasible reason to not see Lord Brentwood. And the worst part was that she wanted to see him again. She didn't know what he was going to say, but she refused to go easy on him. If he wanted a war with words, he had one.

Malcolm was pacing back and forth on the veranda as he watched Lord Roswell and Rosamond converse. He had pleaded with his friend to convince Rosamond to speak to him. It took much effort on his part, but he knew that would be the easy part. Convincing Rosamond that they belonged together would take much more work. He might even have to grovel, which he wouldn't have even considered before Rosamond came into his life. He knew what was at stake, and he was scared.

Rosamond exited the townhouse with Lord Roswell close behind. In the moonlight, her blonde hair gleamed, and her eyes shone more than all of the stars in the sky. She was so beautiful that his breath caught. But it wasn't just her beauty that entranced him. No, it was so much more than that. She was beautiful for the way she could make people smile, even if she was sad. She was beautiful for the way she encouraged others to be a better version of themselves. He doubted that she even knew how beautiful she was to him.

He stopped pacing as Rosamond approached him. She didn't look pleased to see him by the pursing of her lips, but she was here. And that was all that mattered.

Rosamond gave him an expectant look as she came to a stop in front of him, but she didn't say anything. Not that he expected her to do so. He had rehearsed his speech, over and over, and he was prepared. Or so he thought. Now that she was in front of him, his mind went blank.

He bowed. "Thank you for agreeing to see me."

"Was recruiting Lord Roswell truly necessary?" she asked.

"It was, considering your butler repeatedly turned me away today," Malcolm replied.

Rosamond placed a hand on her hip. "Did you expect me to roll out the red carpet for you after our last conversation?"

"I did not, but I am grateful that you are here, right now."

With a glance over her shoulder at Lord Roswell, who was standing by the French doors, she said, "I am here, but my presence will be noticed shortly. I'm afraid I can't stay for long."

"I understand." He took a deep breath, gathering the courage to say what needed to be said. "I am sorry for hurting you. That was never my intention."

She removed her hand off her hip. "Then what was?" she demanded.

"I removed my suit because I wanted you to find a love match," he replied. "It is no less than you deserve."

Was it him or did her eyes just dim? "That was kind of you," she murmured, unconvincingly.

"But, I made a mistake," he replied.

"Which was?"

He took a step closer to her and knew it was time to tell her the truth. "I fell in love with you," he said.

"You did?"

"I did," he replied.

She tilted her head to look up at him. "Why was that a mistake?" she asked, her eyes roaming over his face, no doubt in an attempt to look for answers.

Malcolm hoped that Rosamond would forgive him for what he was about to reveal. "I initially pursued you because of your dowry, not because I thought we would suit," he said. "My family is on the brink of ruination, and a marriage to you was the obvious solution."

"You are a fortune hunter?" she asked, the hurt evident in her voice.

He winced at the truthfulness of her words. "I am, at least I was," he admitted. "I knew I couldn't trap you in a marriage of convenience and that is why I withdrew my suit."

Rosamond took a step back with a crestfallen look on her face. "Was any of it real?" she asked.

"Not at the beginning, but at some point, I stopped pretending," he replied. "You beguiled me, body and soul, and I knew there could never be a future between us unless I told you the truth."

"How do I know this isn't an elaborate ruse to convince me to marry you?" Rosamond asked.

"I wouldn't do that to you."

"But you had no qualms before?"

"That was before I got to know you." He took a step closer to her, and she took a step back, causing his heart to drop. "Please, Rosamond, you must know that I care for you."

"I don't know what to think right now."

Malcolm ran a hand through his hair. "You are all I think about, and I can't lose you. You came into my life and disrupted everything, for the better."

As Rosamond went to respond, a couple stepped out of the townhouse and came to a stop on the veranda.

He gestured towards the path that led to the gardens. "Can we continue this conversation as we tour the gardens, please?"

Rosamond looked unsure and he feared that she would turn him down. Fortunately, after a long moment, she nodded her acceptance.

He offered his arm, but she walked right past him, stepping onto the gravel path. This was not going well, he mused.

Malcolm easily caught up to her and matched her stride. "Dare I ask what you are thinking?"

"I don't think you want to know," she replied.

"If you give me the chance, I will spend the rest of my life making this up to you," Malcolm said.

Rosamond stopped on the path and turned to face him. "How can you think I would ever trust you again?" she asked. "I will always wonder if you loved me for who I am or my dowry. I will never know if I was enough for you."

"You are enough for me," he rushed to assure her.

"So say you," Rosamond said.

Malcolm looked heavenward. What could he possibly say that would convince Rosamond that this wasn't just a passing whim. He loved her, completely, and with every fiber of his being. The only thing he could offer her was his heart, but was it enough?

He knew the time to be bold was now. He reached for her hand, and he was pleased when she didn't pull away. "I am not a perfect man by any means, and I have flaws; lots of them. But I never thought I would ever fall in love. I was against it, actually."

"That is a lovely sentiment," she muttered.

He brought her gloved hand up to his lips. "The truth is that you are the reason I believe in love, but it terrifies me."

With apprehension in her voice, she asked, "Why is that?"

"I have seen what happens when love is corrupted and it is ugly," he replied. "To save myself from that suffering, I vowed never to open my heart to another. But it all changed when you came into my life."

She looked at him with sadness in her eyes. "I want to believe you, but I am scared," she said dejectedly.

"You are still here, with me, and that is enough, for now."

Malcolm lowered her hand but kept hold of it. He didn't ever want to let her go, but he knew that he couldn't rush her. It wouldn't be fair of him to do so. Regardless, he would wait for her as long as it took.

"Why didn't you tell me the truth earlier?" she asked.

"If I had, I doubt you would be standing here right now," he replied.

"I daresay that you underestimated me, then. I care little for the pomp of high Society."

"I know, and that is one of the reasons why I find you so fascinating." He paused as he gently caressed her hand with his thumb. "I wanted to tell you, many times, but I was afraid I would lose you over my secret."

261

Rosamond bit her lower lip as she lowered her gaze to the lapels of his jacket. "I understand that all too well."

"How could you?" he asked. "I doubt you would harbor such a secret."

Bringing her gaze up, she said, "I am not who you think I am."

"I know precisely who you are."

"No, you don't," she insisted with a shake of her head.

"Then tell me, who do you think you are?" he asked.

He watched as a myriad of emotions crossed over Rosamond's face and he would have given anything to know what she was thinking at that exact moment.

As she was about to respond, Mr. Davidson appeared by her side with a pistol in his hand, and it was directed at Malcolm.

"Unhand the lady," Mr. Davidson ordered.

"Absolutely not!" he exclaimed.

Mr. Davidson smirked. "Let's not make this any harder than it has to be," he said. "If you don't release her, I will shoot you and then who will help Miss Hendre?"

"What do you want with Miss Hendre?" he demanded.

"Mr. Longbourn thinks it is only fair that he holds on to Miss Hendre until you produce his wife," Mr. Davidson revealed.

"And if I refuse to let you take Miss Hendre?" Malcolm asked.

Mr. Davidson cocked his pistol. "I think you already know that answer."

Malcolm felt panic well up inside of him and he couldn't think of a scenario where he came out alive from this. But he couldn't let Rosamond go with this man. There had to be another way.

Rosamond slipped her hand out from his and said, "It will be all right." Her voice was calm and reassuring.

"Yes, listen to your lady," Mr. Davidson mocked as he

grabbed her arm. "You have three hours to retrieve Lady Enid and her child. We will meet up at the south entrance of Hyde Park. If you fail to do so, then I will have no choice but to kill Miss Hendre."

"I won't let you take her," Malcolm said. "I don't care if you kill me."

Mr. Davidson chuckled. "Surely you cannot be this foolish?" he asked. "Do you truly think I came alone?"

Malcolm's eyes roamed over the trees but he saw no one. Was Mr. Davidson bluffing? As he debated about what he should do, he heard a cocking of a pistol and saw a shadowed figure emerge from behind one of the trees.

His heart sank. Mr. Davidson wasn't alone and he knew he couldn't save Rosamond.

Mr. Davidson took a step back, jerking Rosamond with him. "If you try to follow me, I will kill Miss Hendre."

"I thought you needed Miss Hendre."

With a shrug, Mr. Davidson said, "Frankly, I don't care if she lives or dies. But I bet you do, my lord," he drawled.

Mr. Davidson didn't wait for Malcolm's reply before he led Rosamond towards the shadow of the trees. It only took him a moment to realize that he couldn't let Mr. Davidson take Miss Hendre. It didn't matter if he would be killed.

He ran towards where he last saw them and saw a gate had been left open. As he approached the gate, he saw a coach speeding down the street.

Blazes. What was he going to do now? He refused to turn his sister over to her husband, but if he didn't, then Rosamond would be killed.

Lord Roswell's voice came from behind him. "Where is Miss Hendre?"

"Gone," he replied, not bothering to turn around.

"What do you mean she is gone?"

Malcolm gestured towards the street. "Someone abducted her," he revealed. "It was all my fault, too."

Lord Roswell came around to face him and his voice was calm and precise. "Tell me exactly what happened."

"My sister's husband, John Longbourn, hired a man to pose as a Bow Street Runner so he could find Enid. He showed up tonight and wants to swap Miss Hendre for my sister."

"When?" Lord Roswell asked. "Where?"

"I have three hours to collect Enid and her child and meet at the south entrance of Hyde Park," he replied.

Lord Roswell removed his pocket watch and looked at the time. "That doesn't give us much time," he said. "I saw Mr. Campden inside. I propose we go speak to him about this matter."

"Let's go," Malcolm responded as he took purposeful strides towards the townhouse. Once he stepped into the ballroom, his eyes roamed over the hall until they landed on Mr. Campden. He was speaking to a dark-haired young lady and a woman he supposed was her mother.

Malcolm brushed past the patrons in the crowded room and came to stand next to Mr. Campden. "I must speak to you," he stated, not bothering to acknowledge the ladies. He knew he was being rude, but he didn't have time for pleasantries.

Mr. Campden's eyes flashed with annoyance as he barely acknowledged Malcolm. "Can't you see that I am busy, my lord?" he asked tersely.

"I do, but I must insist," Malcolm asserted.

Mr. Campden smiled at the ladies before he bowed. "My apologies, but I shall return shortly," he said before he walked away.

Malcolm followed closely behind the Bow Street Runner and Lord Roswell was next to him. He knew that Mr. Campden did not appear eager to see him, but he didn't care. He needed the Runner's help to get Rosamond back, unharmed.

Mr. Campden found a break in the crowd and spun back around. "This better be important," he said, his low tone holding a warning.

Lord Roswell matched Mr. Campden's tone. "Miss Hendre has been abducted and they want to trade her for Lady Enid," he informed the man.

"I must assume this is Mr. Longbourn's doing," Mr. Campden said.

"Yes, it is," Malcolm replied. "We are to bring Enid and her child to the south entrance of Hyde Park in three hours. If we don't, they threatened to kill Miss Hendre."

Mr. Campden's alert eyes roamed over the room. "We need to inform Miss Hendre's family at once and ask them discreetly to leave. We can't risk anyone noticing that Miss Hendre is no longer at the soiree."

Lord Roswell tipped his head. "I shall see to that," he said before he disappeared into the crowd.

"What can I do?" Malcolm asked.

Mr. Campden brought his gaze back to meet Malcolm's. "I have an idea, but you are not going to like it."

"Why is that?"

"Because it involves us turning your sister over to her husband."

Chapter Eighteen

Malcolm sat in the darkened coach as he traveled to retrieve his sister and he was stewing over Mr. Campden's proposed plan. He refused to just hand his sister over to her husband and hope the course of action worked. Lives were at stake, and he was scared.

He didn't want to imagine a life without Rosamond in it. He couldn't. He knew they still had much to resolve but he would do whatever it took to convince her that they belonged together. But first, he had to get her back.

Mr. Campden spoke up. "I need you to be in agreement with this plan or else it could have dire consequences."

"It is a terrible plan," Malcolm muttered.

"I have had worse," Mr. Campden responded.

Lord Roswell interjected, "It is true. His last plan involved just knocking on a door and hoping a murderer would let us in."

"He wasn't a murderer, and I banked on that," Mr. Campden said. "Besides, the plan ultimately worked, did it not?"

"It did, but someone still died," Lord Roswell remarked.

Malcolm had so many questions and he didn't know

where to begin. He glanced between the two men and asked, "When was this?"

"It matters not," Mr. Campden replied dismissively.

Lord Roswell looked amused. "I assisted Mr. Campden on one of his cases—"

"No, you refused to listen to reason and insisted on going," Mr. Campden said, cutting him off.

"It was a good thing I went along," Lord Roswell stated.

Mr. Campden shrugged. "You did prove yourself useful, in the end."

Malcolm couldn't believe that his carefree friend had been useful in one of Mr. Campden's cases. Lord Roswell had a serious side to him, but it was rarely seen.

The coach came to a stop in front of Marjorie's townhouse and he didn't wait for the footman to open the door. He stuck his hand out of the window and pushed down the handle.

Once he stepped out of the coach, he headed straight for the main door. He didn't bother to use the knocker and pounded on the door with his fist.

The door promptly opened and the butler asked, "May I help you, my lord?"

"I need to see my sister," he replied.

The butler opened the door wide and indicated that he should come in.

Malcolm stepped into the entry hall and waited for Mr. Campden and Lord Roswell to do the same.

Once the door was closed, the butler said, "If you will wait here, I will announce you."

"That won't be necessary," Malcolm said as he walked towards the drawing room. He knew that he was being rude but he didn't care. He had more important things to worry about at the moment.

As he stepped into the drawing room, he saw his sister was sitting next to Marjorie on the settee. She was dressed in a lovely blue gown and her hair was pulled back into a chignon at the base of her neck. All the evidence of her living at a workhouse had been scrubbed off and she seemed much more relaxed.

His sister rose when she saw him. "What is wrong, Malcolm?"

Not wanting to mince his words, he replied, "We have a problem."

"Which is?"

Mr. Campden spoke up from behind him. "Your husband abducted Miss Hendre and he wants to trade her for you and Marigold."

Enid gasped and brought her hand up to her mouth. "Good gracious," she said. "I didn't think he would stoop so low to get me back."

Marjorie interrupted, "We must call the constable. He will sort this out."

"Constables are useless," Mr. Campden asserted. "I assure you that I am more than capable of handling this."

"You?" Marjorie asked as her eyes roamed over his fashionable clothing. "But you are a gentleman."

"I am, but I am also a Bow Street Runner," Mr. Campden revealed.

If Marjorie seemed surprised by his admission, she did not show it. She nodded in approval. "I see that you are a man with secrets, and I find that admirable."

Enid placed her hand to her stomach as she said, "I shall go collect Marigold and we can be on our way."

"Leave the child," Mr. Campden ordered.

"But I thought John wanted me and Marigold to trade for Miss Hendre," Enid said with confusion in her voice.

Mr. Campden gave her an understanding nod. "I assure you that Mr. Longbourn is going to be leaving disappointed this evening."

"How?" Enid asked.

"You must trust me, but if everything goes according to plan, you will be home in a few short hours," Mr. Campden replied.

Enid grew silent as she watched Mr. Campden. In a calm voice, she said, "I do trust you, sir."

Mr. Campden's face softened, something Malcolm never thought he would witness. "That means a great deal to me, my lady."

Lord Roswell spoke up. "Not to be a naysayer, but we have much to discuss and not much time to do it."

Malcolm knew that his friend spoke true. A lot still had to be said, and he hoped that his sister was up to it. Her participation was the most important part.

Marjorie gestured towards the chairs and asked, "Why don't you take a seat and lay out your plan?"

They all waited until Enid returned to her seat before they sat down.

Mr. Campden met Enid's gaze and said, "The plan is simple. Lord Brentwood will pretend that he intends to hand you over to your husband. Once we confirm that Miss Hendre is safe, Lord Roswell and I will move in and force them to return Miss Hendre to us."

Mr. Westcott's voice came from the doorway. "What did I miss?" he asked as he walked further into the room.

"Good, we have one more lord to help us," Mr. Campden mocked. "But at least you proved that you aren't entirely incompetent."

"That is high praise coming from you," Mr. Westcott said.

Malcolm turned towards his sister and Marjorie and explained, "I hope that you do not mind that I told Mr. Westcott where to find us. He is married to Miss Hendre's cousin and he is heir presumptive to Lord Ashington. Lord Roswell was insistent that he would prove himself useful and I thought it would be for the best."

Marjorie bobbed her head. "He is more than welcome,"

she said before turning to her attention towards Mr. Westcott. "I thought I recognized your name from the Society pages. You were recently married, were you not?"

"I was," Mr. Westcott said.

Mr. Campden rose. "If we are in agreement, we can travel to Hyde Park early so we can get into position."

Rising, Enid said, "If you will excuse me, I just need to see to one thing."

Once Enid had departed from the room, Marjorie grew solemn. "Your plan is hardly flawless and, frankly, it sounds a little foolhardy."

"I'm afraid it is our only option, my lady," Mr. Campden responded. "But do not fret. I assure you that I will return Lady Enid, unharmed."

"Do not promise things you cannot deliver," Marjorie urged.

"I'm not," Mr. Campden asserted.

Marjorie's critical eye swept over him before saying, "Very good. I have grown rather fond of Lady Enid and Marigold. I do not wish any harm to befall them."

"And none shall," Mr. Campden insisted.

The conversation came to a halt as they waited for Enid to return to the drawing room. Everyone seemed to retreat to their own thoughts, knowing what was at stake. If they made any errors, there was a real chance that people could end up dead.

As Enid stepped into the room, her shoulders were square and she had an air of confidence about her that had been missing since she'd first arrived home seeking Malcolm's help.

"I am ready," she informed them.

Malcolm approached her and said, "Thank you for doing this."

"I have no choice since it is the right thing to do," Enid responded. "I refuse to let Miss Hendre pay for my mistakes."

He offered his arm. "We will keep you safe."

"I know, but with any luck, this will end tonight, and John will never be able to hurt me again," she said in a calm, collected voice.

Malcolm couldn't help but wonder how Enid was so calm about her situation. She was about to face her husband- her abuser- yet she held her head high, as if she were on her way to a social event. It was odd and, frankly, he found it disconcerting. Perhaps she was just trying to be brave for him.

He led her towards the coach and assisted her inside. Once she was situated, he went to sit next to her. Lord Roswell and Mr. Campden sat across from them.

Malcolm glanced out the window and saw that Mr. Westcott's horse was being led away by a groom, prompting him to ask, "Is Mr. Westcott not joining us?"

"He is on the perch with the footman," Lord Roswell informed him.

He lifted his brow. "He agreed to that, willingly?"

"He did," Lord Roswell replied. "Miss Hendre is family and he will do whatever it takes to protect his own."

Malcolm had to admit that his respect for Mr. Westcott had grown immensely.

The coach started rolling down the street and they were being jostled back and forth. As his eyes roamed over the inhabitants, he saw that everyone had a determined look on their faces. Mr. Campden was not a man that he would want to cross, and he had great confidence in his abilities. Lord Roswell was full of surprises, and he hoped that would continue this evening.

Mr. Campden's voice broke through the silence. "I see that residing with Lady Sherborne suits you, my lady."

Enid smiled. "It has been quite the adventure," she admitted. "Marjorie may be eccentric, but she has a kind, loving heart."

"I have no doubt," Mr. Campden said.

"Marigold has really taken to her, as well," Enid shared. "But she prefers that Marigold remain in the nursery."

"Is that an issue?" Malcolm asked.

Enid shook her head. "No, but I am used to having Marigold with me wherever I go. It has been an adjustment to say the least."

"It is good that you are taking some time for yourself, especially after everything that you have been through," Malcolm said.

Enid's smile dimmed. "I have so much to be grateful for but knowing that John is still out there makes me realize that I will never be free of him."

"You mustn't dwell on that," Malcolm encouraged. "I will take care of it."

"How?" Enid asked, shifting on the bench to face him. "John will always be there, looking for me, and finding new ways to torment me."

"Then we will petition for divorce," Malcolm said.

Enid huffed. "They will never grant it to me. I am not important enough for them to even waste their time on."

"With Father's help—"

"He will never help me," Enid asserted, speaking over him. "He disowned me long ago and you must accept that. I have."

Malcolm knew that his sister wasn't wrong. Their father was stubborn to a fault, and not even their mother could get him to change his mind. But he refused to give up on his sister and Marigold. He would find a way to make this right.

Enid gave him a sad, resigned look. "You can't fix this."

"I can try."

"Just focus on the things that you can change," Enid encouraged. "I will be fine with Marjorie. She has asked me to stay on as her companion."

"That was most kind of her," Malcolm said.

Enid nodded before she turned to look out the window.

With every rotation of the wheels, Malcolm knew they were getting closer to Hyde Park, and he found himself growing increasingly anxious. He hoped that he walked away alive from this, but he would gladly give his life to ensure Miss Hendre and Enid were safe.

———————⁓———————

Rosamond sat quietly in the darkened coach as two strangers stared back at her. Her shoulders were slumped, hands firmly clasped in her lap, and she would let out the occasional sniffle. By all accounts, she appeared to be terrified, yet she was anything but. She was biding her time and waiting for her opportunity to escape.

These men were hardly a match for her. They both carried pistols, which was a problem, but that didn't stop her plotting. The taller man had been called Mr. Longbourn by her abductor and he had made a few references to Enid being his wife. He seemed to be the mastermind of this scheme. But he didn't seem to be very bright. Did he truly think that Lord Brentwood would just hand over his sister to the likes of him?

Lord Brentwood was a capable man, and she was sure that he had made some provisions. At least, she hoped he had. She doubted that he had ever been in this situation before. Sadly, this wasn't the first time she had been held captive. The first time ended poorly when her ex-fiancé was shot, but with any luck, no one would be killed this time.

They had been waiting in this coach for what felt like hours and she knew she needed to make her move soon. Her abductor had told her that she wouldn't be hurt if Lady Enid was delivered to them, but she had her doubts. Criminals tended to say things that were convenient at the time and not necessarily the truth.

Her abductor groaned. "I need to stretch my legs," he said as he reached for the handle.

"Do you think that is wise?" Mr. Longbourn asked.

"Why?" her abductor asked as he gestured towards her. "What do you think this chit is going to do?"

In response, Rosamond swiped at her cheeks as if she were crying.

"You are right," Mr. Longbourn said. "I believe I will join you."

Rosamond brought her gaze up. "You aren't going to leave me in here alone, are you?" she asked, her voice shaking.

Mr. Longbourn leaned forward and grabbed her chin. "We will be right outside the door. You better not try anything funny."

She shook her head.

He must have been satisfied with her response because he dropped her chin and stepped out of the coach. Once the door was closed, Rosamond reached under the bench to search for any weapon she could use to defend herself. But there was nothing.

Drats. What was she going to do now?

She could hear the men talking and knew it would only be a matter of time before they checked in on her. She pushed back the drapes and saw the path was lined with woodlands. If she could just get to the trees undetected, then she could hide from them. However, that was easier said than done. Once she exited the coach, she would only have a small window before someone might spot her.

Rosamond shifted on the bench and pulled back the drapes on the side where the men were standing. They had their backs to the coach and were talking loudly. It was evident they hadn't even considered her a threat. That would be their mistake.

Now that she confirmed that the woodlands were on both sides of the path, she could make her plans. She had an idea, but it was risky. Frankly, she wasn't entirely sure if it would work, but it was her best shot of escaping.

She knew she couldn't escape on the side of the coach where the men were, so that left her only one option. She reached for the handle and opened the door. Then, ever so quickly, she climbed down and closed the door behind her. She got down onto her hands and knees and went to lay under the coach.

Rosamond stared up at the undercarriage and prayed that the horses did not spook easily. She laid perfectly still and tried to ignore the rocks that were digging into her back. It was deucedly uncomfortable, but it was better than the alternative.

It wasn't very long before she heard Mr. Longbourn say, "It is almost time. Get Miss Hendre out of the coach."

The coach shook slightly as the door was opened and it was followed by her abductor saying, "She is gone."

"Gone!" Mr. Longbourn exclaimed. "Where did she go?"

"She must have snuck out on the other side of the coach," the abductor said.

"Well, go find her!" Mr. Longbourn ordered.

The abductor's boots ground on the dirt. "Aren't you coming, too?"

"Why? Are you afraid of the dark?" Mr. Longbourn mocked.

"No, but it would be much faster if we both were looking."

Mr. Longbourn grunted. "Stupid chit! I just had these boots polished," he said before he took off for the woodlands on the other side of the path.

Rosamond waited for a long moment and heard them calling her name. If they were expecting her to respond, they would surely be disappointed. As they went deeper into the woodlands, their voices became more distant, and she knew it was her chance.

She crawled out from under the coach and started running

towards the woodlands, which was proving to be quite difficult in her muslin gown.

The driver shouted out, "Mr. Longbourn! I see her!"

Rosamond didn't slow her pace and entered the safety of the trees. She kept running further into the woodlands and didn't dare look over her shoulder for fear that it might cause her to lose her footing. When her breathing became labored, she knew she couldn't keep running forever so she needed to find a place to hide or, at the least, something to protect herself with.

An oak tree loomed ahead, and she figured she could hide behind the trunk, if only to catch her breath. Her eyes roamed over the ground and they landed on a thick branch. It wouldn't kill her attackers, but it could definitely hurt them, giving her time to run away.

She picked it up and had her hand adjust to the weight. She chided herself on not bringing her muff pistol with her. She always took it with her everywhere she went but Lizette had insisted that she didn't need it at a soiree. How wrong her sister had been.

Rosamond could hear someone approaching and she clutched the branch in her hands. The footsteps were getting closer, and she got to her feet. She needed all the momentum that she could get if she wanted to ensure the hit stunned her attacker.

The footsteps stopped a short distance away and Rosamond felt her heart pounding in her chest. Boldly, she peeked out from behind the tree and saw the shadow of a man, his back to her. Could she hit him before he knew she was there?

She had to try.

With quick steps, she approached the man and reared the stick back. Then she hit the man in the back, causing him to drop to the ground and let out a groan.

Rosamond dropped the stick and started to run away. She didn't want to wait around for the man to regain his senses.

A familiar voice called out to her. "Rosamond," he said in a low voice.

She stopped and spun back around. "Lord Roswell?" she asked.

Lord Roswell brought his hand to his back. "Why did you hit me?" he asked.

"Why were you lurking in the woodlands?" she challenged.

He winced. "I'm here to save you," he replied.

"Well, as you can see, I am not in need of saving." She paused. "But since you are here, can you take me home?"

Lord Roswell's smile was tight as he said, "We still need to save Malcolm and Enid."

"How do you propose we do that?"

Reaching behind him, he pulled out a pistol and extended it towards her. "Use this to protect yourself. It is much more practical than a tree branch."

Rosamond accepted it and gripped it tightly. "Thank you."

"How did you escape?"

She shrugged one shoulder. "Those men underestimated me and that was their mistake."

"That it was," Lord Roswell agreed.

"Who else is here?" she asked.

"Tristan and Mr. Campden," he replied.

With a nod, Rosamond said, "That should be sufficient to stop those dunderheads."

"I see that you are not fond of your captors," Lord Roswell joked.

"Not in the least."

In the distance, she could hear her name being called and Lord Roswell brought his finger up to his lips. Then he indicated that she should follow him.

As she trailed behind Lord Roswell, she found immense

relief that he was with her. At the least, she knew he was a good shot.

Lord Roswell put his hand up and crouched down behind a tree. Up ahead, Rosamond saw Mr. Longbourn in the center of the path as a coach approached him.

In a hushed voice, she asked, "Lord Brentwood doesn't intend to turn over his sister to her husband, does he?"

"Not if we can help it," Lord Roswell said.

The coach came to a stop a short distance away and the door promptly opened, revealing Lord Brentwood. Her breath hitched at the sight of him. There were still so many things that still needed to be said between them, but she felt buoyed by the fact that he loved her. She felt her lips curve into a smile at that thought, which was entirely out of place considering the circumstances. But she didn't care. He loved her, and she loved him.

Once Lord Brentwood was on the path, he closed the door behind him.

"Where is my wife?" Mr. Longbourn demanded.

Lord Brentwood remained standing by his coach. "Where is Miss Hendre?" he asked.

Mr. Longbourn gestured towards his coach. "She is in the coach, and she will be released only after I get my wife."

Rosamond couldn't believe that Mr. Longbourn was lying, but what did she expect? She figured that he would say just about anything to get his wife back. Should she make herself known and end this charade?

As she debated about what she should do, Lord Roswell put his hand on her sleeve and said, "Don't go."

How did he know precisely what she was thinking? But she couldn't just stay back and let Lady Enid get taken by her husband.

Lord Brentwood's voice drew her attention back to the situation at hand. "How do I know that you will release Miss Hendre?"

Mr. Longbourn put his arms out. "You will just have to take my word for it."

"Your word means nothing to me."

"You wound me, my lord," Mr. Longbourn mocked. "I thought we could be civil about this."

"There is nothing civil about this situation."

Mr. Longbourn let out a dry chuckle. "You are right, and that is why I will take great pleasure in killing you this evening," he said. "Mr. Davidson, if you please."

Mr. Davidson stepped out from behind the coach and pointed a pistol at Lord Brentwood. "Hello, again," he said.

"While you were rambling on, my associate was able to get into position," Mr. Longbourn shared. "Now, if you don't mind, give me my wife."

"But I do mind."

"You are hardly in a position to argue."

Lord Brentwood stood tall and didn't appear too affected by a pistol being pointed at the back of his head.

Rosamond turned to Lord Roswell and said, "We have to help him."

"In due time," Lord Roswell replied.

"When?" she asked. "After he is shot?"

"Patience, Rosamond."

She pressed her lips together, knowing that patience had never been one of her strong suits. How much longer did Lord Roswell expect her to stay here when Lord Brentwood's life was on the line?

"Open the coach," Mr. Longbourn demanded.

Lord Brentwood did as he was instructed and he assisted his thin, brown-haired sister out of the coach. She removed her hand from her brother's and clasped them in front of her. In a voice that held no hint of fear, she said, "Hello, John."

"I see that you got a new gown."

"I got a whole new wardrobe," Lady Enid said.

Mr. Longbourn's voice grew gruff as he asked, "Where is Marigold?"

"She is somewhere safe."

"The deal was Miss Hendre for you and Marigold," Mr. Longbourn said gruffly.

Lady Enid tilted her chin stubbornly. "You will never see our daughter again, if I have my way. You lost that right when you started abusing her."

"We shall see," came Mr. Longbourn's response.

Mr. Davidson spoke up. "Now that you have Lady Enid, what do you want to do with Lord Brentwood?"

"Kill him," Mr. Longbourn said. "I care little if he lives or dies."

Rosamond gasped and knew that she had to help Lord Brentwood. Before she fully thought through the repercussions of her actions, she rose and hurried out of the safety of the trees.

Mr. Longbourn turned to face her. "Have you come to die, too?" he sneered.

"No, I have come to barter." She pointed the pistol at Mr. Longbourn and cocked it. "Lord Brentwood's life for yours."

Chapter Nineteen

Malcolm's heart sank when he saw Rosamond exit the woodlands and he couldn't help but wonder what she was thinking. She had been safe. So why did she come back for him?

Rosamond may be many things, but she was no match for these men. She was good and kind, and they were not. He had no doubt that they would kill her at their first opportunity, without blinking an eye. Yet he had to admire her strength. Her eyes held no hesitation as she pointed the pistol at Mr. Longbourn. But she was no killer. He was sure of that.

Mr. Longbourn didn't seem to take Rosamond seriously by his relaxed stance. "We both know that you aren't going to kill me," he said.

"How can you be certain?" Rosamond asked.

"You are just a stupid chit that somehow acquired a pistol." Mr. Longbourn held his hand out. "Give me the pistol before you do something you might regret."

Rosamond stood her ground. "I think not."

"You may have fooled us once by your escape, but your luck has run out," Mr. Longbourn said. "Although I do find it admirable that you are trying to help Lord Brentwood. Mr. Davidson told me that you two have gotten rather close."

Mr. Longbourn took a step towards her. "It would be a shame if you both didn't walk out of here alive. If you give me the pistol, I will let you and Lord Brentwood leave, together. Isn't that what you want?"

"It is," Rosamond replied, "but if you take a step closer, I will shoot you." Her voice held a warning.

"But what will become of your precious Lord Brentwood if you shoot me?" he asked. "If you did something so foolish, then my associate would kill him."

Rosamond's lips twitched, as if she were privy to a secret. "I will take my chances."

Mr. Longbourn studied her for a moment before he said, "I will just take what is mine and we can depart from here."

"About that," Rosamond started, "I can't let you take Lady Enid."

With a scoff, Mr. Longbourn declared, "She is my wife. I will do with her as I please."

Enid spoke up. "I am not going anywhere with you, John," she said. "You go live your life and I will live mine." Her words were soft at first, but they grew with confidence with each passing word.

Mr. Longbourn's eyes narrowed. "Surely you do not think I will let you go so easily."

"You only married me for my dowry," Enid said. "You never truly cared for me."

"It doesn't matter because once I have you, I will have you locked up in an asylum," Mr. Longbourn revealed.

"Why would you do something so cruel?" Enid asked.

Mr. Longbourn smirked. "Your great aunt left you a generous inheritance, but the solicitor won't release the funds until I produce you. Once that is done, I already have two doctors that are willing to testify of your madness."

"I am not mad," Enid said.

"What woman would willingly choose to live in a work-house rather than with her husband?" Mr. Longbourn tsked.

"Clearly, these doctors have never lived with you," Enid retorted.

Mr. Longbourn frowned. "I see that you have regained your sharp tongue with your newfound freedom."

"Among other things," Enid replied.

Malcolm had had enough of Mr. Longbourn, especially after what he had revealed as his true intentions for wanting Enid back. "I am not going to hand over Enid to you, not now, not ever."

"You have no choice in the matter," Mr. Longbourn said. "Mr. Davidson will kill you if you don't."

Malcolm's eyes roamed over the woodlands and he hoped that his friends were in their positions. If not, he had just signed his own death warrant.

"I propose we just walk away and pretend this never happened," he said.

Mr. Longbourn shook his head. "I am not going to let you take Enid. I need that money."

To Macolm's horror, Enid took a step closer to her husband. "Was any of it real?' she asked.

"None of it," Mr. Longbourn replied.

Enid shrank back slightly. "You made me believe that you loved me. I gave up everything to be with you."

Mr. Longbourn shrugged. "We would have been happy if your father had released your dowry."

"Would we have?" Enid demanded. "Would that have stopped you from striking me and Marigold?"

"You made me hit you," Mr. Longbourn replied. "I took no pleasure in it."

"No, you are a monster."

Mr. Longbourn's face contorted with anger as his nostrils flared. "How dare you speak to me like that!" he shouted.

"I will speak to you however I see fit," Enid said, her shoulders squared. "It is about time that I did."

"I'm beginning to think sending you to an asylum is too kind for you. Perhaps I will just kill you with my bare hands," Mr. Longbourn growled.

Enid slipped her hand into the folds of her gown and removed a muff pistol. "I am not going to let you hurt me or Marigold ever again."

Malcolm saw the determined look on his sister's face and he knew what she was planning. She had every reason to hate John, but he couldn't let her kill him. It would destroy her.

He turned towards her. "Enid... you don't have to do this."

"Yes, I do," Enid replied, her eyes remaining on John. "I will never be free of him as long as he is still alive."

"I will keep you safe," Malcolm insisted.

"You can't promise that," Enid said. "John won't stop until I am dead. We both know that."

Mr. Longbourn huffed. "You don't even know how to use a pistol, Dear. You are embarrassing yourself."

In response, Enid pointed the pistol at her husband and cocked it. "I was recently taught by a friend."

Malcolm was unsure of what he should do. He didn't dare take the pistol away from Enid, but he couldn't just stand by and let her shoot Mr. Longbourn.

Mr. Davidson spoke up from behind him. "What do you want to do, Boss?" he asked. "Should I shoot Lord Brentwood or Lady Enid?"

"Don't kill Enid because I need her to collect the money, then we will dispose of her," Mr. Longbourn said. "Feel free to kill Lord Brentwood."

Rosamond interjected, "If anything happens to Lord Brentwood, I promise that you will suffer the same fate."

"Then we are at a standoff," Mr. Longbourn declared.

A rustling came from the bushes before Mr. Campden

stepped out from the woodlands. He held a pistol in his hand, and it was pointed at Mr. Longbourn.

"Ah, Mr. Campden, it is you," Mr. Longbourn said with relief in his voice. "You are right on time to help me with this situation."

"I'm afraid not," Mr. Campden responded. "I overheard your confession. I can promise you that you will never see a farthing of that inheritance."

"But you work for me!" Mr. Longbourn exclaimed.

"Our contract was terminated the moment I realized your intentions weren't honorable," Mr. Campden explained.

Mr. Longbourn turned towards Malcolm and said, "You think you were so clever to involve a Bow Street Runner but even he won't be able to save you now."

Malcolm grinned. "I didn't just bring him."

Glancing towards the woodlands, Mr. Longbourn asked, "Who else did you bring with you?"

Before Malcolm could reply, he heard a thud behind him and he turned around to see Mr. Davidson laying on the ground, unconscious. Mr. Westcott was standing over him with the butt of the pistol in his hand.

"I thought it might be best to eliminate this threat," Mr. Westcott said. "After all, it is in bad form to shoot someone in the back."

"Thank you," Malcolm responded before he turned back to face Mr. Longbourn. "You have lost. You are outnumbered, outmanned, and outgunned. Just walk away with your life and never contact Enid again."

"She is my wife," Mr. Longbourn shouted. "You have no right to keep her from me."

"I am going to petition Parliament for a divorce between you two," Malcolm said.

"They will never grant it."

Malcolm smirked. "I think once I explain the torment you have caused her, they will be more inclined to grant it."

"They won't believe you," Mr. Longbourn said smugly.

Lord Roswell stepped out from the woodlands and kept his pistol trained on Mr. Longbourn. "No, but they will believe my father when he vouches for Lady Enid."

"Why would he vouch for her?" Mr. Longbourn asked.

"Because you will be transported by then," Lord Roswell said. "You can't abduct Lord Ashington's ward without some repercussions."

Mr. Campden interrupted, "It is true. If I have my way, you will be on the first ship out of England."

"This is lunacy!" Mr. Longbourn exclaimed, his eyes darting between the men.

"No, what is lunacy is that you actually thought you could get away with hurting so many people," Lord Roswell said.

Mr. Longbourn's eyes narrowed as he turned his attention to Enid. "This is all your fault," he snarled. "You should have never left me."

Enid held his gaze, her eyes ablaze. "You gave me no choice. I had to leave or else you would have eventually killed me."

Mr. Longbourn's face grew red, splotchy as he stared at Enid; the hate evident in his eyes. "Fine," he said as he went to raise his hands. "I guess I only have one option..." His voice trailed off as he flicked his right wrist and produced a muff pistol that had been up his sleeve.

As he went to aim at Enid, multiple pistols discharged, the sound echoing in the night. Mr. Longbourn dropped to his knees before he fell face-first into the dirt.

Malcolm turned towards his sister and saw that she was holding a smoking pistol. Her eyes were fixed on her husband.

"Give me the pistol, Enid," he said in a soft voice.

She blinked before saying, "I had to shoot him. He had a pistol."

"I know," he replied.

Enid extended him the pistol as a tear slipped down her

cheek. "It is over, isn't it?" she asked. "He will never be able to hurt Marigold again."

"Or you."

Malcolm held his arms out and she stepped into them. He wrapped his arms around her and held his sister tightly. She had been through so much at the hands of her husband and she was finally free of him.

Mr. Campden walked closer to the body. "Who else took a shot?" he asked, his eyes roaming over the group.

Lord Roswell, Rosamond and Enid put their hands up.

"Blazes," Mr. Campden muttered. "How am I ever going to explain this to the magistrate?"

"If it would help, I can testify as to what happened," Lord Roswell said.

"It would, greatly," Mr. Campden remarked. "The rest of you need to go home and never speak of this again."

Enid stepped out of Malcolm's arms and looked up at him. "I am all right," she said. "Why don't you go see how Miss Hendre is faring?"

Malcolm didn't need to be told twice. He closed the distance between them and came to a stop in front of her. He didn't say anything at first, but his eyes took in her disheveled hair, soiled dress and dirty streaks on her face. He wasn't quite sure what she had endured, but he wanted to know every painstaking detail.

As he opened his mouth, she smiled, making him forget everything that he had intended to say. How could a single smile from her affect him so profoundly? One touch from her and he was undone. It was terrifying to think of how much power Rosamond had over him.

"I am all right," she assured him. "Nothing that just a good soak won't take care of."

He reached for her hand. "What were you thinking coming to save me?" he asked. "You could have been hurt."

"I knew the risks, but I couldn't let anything happen to you."

Malcolm felt his heart take flight. Did this mean that she cared for him as he did for her? After all, she did risk her own life to save his. His finger caressed her torn gloves. "Rosamond…" he started.

"Yes?"

Mr. Westcott's voice came from next to them. "It is time to go home, Rosamond," he said. "I was able to convince the driver of Longbourn's coach to give us a ride home."

"How did you do that?" Rosamond asked.

"I asked nicely," Mr. Westcott said with a shrug.

Rosamond didn't look convinced. "Tristan, what did you do?"

Mr. Westcott sighed. "Fine, I may have threatened him to do so," he responded. "I have no doubt that Lizette is worried sick about you."

Rosamond slipped her hand out of Malcolm's and gave him a sad smile. "I need to go home and inform everyone that I am all right."

Malcolm didn't want to let her go, to leave his side, but he knew he must say goodbye… for now. "I understand."

"Perhaps you can call on me tomorrow," she asked, hopefully.

"I have every intention to."

As Rosamond walked away, Malcolm knew he didn't know what the future held, but he knew who held his future.

Rosamond sat in the coach as it traveled back to Lord Ashington's townhouse. Tristan sat across from her and she was grateful that he didn't feel the need to engage in useless chatter. Quite frankly, she wasn't in the mood to talk.

She had never shot someone before and that weighed heavily on her conscience. Not that she regretted her actions. Mr. Longbourn was a terrible person, but that didn't mean he had to die. Why had he been so foolish as to retrieve a pistol? Why couldn't he have just gone with Mr. Campden, knowing the odds were stacked against him?

The coach came to a stop and Tristan opened the door. Once he stepped down onto the pavement, he assisted her out of the coach.

"Thank you," she murmured as she slipped her hand out of his.

Tristan remained rooted in his spot with a solemn expression. "I just want you to know that you did nothing wrong."

"I know, but I wish it had ended differently."

"As do I. But I do believe Mr. Longbourn knew what he was doing," he said. "He didn't want to be transported."

"But he would have been alive."

"To some, transportation is worse than death."

Rosamond nodded her understanding. She knew that Tristan was trying to comfort her but she just needed time alone to process what she had done. Fortunately, she hadn't been the only one that had taken a shot.

Tristan offered his arm. "Shall we go inside?" he asked. "I have no doubt that everyone is waiting up, anxious for your return."

"Most likely," she replied, accepting his arm. She said her words lightly, but it felt good that there were so many people that cared about her. It made her grateful for the things that she did have in her life.

Tristan led her up the stairs and opened the door. He dropped his arm and indicated she should go first. She had just stepped into the entry hall when Lizette came rushing out of the drawing room.

"You are home!" Lizette exclaimed before she threw her arms around Rosamond. "I was so worried."

Rosamond embraced Lizette before she said, "There was no reason to worry about me. I can take care of myself."

Lady Anne came to stand in the entry hall. "You are filthy, Child," she chided lightly. "You will need a good soak at once."

"That sounds divine," Rosamond admitted as she took a step back.

"I fear that gown will need to be thrown out." Lady Anne approached Rosamond and her face softened. "I am most relieved that you are back home where you belong."

Rosamond felt her lips curve into a smile at that thought. She did belong here and that filled her heart with joy.

"But you must not let yourself be abducted again," Lady Anne said with a pointed look. "Fortunately, no one noticed your disappearance at the soiree."

"I promise," Rosamond responded.

Tristan chuckled. "I doubt that is something one can plan."

Lady Anne gave him a haughty look. "And yet, I have never been abducted, young man." She turned towards Brownell, who had been standing back. "Can you see to Rosamond's bath at once?"

The butler tipped his head. "Yes, my lady," he replied before he walked off to do her bidding.

"Now that we've handled that, my father would like to see you in his study," Lady Anne said.

Lizette looped her arm through Rosamond's. "I will take her."

Lady Anne nodded approvingly. "Run along, then," she responded. "I have no doubt that my father is terribly worried."

As Lizette began to lead her down the hall, she leaned in and said, "My grandfather said he wasn't worried at all and he told us to inform him once you returned home."

Rosamond wasn't sure how she felt about that. Lord Ashington wasn't worried at all about her?

Lizette continued, unaware of her thoughts. "He said that whoever abducted you made a grave mistake since you are more than capable of taking care of yourself."

"He said that?"

"Yes, my grandfather thinks very highly of you," Lizette said with a glance at her. "Surely you know that."

She didn't have time to respond since they arrived at Lord Ashington's study. They stepped inside and saw the aged marquess sitting at his desk, his head bowed over the ledgers.

"Grandfather, Rosamond is home," Lizette announced.

Lord Ashington's head shot up. "You startled me," he declared. "I didn't hear you come in."

"You startle entirely too easily," Lizette remarked.

He shoved back his chair and rose. "Regardless, I am pleased to see that Rosamond has returned home." His eyes twinkled with merriment as he shifted his gaze to Rosamond. "You did have me worried since I expected you home hours ago."

"There were some complications," Rosamond said.

"There always are." Lord Ashington walked over to her and embraced her. "I do not think my old-man heart can take it if anything happened to you or Lizette."

"You are not old," Rosamond attempted.

Lord Ashington chuckled as he dropped his arms. "Thank you for that, but we both know that isn't true," he said. "Now, tell me, how did you escape?"

"I had some help," Rosamond replied as she shot a grateful look at Tristan, who had followed them into the study. "If it weren't for them, I might not be standing here."

Tristan interjected, "I do believe you are selling yourself short since you had already escaped before we arrived."

"Those men weren't the brightest," Rosamond said.

"Although, Rosamond did put herself in harm's way when Lord Brentwood's life was threatened," Tristan revealed.

"Why would you do such a thing…" Lord Ashington's voice trailed off as realization dawned. "You love him, don't you?"

Rosamond knew there was no point in lying, not to her family. She smiled at that thought. This was her family. She was home.

Tristan leaned closer to Lizette and asked, "Why is she smiling?"

"Because she is in love," Lizette whispered back.

Rosamond laughed. "That is not why. I just realized that I am home."

Lizette gave her a blank look. "Of course you are home," she said. "Did you get hit over the head when you were abducted?"

"No," Rosamond said. "I finally found where I belong."

Lord Ashington placed his hand on her sleeve. "I am happy to hear that," he said. "But that didn't answer my question. Are you in love with Lord Brentwood?"

"I am," Rosamond said. "I am wholly, unequivocally, in love with him."

"Wonderful!" Lord Ashington exclaimed, clasping his hands together. "I had anticipated this outcome since Lord Brentwood withdrew his suit."

"Why was that?" Rosamond asked.

"It was evident that you two belonged together, but we had to wait until you came to the same conclusion," Lord Ashington explained.

Rosamond bit her lower lip as she decided to be honest with her family. She didn't want any more secrets between them.

"Lord Brentwood did inform me that his family is on the verge of ruination and he only intended to marry me for my dowry," Rosamond said.

Lord Ashington tensed, and his voice grew terse. "I hadn't realized that Lord Brentwood was a fortune hunter."

"He was, but that is why he withdrew his suit," Rosamond shared. "He wanted to do the honorable thing and let me find a love match. But he had made a mistake."

"Which was?" Lord Ashington asked.

"He fell in love with me," Rosamond said.

"He told you this?"

Rosamond nodded.

"Do you believe him?" Lord Ashington questioned.

Tears came into her eyes as she replied, "With my whole heart." She paused as she walked over to the window. "And that is the problem."

Lizette spoke up. "What is the problem?" she asked. "You love him, and he loves you. Isn't that what you want?"

How did she make them understand that even though she dressed and acted like a lady, she was still the daughter of a seaman? She couldn't keep that part of herself hidden if she ever wanted to have a future with Lord Brentwood.

Rosamond wrapped her arms around her waist. "I want to tell him the truth of who I truly am," she said.

"Do you think that is wise?" Lizette asked.

"I know I am asking a lot of you since our pasts are intertwined, but I can't keep hiding who I am from him," Rosamond replied.

Lizette exchanged a glance with Tristan before saying, "Then you should tell him."

"Do you mean that?" Rosamond asked.

"I do," Lizette said. "Secrets have no place in a marriage."

Tristan stepped closer to his wife and slipped his arm around her waist. "If Lord Brentwood loves you as much as I suspect he does, he will care little about your past. He will only care about sharing a future with you."

"I hope so," Rosamond said.

Lord Ashington sighed. "I do not like the thought of

someone else knowing our family secrets, but I do agree that it is necessary to bring Lord Brentwood into our confidences."

A knock came at the door and Brownell stepped into the room. "Pardon the interruption, but Miss Hendre's bath is readied."

"Thank you," Rosamond acknowledged.

Brownell gave her one of his rare smiles. "It is good to have you back home, Miss," he said.

After the butler left, Lord Ashington encouraged, "Go enjoy your soak and change out of that filthy gown."

Not needing to be told twice, Rosamond headed out of the study and hurried up the steps. She opened the door to her bedchamber and saw her Aunt Betsey placing her wrapper onto her bed. Her eyes lit up when they landed on her.

"You are home, my dear," Aunt Betsey said as she rushed over and embraced Rosamond. "I was so relieved when Brownell said that you had returned."

"It was an adventure, to be sure," Rosamond responded as her aunt held her tightly. She didn't mind, though.

Aunt Betsey dropped her arms and stepped back. "I want to hear all about it, but first, you need to take a long soak and get some rest."

Rosamond's eyes wandered over to the basin that was near the hearth where a fire had been prepared. "You will hear no objections from me," she sighed.

Chapter Twenty

"This is madness," Enid said as she held Marigold on her lap in the coach. "Father hates me and nothing will change that."

"He does not hate you," Malcolm assured her.

"Typically, when someone disowns a family member, it means that they have at least a great disdain for them."

"Father is just confused."

"Confused?"

"All right, I will admit it. This won't be easy, but it is something I should have done a long time ago."

Enid smoothed back her daughter's hair. "I appreciate what you are trying to do, but Marjorie wants me to stay on as her companion."

"I am most grateful for that, but you can do more with your life than just be a companion."

"Considering my circumstances, I am most fortunate to even have that opportunity," Enid asserted. "I don't want to squander it."

Malcolm knew that his sister spoke true, but he wasn't ready to let her waste her life as a companion. What would become of her when Marjorie didn't require her services anymore? She needed to be back with her family, where she belonged. It just took him a long time to realize that.

The coach came to a stop in front of their townhouse and he gave Enid an encouraging smile. "Are you ready?"

"No," came her prompt reply. "I will be lucky to get past the front door."

Malcolm retrieved his pocket watch from his waistcoat pocket and saw the time. "Father and Mother are most likely having breakfast in the dining room."

"It isn't too late to return us to Marjorie's townhouse and forget you had this ridiculous idea of reconciliation," Enid said as she tightened her hold on Marigold.

"Where is my sister that bravely confronted her husband last night?" Malcolm asked.

"It was different."

"How?"

"I had a pistol in my hand." Enid grinned. "Perhaps you will give me a pistol while I speak to Father."

Malcolm shook his head. "That would be a terrible idea."

Enid shrugged one shoulder. "It would make me feel better."

A footman opened the door and stood to the side as Malcolm exited the coach. Once he was on the pavement, he extended his hand to assist his sister.

"This is madness," Enid muttered as she withdrew her hand.

With a glance at his sister, he said, "You already said that."

"It makes it no less true."

Malcolm knew that his sister had a reasonable concern, but he had no intention of letting his father disrespect her. It was time to prove the type of man that he was. Or at least that he hoped to be.

As they walked up the three stairs towards the main door, it opened and Osborne stood to the side to let them enter.

"It is good to see you looking so well, my lady, and if I do say so, back where you belong," Osborne said.

Enid ran a hand down her pink gown. "Thank you, Osborne," she greeted. "It is nice to be home."

"Where are my parents?" Malcolm asked.

"In the dining room," Osborne informed them. "Would you care for me to announce Lady Enid?"

"No, I think it would be best if we surprised them," Malcolm said.

"Yes, because Father loves surprises," Enid muttered as she placed Marigold onto her hip.

Malcolm smiled. "This one, he will." He gestured towards the hall that led to the dining room. "After you."

Enid turned to address Osbourne. "You might as well keep the door open. I have no doubt my father will throw me out the moment he sees me."

"Oh, ye of little faith," Malcolm teased.

With her head held high, Enid started to walk down the hall and Malcolm met her stride. The sound of their father's harsh voice could be heard coming out of the dining room.

Malcolm turned towards his sister and saw that she had a look of trepidation on her face. "It will be all right," he encouraged.

"This is pure and utter madness," Enid said. "It is not too late to return me to Marjorie and forget this ever happened."

"Where would be the fun in that?" he asked.

Enid stopped short of the door. "I do hope you are not taking joy in my discomfort. That is very ungentlemanly of you."

"I am trying to be encouraging."

"Will you stop it?" she asked. "It is infuriating."

"Duly noted."

Enid adjusted the ruffled collar on Marigold's white dress. "Will you go first?" she asked. "Perhaps it would be for the best if I wasn't the first thing that Father saw."

Malcolm placed a comforting hand on her sleeve before he stepped into the room.

His father glanced up from the table. "Where the blazes have you been?" he demanded. "I haven't seen you since you stormed out. Have you finally come to your senses and done your duty to this family by convincing Miss Hendre to marry you?"

"I have every intention of marrying Miss Hendre, not because of this misplaced duty you are speaking of, but because I love her," Malcolm said.

His mother smiled brightly. "I am so happy to hear that."

"I don't care what your reasons are so long as you do it," his father grumbled.

Malcolm glanced over at the door and saw his sister standing back. He hoped he wasn't wrong about involving his sister. He didn't want to hurt her, especially since she had already gone through so much at the hands of her husband. The man that was supposed to be her protector and love her above all else.

"I brought along someone with me," Malcolm said.

His mother cast a worried look at her father and he suspected she already knew who it was.

Malcolm waved his hand, encouraging Enid forward. "I thought it was time that we be a family again."

Enid stepped into the room, holding Marigold tightly against her.

His father jumped up from his seat. "What is she doing here?" he demanded. "She is not welcome here."

"Sit down, George," his mother said.

He turned his glare towards his wife. "I beg your pardon?"

With pursed lips, she repeated her words. "I said 'sit down'." Her words were uncharacteristically firm.

To his surprise, his father slowly returned to his seat with a stunned look on his face.

The silence was deafening as his mother rose from her seat

and approached Enid. "May I?" she asked, holding her hands out.

Enid nodded as she extended Marigold towards her mother.

Tears came into their mother's eyes. "I have never seen anything so precious before," she said. "What is her name?"

"Marigold Diane," Enid replied.

His mother kissed the top of the child's head. "You named her after me?"

"I did," Enid replied.

His father spoke up. "You bringing your child here doesn't change anything. You left us and eloped with that terrible excuse for a human."

"You are right," Enid admitted. "I should have listened to you about John and I am sorry. He was not the man that I thought he was."

His father was visibly taken aback by Enid's words. "Yes, well, I tried to warn you, and you refused to listen."

"I know, but I wouldn't change anything, because that path led me to having Marigold," Enid said. "She has been my saving grace."

"She is perfect," his mother murmured as she hugged Marigold tighter.

"I think so," Enid agreed.

His father came around the table. "Regardless, you made your choice and now you must face the consequences. You are married…"

Malcolm spoke over him. "She is a widow, now."

"Since when?" his father asked.

Enid tilted her chin. "Since I shot John last night."

His father's eyes grew wide. "You murdered your husband?" he exclaimed. "And you dared to come to my home?"

Malcolm put his hand on his father's chest, stilling him.

"You know not what you are speaking of," he said, "and I urge you to keep your voice down."

"Enid should be in jail," his father countered.

"No, she was defending herself and Miss Hendre," Malcolm said as he lowered his hand. "Mr. Longbourn abducted Miss Hendre so I would turn over Enid to him. When he faced the threat of transportation, he tried to shoot Enid."

His father's hard expression slipped ever so slightly. "I am relieved she is not hurt but the coroner might see the facts differently."

"I don't believe so, considering a Bow Street Runner was present to witness his confession," Malcolm explained. "Lord Roswell and Mr. Westcott are also willing to testify, if called upon."

Marigold started babbling and he could tell that his mother was entranced. She kept staring at the child as if she might disappear at any moment.

His father crossed his arms over his chest. "Give the child back, Diane," he ordered. "It is time for Enid to leave."

Instead of following his command, his mother turned towards her husband. "Do you want to hold her?"

"Absolutely not!" his father declared. "That child is not welcome here."

"This 'child' is your granddaughter, and you need to stop being so obstinate," his mother said. "Enid made mistakes, but we all did."

"I will not yield on this," his father declared.

Malcolm slipped his arm over Enid's shoulders. "I thought you might say that," he said. "Which is why I intend to take Mother and Enid to live in the country house after I wed Miss Hendre."

His father dropped his hands in a huff. "That is my country house and I forbid it."

"Forbid it all you want, Father, but it won't change my

mind," Malcolm said. "After I marry Miss Hendre, I will control the funds and you will have to come to me for money."

"You cannot be in earnest!" his father shouted. "That is my money."

"No, it will belong to me and Miss Hendre," Malcolm corrected. "I would be foolish not to heed her advice from this time forward, in all matters.

His father turned towards his wife. "You wouldn't leave with Malcolm, would you?" he half-demanded, half-asked.

"I think I would," his mother replied. "We haven't been happy in quite some time."

"You would leave me?" his father asked in disbelief.

Keeping hold of Marigold, his mother responded, "I kept hoping you would return to the man I fell in love with, but now I see that was wishful thinking on my part."

His father grew silent. "If I let Enid come home, will you stay?"

"It would be a start," his mother replied.

Malcolm removed his arm from Enid's shoulders and said, "It is time that we start healing as a family… together."

In a gruff tone, his father declared, "Enid can stay, for now. I will notify Osborne to prepare her bedchamber and have the nursery opened."

His father spun on his heel and departed from the dining room without saying another word.

With tears in her eyes, his mother said, "Thank you, Malcolm."

"It was time that I did the right thing," he responded. "And I do believe that Father will come around."

"As do I," his mother agreed.

Enid leaned in and kissed his cheek. "Thank you, Brother."

"I hope you aren't terribly disappointed about not being Marjorie's companion," he said.

Her eyes roamed over the room, and he could see the faint smile on her lips. "No, I am much happier being home."

"I am happy to hear that because I'm afraid I must leave you both. It is time I called upon Rosamond and beg her to marry me."

Marigold let out a cry as she reached for Enid. As his mother handed the child off, she said, "I never thought I would see the day that my son would beg for anything, much less a woman."

"You will see why I was willing to do so when I introduce you to Miss Hendre."

"Then go get your bride," his mother encouraged.

———

Rosamond stared up at the canopy of her bed as she laid there. The sun streamed through her windows, brightening her bedchamber, but it was doing nothing to affect her mood. She knew Lord Brentwood would come to call today and offer for her, but she had no idea how he would react once she told him the truth about her past.

And that is what frightened her.

She loved Lord Brentwood with her whole heart, but she couldn't marry him, not without revealing her secrets- secrets that should never be spoken of. But she didn't want to hide a part of herself from him. Not anymore. She may look and act the part of a lady, but she was still the daughter of a seaman. She wasn't ashamed of it either.

Rosamond knew that he cared for her, loved her, even, but would that be enough? Despite everything that had happened, she still believed that love could conquer all.

Her door opened and Aunt Betsey walked into the room with a tray. "You missed breakfast so I took the liberty of having a tray made up for you."

"Thank you," Rosamond said as she moved to sit up.

Aunt Betsey placed the tray down onto a table and remarked, "It is not like you to sleep in, but you did go through a terrible ordeal last night."

"I have been awake for hours," Rosamond admitted.

"Then why did you not ring for me?" Aunt Betsey asked.

Rosamond leaned her back against the wall as she let out a sigh. "Lord Brentwood is going to call on me today and I have yet to figure out what to say to him."

"I suspected as much." Aunt Betsey moved to sit on the edge of the bed. "Just follow your heart and you will know what to do."

Her heart? Surely it couldn't be that simple, she thought. "My heart is what got me into this situation," she said.

"You speak of love as if it were a sickness."

"No, but I do hope Lord Brentwood loves me enough to accept my past," Rosamond said.

"If he doesn't, then he is not the one for you."

Rosamond sighed. Her aunt was always so encouraging, almost to a fault. A part of her was envious of her aunt, though.

Aunt Betsey reached for Rosamond's hand. "I know it is scary to be so vulnerable with someone, but I do believe that Lord Brentwood will protect your heart- and secrets- with his life."

"I do hope so because I love him so much," she admitted.

"I know, Dear," Aunt Betsey replied.

A knock came at the door before a young maid slipped into the room. "Lord Brentwood has come to call, Miss. Are you taking callers?"

Rosamond perked up. "I am," she replied. "Please inform Lord Brentwood that I will be down shortly."

"Yes, Miss," the maid said before she departed from the room.

Aunt Betsey rose from the bed. "It would appear that Lord

Brentwood is rather eager to see you this morning." She walked over to the wardrobe. "Shall we dress you?"

A thought came to Rosamond and she asked, "Is the pink dress that I wore when I first arrived here still in the wardrobe?"

"Yes, but why would you wish to wear that simple gown?" Aunt Betsey asked.

Placing her feet over the bed, Rosamond replied, "I want Lord Brentwood to see me for who I truly am."

"A dress does not reflect who you are."

"Perhaps, but it is a start."

Aunt Betsey retrieved the simple gown and held it up. "If you are sure..." Her voice trailed off.

"I am."

"Then let's get you dressed."

A short time later, Rosamond stepped out of her bedchamber with her hair neatly coiffed and dressed in a gown that scratched at her skin. It was a far cry from the muslin gowns that she wore now, but she knew she had to do this.

She descended the stairs and tipped her head at Brownell, who was watching her with mild curiosity. "Good morning," she greeted.

Brownell replied in kind.

The sound of Lord Brentwood's voice drifted out of the drawing room and she felt her heart start racing. She placed a hand on her stomach to calm her growing nerves. She could do this, she told herself. There was nothing to fear, but she knew what was at stake.

Rosamond squared her shoulders and she hoped she looked more confident than she felt. She stepped into the drawing room and Lady Anne's eyes roamed over her gown with disapproval.

Lord Brentwood placed his teacup down onto the table

and rose. He bowed. "Miss Hendre, you are looking lovely," he said.

"Do you like my gown?" Rosamond asked, holding out the skirt. "I made it myself."

Lady Anne bristled. "Yes, and I thought we disposed of that gown when you arrived."

"As did I. But thankfully, my lady's maid found it for me in the wardrobe."

"Yes, thankfully," Lady Anne muttered.

Rosamond did not take offense by Lady Anne's reaction. Frankly, she had expected it. A ward of a marquess did not wear such simple gowns, but a daughter of a seaman did. And she was caught between both worlds.

Lord Brentwood smiled at her, and she returned his smile, and, just like that, everything seemed perfect.

"May I be so bold as to ask to speak to you privately?" Lord Brentwood asked.

"Yes," Rosamond rushed to reply. But she stopped and gave Lady Anne a sheepish smile. "Assuming it is all right with Lady Anne, of course."

Lady Anne rose from her seat. "I will allow it, just this once," she said. "I will be standing right outside of the door so I expect you both to behave."

Once Lady Anne stepped out of the room, Lord Brentwood turned his gaze towards her and she saw an intensity in his eyes that she had never seen before.

"Thank you for agreeing to see me," he said as he closed the distance between them. "I have a question that I must ask you."

Rosamond bit her lower lip, knowing what she must do. "Before you do, there is something that I must tell you."

"Can it wait?"

"No, it can't." She held his gaze as she said, "I am not who you think I am."

"You are exactly who I think you are."

"But I am not," she asserted. "You know me as the ward of a marquess, but I had a whole other life before Lord Ashington took me in."

"That doesn't matter to me."

"It does to me," Rosamond said. "I was not raised wealthy, I made my own clothing, and we lived in a small manor in a village that most people just passed through."

"There is no shame in being a poor relation."

Rosamond turned away from him and walked over to the window. "That is the problem, I am not related to Lord Ashington."

Lord Brentwood furrowed his brow. "Then how did you become his ward?"

She knew it was time to tell him the truth and she hoped he wouldn't betray her. "I am a twin, and Lady Lizette is my sister."

Silence.

After a long moment, Lord Brentwood said, "I'm afraid I don't understand."

"Lord and Lady Crewe raised Lady Lizette as their own when their baby was a stillborn," Rosamond explained. "By doing so, they provided my mother funds so she could live comfortably for the remainder of her days, with the understanding that we would never learn about one another."

Rosamond wrapped her arms around her waist as she continued. "But I made a mistake. My mother confessed the truth to me on her death bed and I foolishly told my fiancé. He took it as an opportunity to become rich and he abducted Lady Lizette with the intent of ransoming her. Sadly, he was killed when we rescued my sister."

"We?" Lord Brentwood asked.

"Yes, I came to Town to convince George to do the right thing and he held me captive, as well. Fortunately, Tristan brought along Lord Roswell and Mr. Campden to retrieve Lady Lizette. I tried everything I could to save George, but he threatened to kill me and my sister. It was as if he became a different person."

Lord Brentwood ran a hand through his hair. "So you have been abducted two times?"

"I have."

"That would explain how you handled yourself with such confidence last night," Lord Brentwood said.

"I couldn't watch you die, no matter what, and I do not regret my actions one whit." She hesitated before saying, "There is one more thing that I must share with you."

With a lifted brow, Lord Brentwood asked, "There is something else?"

Rosamond nodded. "I am a daughter of a seaman."

Lord Brentwood stared at her, his expression giving nothing away, before saying, "I do appreciate your honesty, but this changes nothing for me."

"How could it not?" Rosamond asked. "I do not belong in your world."

"Then we will create our own world, together." He approached her and came to a stop in front of her. "I fell in love with you, not your standing in high Society."

Rosamond's mind spun. "But what of all my secrets?"

"Who am I to judge you for keeping secrets to protect your loved ones?" Lord Brentwood asked. "I am just thankful that you trust me enough to share them with me."

"I don't know what to say," she said. And for once, she didn't. He was offering her the acceptance she had hoped for. Did she dare accept it?

Lord Brentwood cupped her right cheek. "Your past will always be a part of you, but I am much more interested in your future. I hope to be in it."

Rosamond felt tears prick at the back of her eyes. "You love me, despite my past?"

"No, I love you, *because* of your past," he asserted. "I have never met a more resilient, stubborn, and utterly captivating woman before. Your experiences, good and bad, have made you the woman you are today; the only woman that I have ever loved."

There was only one thing that she could say that could express what she was feeling now. It was time she confessed her true feelings to him, knowing that he would be the protector of her heart that she had so longed for. "I love you, too."

"I was hoping that you would say that," he said as he leaned in and pressed a kiss to her lips. It was a kiss that was free of secrets, worries, and questions. She felt light and whole, and she knew she could fully give herself, all of her, to this man.

A clearing of a throat came from next to them, causing them to jump apart.

Rosamond brought her hand up to touch her kissed lips as she met Lady Anne's disapproving gaze.

"I did not hear much talking out in the entry hall so I decided that my presence was required in here," Lady Anne said. "Dare I hope that you two are engaged?"

Lord Brentwood gave her a sheepish smile. "I hadn't gotten to that part yet," he admitted.

"Typically, that comes before the kiss, young man," Lady Anne remarked. "Go on, then. Say it properly or she won't answer unless you are down on one knee and everything."

Turning to face her, Lord Brentwood reached for her hand and lowered himself down onto one knee. "Miss Rosamond Hendre, will you do me the honor of becoming my wife?" he asked, his lips curling into a smile.

"Yes," she replied without the slightest hint of hesitation. "Yes, I will marry you."

Lord Brentwood jumped up to his feet and pulled her towards him. He brushed a kiss over her lips. "You have made me the happiest of men."

"Yes, yes, you love her, but it is time for you to go," Lady

Anne said with a wave of her hand. "We have a wedding that we must start planning."

"Does Lord Brentwood have to go so soon?" Rosamond asked with a pout on her lips.

Lady Anne gave her an exasperated look. "A wedding does not simply plan itself."

With a chuckle, Lord Brentwood said, "I shall leave you to it, but I will call upon you tomorrow."

"Promise?" Rosamond asked.

Lord Brentwood took her hand and brought it up to his lips. "Nothing can keep me away from you, my love."

And she knew he spoke true. For she felt the same way.

Epilogue

Three weeks later...

Malcolm stood in front of his friends and family as he said his vows to love, honor and cherish Rosamond. Which he had every intention to. She had not only saved him from himself, but her dowry had gone to save his entire family from ruination. He would spend the rest of his life proving to her how grateful he was that she had taken a chance on him.

He still couldn't quite believe that he was here, marrying the love of his life. He had vowed never to fall in love, but he had said a lot of things before he had met Rosamond. She had helped him to see a new way of life- a better way of life.

Rosamond glanced over at him with a smile on her lips and he was lost all over again. How was he expected to listen to the vicar when he just wanted to kiss his wife. His wife. He quite liked the sound of that.

A cheer went up around the chapel and Malcolm realized that the vicar had pronounced them man and wife. How had he missed that?

Malcolm turned to face Rosamond. "Hello, Wife."

"Hello, Husband," Rosamond replied.

Leaning in, he brushed a kiss over her lips. "I am looking forward to getting you alone later today," he whispered.

An adorable blush came to Rosamond's cheeks as she responded, "You shouldn't speak of such things."

"But we are married now," he said before he led them down the center of the chapel and out the doors.

Once they were outside, Malcolm went to assist her into his black coach. He waited until Rosamond was situated before he climbed in next to her, closing the door behind him.

"I hope you have no regrets, my love," Malcolm said.

"None."

"You seem rather sure of your response."

Rosamond's eyes grew mischievous. "Perhaps it is because I know how truly lucky you are to marry me."

He chuckled. "I won't disagree with you there."

With a glance out the window, Rosamond said, "It is odd to me that I am a viscountess. I do hope I won't make a misstep."

"You will be a viscountess unlike any other."

She looked unsure. "Is that a good thing?"

Malcolm reached for her hand and rushed to reassure her, "It is. Besides, I will be there to guide you, as will my mother."

"That is a relief."

He shifted on the bench to face her. "I never want you to feel that you need to change any part of you to fit in. You are perfect, just the way you are."

"To you, perhaps."

"Who else matters?" Malcolm asked. "It's you and me against the world."

"I like the sound of that."

The coach came to a stop in front of Lord Ashington's townhouse and a footman stepped off his perch to open the door.

As Malcolm went to exit the coach, Rosamond said, "Stop."

"What is it?" he asked.

She leaned forward and pressed her lips against his. It only took him a moment before he realized that he wasn't doing anything about it. He only deepened the kiss a little while his hands wrapped around her, pulling her close.

This was to be his life now. A glorious life where he could kiss Rosamond whenever he so desired. Could he have envisioned such a perfect future?

He broke the kiss and remained close. "I love you," he said.

"I love you, too."

"Shall we go inside?" he asked.

Rosamond looked put out. "Do we have to?"

Malcolm kissed the tip of her nose. "I daresay that Lady Anne might have me drawn and quartered if I allow us to miss the luncheon."

"That would be rather drastic of Lady Anne, but you might not be wrong," Rosamond said lightly.

"Then we are in agreement?"

Rosamond nodded. "We can go inside."

Malcolm stepped out of the coach and assisted her onto the pavement. Then he slipped her hand into the crook of his arm.

The main door opened and Brownell stepped back to allow them entry. "Good morning, my lord and lady," he greeted.

"That might take some time to get used to," Rosamond admitted.

His sister met him in the entry way with a smile on her face. "It is about time you got here," she teased.

"We came straightaway from the chapel," Malcolm said. "How did you manage to arrive first?"

Enid gave him a knowing look. "It could be because I

didn't stop to engage in extracurricular activities, such as kissing," she replied.

"Pity," Malcolm said. "Are Father and Mother here?"

"They are, but they are already in the drawing room," Enid responded. "I just wanted to offer my best wishes before you are inundated with your guests."

"That is most kind of you," Rosamond said.

Enid approached Rosamond and embraced her. "I have always wanted a sister," she shared. "I am glad that it is you." She turned towards her brother, her next words holding a warning. "Do not mess this up."

"I have no intention of doing so," Malcolm stated as his sister embraced him.

As his sister took a step back, the door opened and Mr. Campden walked into the entry hall. His eyes landed on Enid, and he looked uncertain, which was in stark contrast to how he usually was.

"Lady Enid," he greeted with a bow.

She dropped into a curtsy. "Mr. Campden."

The Bow Street Runner lowered his voice. "I know this is not the time to speak of such things, but Lady Enid has been cleared of all wrongdoing in the death of her husband."

"That is wonderful," Enid gushed, clasping her hands together. "How did you manage such a feat?"

"It took some effort on my part, but Lord Roswell's testimony went a long way in proving your innocence," Mr. Campden explained.

"Thank you for all that you did for me," Enid said.

Mr. Campden's eyes crinkled around the edges. "You are most kindly welcome, my lady," he responded, holding her gaze. "May I escort you into the drawing room?"

"Thank you," Enid replied as she accepted his proffered arm.

Rosamond watched their retreating figures and said, "I think it would be for the best to get this over with."

Malcolm gave her an amused look. "That is the spirit, my love."

The main door opened and his friends, Mr. Moore and Mr. Whitmore, stepped into the entry hall, both with smiles on their faces.

Whitmore approached them and performed an exaggerated bow in front of Rosamond. "You have done the impossible, my lady," he said. "You made an honest man out of Malcolm."

Malcolm shook his head at his friend's antics. "I do apologize, but Whitmore is an idiot."

"How dare you, sir!" Whitmore exclaimed. "I merely came to offer my best wishes and you manage to insult me soundly."

Rosamond looked amused. "I apologize if my husband offended you. I doubt that was his intention."

"No, it was precisely my intention," Malcolm quipped.

Moore smiled at Rosamond. "I do hope you will not live to regret your choice of husband. He can be rather ornery at times."

"I am well aware," Rosamond replied good-naturedly.

Shifting his gaze towards Malcolm, Moore said, "You do not deserve such a beautiful young woman. Her smile is brighter than any star in the sky."

Malcolm chuckled. "I should note that Moore's talent is wasted as a barrister. He should be writing sonnets."

"I think he is charming," Rosamond remarked.

Moore puffed out his chest. "She is as wise as she is beautiful."

Whitmore interjected, "I do believe it was I that said that Rosamond was perfect for Malcolm."

"No, you advised Malcolm not to fall prey to the parson's mousetrap," Moore corrected. "I was the voice of reason."

Malcolm sobered. "And I do thank you for that."

Lady Anne stepped out of the drawing room with an

expectant look on her face. "Are you two just going to dawdle there all day or are you going to join your other guests in the drawing room?"

"Do we have a choice?" Rosamond joked.

With a frown, Lady Anne replied, "I see that marriage has not changed that quick wit of yours. What a shame."

Malcolm offered his arm. "We can do anything as long as we are together," he said, knowing nothing in his life had been this perfect before.

The End

If you enjoyed A Beguiling Ruse, check out the next book in the series

He is determined not to lose her, but is her heart too shattered to ever try again?

Greyson, the Viscount of Rushcliffe, is content with his life as a Bow Street Runner, but it all comes to a jarring end when his older brother is murdered. He is now an heir to an earldom- a position he never wanted. As he is trying to come to grips with the newfound shackle on his life, Lady Enid- the only woman that he is inexplicably drawn to- comes to him for help to let his brother's murderer go free.

In the eyes of London society, Lady Enid Longbourn is ruined. Though the *ton* whispers about how she returned home after the death of her husband, any speculation remains just that: gossip. Her own father doesn't even want her home, but she is determined to give her daughter the future she deserves. However, when her friend is arrested for murder, she knows it must be a terrible mistake and is determined to do whatever it takes to ensure she is set free.

After Enid proves herself to be reckless, Greyson agrees to take the case, but only to keep this vexing woman safe. It should be a straightforward investigation, but it becomes increasingly tangled and confusing, making him question everything. Although, the greatest complication is the one that he didn't see coming: he never thought they would fall in love.

Also by Laura Beers

Gentlemen of London

A Treacherous Engagement

An Unlikely Match

A Perilous Circumstance

A Precarious Gamble

A Deadly Entanglement

A Devious Secret

Proper Regency Matchmakers

Saving Lord Berkshire

Reforming the Duke

Loving Lord Egleton

Redeeming the Marquess

Engaging Lord Charles

Refining Lord Preston

Regency Spies & Secrets

A Dangerous Pursuit

A Dangerous Game

A Dangerous Lord

A Dangerous Scheme

Regency Brides: A Promise of Love

Charming Mr. Blackmore (prequel)

A Clever Alliance

The Reluctant Guardian

A Noble Pursuit

The Earl's Daughter

A Foolish Game

The Beckett Files

Saving Shadow

A Peculiar Courtship

To Love a Spy

A Tangled Ruse

A Deceptive Bargain

The Baron's Daughter

The Unfortunate Debutante

About the Author

Laura Beers is an award-winning author. She attended Brigham Young University, earning a Bachelor of Science degree in Construction Management. She can't sing, doesn't dance and loves naps.

Laura lives in Utah with her husband, three kids, and her dysfunctional dog. When not writing regency romance, she loves waterskiing, hiking, and drinking Dr Pepper.

You can connect with Laura on Facebook, Instagram, or on her site at www.authorlaurabeers.com.

9 781962 703017